# MURDER IN THE GREEK ISLES

*Also by Wendy Church*

*The Jesse O'Hara Novels*

MURDER ON THE SPANISH SEAS *
MURDER BEYOND THE PALE *

*The Shadows of Chicago Mysteries*

KNIFE SKILLS *
TUNNEL VISION *

* *available from Severn House*

# MURDER IN THE GREEK ISLES

Wendy Church

SEVERN
HOUSE

First world edition published in Great Britain and the USA in 2025
by Severn House, an imprint of Canongate Books Ltd,
14 High Street, Edinburgh EH1 1TE.

severnhouse.com

Copyright © Wendy Church, 2025

Cover and jacket design by Piers Tilbury

*British Library Cataloguing-in-Publication Data*
A CIP catalogue record for this title is available from the British Library.

ISBN-13: 978-1-4483-1565-9 (cased)
ISBN-13: 978-1-4483-1566-6 (e-book)

*All Severn House titles are printed on acid-free paper.*

FSC
MIX
Paper from
responsible sources
FSC® C013056
www.fsc.org

Typeset by Palimpsest Book Production Ltd., Falkirk,
Stirlingshire, Scotland.
Printed and bound in Great Britain by TJ Books,
Padstow, Cornwall.

The manufacturer's authorised representative in the EU for product safety is
Authorised Rep Compliance Ltd, 71 Lower Baggot Street, Dublin D02 P593
Ireland (arccompliance.com)

# Praise for the Jesse O'Hara novels

"Fans of Janet Evanovich will enjoy meeting the freewheeling Jesse, and this debut gives an enticing hint of more adventures to come. Armchair travelers and foodies, rejoice. Go, Jesse!"
*Booklist* Starred Review

"Clever, transportive, and laugh-out-loud funny, *Murder on the Spanish Seas* is the perfect book to read poolside—just not on the deck of a luxury ocean liner. I can't wait to read more from this wickedly entertaining new voice"
Andrea Bartz, *New York Times* bestselling author of *We Were Never Here*

"A whip-smart, sarcastic, amateur sleuth and a tightly plotted story that's perfect for fans of Ruth Ware, Catriona McPherson, and Darynda Jones. Readers will want to see Jesse again"
*Library Journal*

"An action-packed debut that's as funny as the heroine is unstoppable. I loved it!"
Nora McFarland, author of the Lilly Hawkins Mysteries

# About the author

**Wendy Church**, PhD, is the author of the Jesse O'Hara Mysteries, the first of which, *Murder on the Spanish Seas*, was named a *Booklist* Top 10 Debut Mystery & Thriller of 2023. She is also the author of the Shadows of Chicago Mysteries. *Knife Skills*, the first in the series, received a Starred Review from *Kirkus Reviews*. She lives in Seattle, Washington with her partner and several animals.

wendyschurch.com
@wendychurchwriter

*For Eleanor Rose and Nolin Scott Church.*
*Welcome to the family!*

# PROLOGUE

The car careened off the narrow road, breaking through bushes and branches on its way down the bank. It slammed to a stop against a boulder.

The crumpled front end of the car did its job, preserving the occupant compartment and the two people inside.

After a few moments the man lifted his head off of the deflating airbag.

"Jenny, are you OK?"

"I think so. What happened?" She pushed away from her own airbag, rubbing her forehead.

"I don't know. That other car came out of nowhere."

The man peered out the window and over the car's hood. "Jesus, look at that."

The boulder they'd crashed into was perched at the edge of a cliff, hundreds of feet above a beach. White-topped waves boomed onto the rocky shore below.

"Oh my God, Matt. We were lucky."

"No kidding." He carefully leaned forward, looking further out in front of the car. "It looks stable, but I don't want to count on it staying that way. Let's get out of here."

He pulled on his door handle. "My door's stuck. How's yours?"

She tried her handle, and the door opened a few inches before it stopped. She looked through the thin opening down to the small patch of ground.

"Mine's stuck, too."

"Do you think you could pry it open, if you had something?"

"Maybe."

"There's an umbrella on the floor in the back seat." He unhooked his seat belt and stretched his arm to the back, feeling for the umbrella. The tips of his fingers grazed the handle.

He shifted in his seat as much as he dared and extended his

arm, bringing his hand just close enough to grab the end. He dragged it toward him and handed it to her.

She slid it into the space between her door and the frame, then used it as a lever to expand the opening.

The door moved less than an inch before the umbrella began to bend.

"It's not working," she said, her voice higher now, barely loud enough to hear over the crashing waves.

He reached across the seats and put his hand on her leg. "Don't worry, we'll be fine. That rock isn't going anywhere. We can just break the windows and crawl out. Besides, what's a honeymoon without a little excitement?"

She managed a small smile. "You're right. Here goes." She pulled the bent umbrella back toward her, turned her face away, and drove the end of it into the glass.

The window cracked, spidery tendrils moving out from the point of impact.

She hit it again in the same place. This time it shattered, showering bits of safety glass on the seat and the ground outside.

"See?" he said. "Easy-peasy. My turn." She handed him the umbrella, and he broke his window on the first try.

He swept the broken glass away from the window frame with his sleeve. "Do you need help out?"

"No, I'm good. I'll meet you by the trunk," she joked, leaning over to kiss him.

She unhooked her seat belt and used her sweater to cushion the window frame. As she started to crawl out, she heard the low rumble of an engine.

"Someone's up there! Does the horn still work?"

He pushed on the horn and the sound joined the rumbling of the waves. "Yes!" He continued to honk, looking up at the road.

"They heard you!"

A black SUV left the road and rolled towards them.

"Thank God." She waved her hand at the car, her shoulders and arms now completely through the window.

She'd almost wriggled her entire body out when the SUV rammed into the side of their car, its grill screeching as it slid across the boulder.

The SUV continued to push the car until it was perched at the edge of the cliff. One last, gentle bump sent it over the precipice.

The SUV idled until the car smashed on the rocks below. Then it backed away, and drove up the bank and onto the road.

# ONE

My phone vibrated in my pocket. I pulled it out and looked at the screen, declined the call and slipped the phone back.

"Is that your dad again?" asked Sam.

"Yep."

"How many is that?"

"Thirty-seven."

"Are you ever going to talk to him?"

"There's nothing to say. He probably wants to make amends or some shit." I took a long sip of my beer. Guinness, the breakfast of champions.

We were sitting in Sam's kitchen, in the main house on the large property she owned in the Old Edgewood neighborhood of Chicago that she currently shared with a pack of rescue dogs and an indeterminate number of cats. And, more recently, me.

"What if he does want to make amends? What would be so wrong with that?"

Sam knew better by now than to try to talk to me about my dad. "Just because you have a great relationship with your parents doesn't mean everyone else does." I adopted a low, gravelly voice. "'Hi Jesse. Listen, I'm sorry for killing your mom. But I'm out of jail now, and ready to continue on with my life of alcoholic narcissism. I'd love to have your forgiveness. And just to save time, for when I eventually do something terrible to your sister, too, can you forgive me for that in advance?'"

"I didn't mean—"

"'Oh, yeah, and your hot friend, Sam? Can you get me her number?'"

"OK, OK, you're right. I'm sorry. Where's he staying?"

"With Shannon." My sister had jumped at the chance to put my dad up when he was let out on parole. She was younger than me, and hadn't experienced the full impact of what he'd done to our family.

We were interrupted by all the dogs barking at once. They ran to the front door in a pack, a large, happy, tail-wagging amoeba. Sam left the kitchen and returned with a familiar brown package in her arms.

"It's for you," she said unnecessarily. She set the package on the counter. "Looks like she's figured out where you live."

I sighed. "Do you still think she's going to forget about me?"

"I suppose not. The usual?"

"Yeah."

I used my Datu boot knife to slice the tape and open the box. Inside was a skull-shaped bottle of Crystal Head Vodka.

The cold, clear eyes stared up at me. No matter how many times I looked at one of these bottles, it never ceased to send a chill up my spine.

I grabbed it and joined Sam outside. We took the short path through her garden to the mini warehouse that housed her makeshift gun range. I placed the bottle on the wooden shelf and joined her on the firing line, then pulled out my phone and started filming.

The thick glass shattered on impact, the sound of breaking glass joined by the crack of the 9mm round leaving Sam's Beretta. We watched the mist of vodka spray from the bottle as it exploded.

"Six for six," I said.

Sam was twenty-five yards away from the line of targets. The remains of five previous bottles were littered on the ground below it.

"This does seem like a waste of good vodka," she said.

"We don't need her vodka. And she's going to love the video I'm going to post on Insta." I turned the phone around and waved at it. "Hi Svetlana. See you never, I hope."

"Do you think she has an Instagram account?"

"Probably not. But she'll hear about it from someone who does."

Sam pushed up her goggles, somehow managing to not disturb a hair on her head. Despite the fact that it was June, and a humid eighty-five degrees, she didn't have a single bead of sweat on her face. I couldn't remember the last time I'd seen her where she didn't look perfect.

"And do you really think it's a good idea to provoke her? Wouldn't it be better to just leave her alone?"

"It's a great idea. I want her to know what we think of her shitty vodka, and that I'm not intimidated."

"For the record, Crystal Head isn't shitty vodka. And you are intimidated. That's why you're staying with me, instead of at your own house."

"Yeah, but she doesn't have to know that."

It was true, I was definitely intimidated by Svetlana. She'd been sending bottles of her favorite vodka to my house regularly since we'd crossed paths with her last year. And I was pretty sure she wouldn't be happy just sending vodka; eventually she'd take her revenge out on me more directly.

Svetlana Ivashchenko was the head of Russia's largest energy company, Rusgaprom. Over the years she'd used her virtually unlimited wealth and power to threaten anyone who got in her way. This included a number of her energy industry competitors, all of whom had somehow met "natural" deaths shortly after making moves that interfered with her corporate hegemony. I'd personally watched her almost blow up a gas plant, murder an accomplice, and nearly succeed in kidnapping my best friend.

Now it was me on her hit list.

I'd relaxed a bit after moving to Sam's place, in the hopes Svetlana wouldn't know where I'd gone, which was completely stupid. Of course she knew. And even though Sam's estate had a state-of-the-art security system, with her resources Svetlana would eventually find a way to get to me.

I heard the sound of a car door, and a few moments later Gideon entered the warehouse.

"Hey you two."

"Hey. To what do we owe this visit?" Gideon worked insane hours during the week, and we rarely saw him outside of weekends.

He closed the door and joined us at the firing line. "Want to go to Greece?"

Sam's eyes lit up. "Always. What's the occasion?"

"I got invited to give a paper at the International Conference on Law Enforcement and Investigation. Well, actually we got invited." He turned to me. "The organizers heard about our work in Spain and Ireland, and they want us to do a session."

"That's exciting," said Sam. "On what?"

"Something to do with how multifunctional teams work together to conduct criminal investigations."

I put my phone away. "You mean, where two people are constantly in harm's way, get the crap kicked out of them, shot at, and almost killed, while the third one is safely at home, sitting in front of a computer, eating popcorn? That kind of team?"

We'd been involved in two high-profile investigations over the last year, and Sam and I, in both cases, had been lucky to get out alive. The biggest threat to Gideon had been carpal tunnel syndrome.

As usual he ignored my sarcasm. "I think it's supposed to be about how people on the ground work in tandem with technical support. They want us to share our process. You have to admit, it was impressive. You're two for two."

"I'd be happy to be one for one, if we'd caught Svetlana."

Our first case had been accidental; we'd stumbled upon Svetlana's bombing attempt in Spain. We'd stopped her, but she'd gotten away, and since then she'd sent a bottle of her favorite vodka to me every month, the remains of which were now scattered around Sam's gun range. Svetlana wanted to let me know she knew where I lived, and make sure I didn't forget about her.

It worked. I hadn't.

"When's the conference?" I asked.

"Two weeks."

"That's really soon," said Sam. "Don't they usually set those things up months in advance?"

"One of the other teams can't make it. They need to fill a spot."

Conferences were a dilemma for me. I actually liked presenting papers, and I wasn't worried about putting something together in two weeks; I could easily show up and completely wing it, if I had to. But the obligatory hand shaking, small talk, and requirement to interact with other people was a real deterrent.

Gideon knew me well, and added quickly, "This is the biggest law enforcement conference in Europe. They're holding it on Crete, in Heraklion. They'll pay for our flight, and put us up in a hotel for four days. We can make a longer vacation out of it."

Sam had been to Greece many times, it was her favorite place to visit, outside of France. "You've never been, have you?" she asked, looking at me.

"No, but I've always wanted to go. You know how I feel about archaeology. And I'm ready, I've done my research."

"I'm almost afraid to ask . . . OK, I have to ask. What did this research entail?"

"Basic internet exploration about the country, augmented by extensive film and TV study to round out my knowledge of cultural elements."

"And what was included in your cultural studies? *Clash of the Titans*? *Troy*? *300*?"

I nodded. "All of them. And, *Remember the Titans.*"

"That wasn't about Greece."

"Yeah, I found that out. Still, not a bad movie. I also watched *Jason and the Argonauts*, twice. Amazing what they could do in 1963 with stop-motion animation. You know it took them over four months to film the scenes with the skeleton warriors, the ones that spawned from the hydra's teeth? Pure cinematic gold. And, obviously, I've seen all six seasons of *Xena: Warrior Princess*, several times."

"You know that *Xena* was filmed in New Zealand, right?"

"The lore is the lore. I've also been through the Lynda Carter *Wonder Woman* series, both Gal Gadot *Wonder Woman* movies, and *Hercules in New York*."

"I managed to miss that last one," Sam said drily. "What about *Zorba the Greek*?"

"No."

"*Zorba the Greek*? It won three Academy Awards."

I shrugged.

"*The Sisterhood of the Traveling Pants*?"

"Nope."

"*Mamma Mia*?"

"I heard the song, I didn't feel the need to see the movie."

"*The Guns of Navarone*? *Dogtooth*? *Eleni*? *Captain Corelli's*—"

"And you know," Gideon interrupted, "a paper at this conference would be a great way for you to promote your new business."

He was bouncing up and down on his toes. I hadn't seen him this excited since *Witcher 3* was released.

"What new business?" I asked.

"Private investigation. You've solved two high-profile crimes in the last year. And you've already got some good name recognition. This invitation is evidence of that."

I wasn't sure I had the kind of name recognition that would be helpful. Two successful investigations couldn't overcome a slew of failed career moves, mostly related to what my previous employer referred to as my "million-dollar brain and ten-cent personality."

Some years ago, I'd started a consulting business investigating corporate financial malfeasance. There was a decent demand for forensic accountants who could not only investigate, but also accurately recall details on a witness stand. My near photographic memory was a huge benefit, and it didn't hurt that I had the requisite résumé, including a PhD in forensic accounting.

I'd been making good money until I'd blown it, on live TV, and in spectacular fashion. I was testifying against a famous corporate asshat who'd caused hundreds of people to lose their jobs. Two days of relentless cross-examination by his highly paid attorneys was getting to me, and I'd finally reached my boiling point, blurting out to the court that the defendant was as "useful as a baby building a space shuttle."

That effectively ended my expert witness career. No one wanted anything to do with a loose cannon on the witness stand.

"I even have the stationery for the new business." Gideon pulled a folded piece of paper out of his pocket and handed it to me.

The blank white sheet was bordered in light blue, with a signature line across the bottom: "Jesse O'Hara, Shuttle Investigations." In the top right corner was a logo of a baby riding a space shuttle.

Sam looked over my shoulder. "Very nice. I think it captures your essence." She turned, and fired one last shot at the largest piece of glass on the ground under the shelf. It shattered into tiny pieces.

The three of us left the building and walked back up the path to the main house, where we were greeted raucously at the door by the dogs, who circled around us as we went into Sam's kitchen.

All of them except Chaz, her Chinese Crested, who was comfortably ensconced on a plush dog bed set on Sam's couch, the stylish bed in sharp contrast to his hairless body, crooked teeth, and drooping tongue that never seemed to make it all the way into his mouth.

Surrounding him on the couch were the remains of my favorite T-shirt.

"You little *bastard*," I said, leaning down to pick up the larger pieces. "Could you be any uglier? She should have named you Medusa. It's a miracle we haven't all turned to stone by now."

Sam picked Chaz up from the couch and gave him a kiss, then gently laid him back down. "It's not his fault. You're the one who leaves your T-shirts lying around. He is a dog, after all."

"He's barely a dog." I got on well with all animals, and was on the best of terms with her other dogs. All but canine Severus.

Sam went to the refrigerator and pulled out a bottle of cava and a can of Guinness, handing the beer to me and pouring her and Gideon each a glass.

"Can I use your Instagram account? You have more followers than I do," I said, looking at the video I'd just taken.

"How many do you have?"

"Two."

"Me and Gideon?"

"Yeah."

"Can we talk about that later?"

"Don't worry, I won't—"

"So, Jesse, what do you think? Can we go to the conference?" Gideon interrupted.

Sharing our work at a conference would be kind of cool. And I'd been unemployed now, going on a year, so didn't have anything better to do.

A subsidized trip to Greece? It was kind of a no-brainer. I really loved archaeology, and Crete was home to some of the oldest civilizations on earth.

"I'll do it, with some conditions: I'm not doing any group dinners, lunches, coffee meet-ups, ice breakers, mingling events, rope courses, bonding exercises, mixers, or speed dating. I'm not putting on a name tag and adding cute stickers to it, and if I'm in the bar and anyone comes up to me and wants to chat, I reserve the right to leave for my room and finish drinking from the mini fridge, on your tab."

"No, no, I know. No problem! That's a yes, then?"

"Yes."

Gideon clapped his hands together. "Great! When should we get started on our paper?"

"Tonight, if you want."

"Terrific! Toast!" He put his glass forward and we clinked drinks.

I couldn't blame him for being excited. He did most of his work in front of a computer, and rarely got to go anywhere.

I was a little excited, too. The presentation would take an hour, and then I'd be free to explore. As importantly, going to Greece right now would give me the opportunity to relax. We'd be in and out of the country before Svetlana even knew we were gone, and it would be nice to get out of town for a while, in a place where Svetlana didn't know where to send her damn skull vodka. I needed a break from her.

The phone in my pocket vibrated and I pulled it out.

Dad again. I swiped left and put it back.

# TWO

Gideon and I worked on our presentation over the next two weeks, then the four of us flew out to Greece the day before we were scheduled to give our paper.

Over my objections, Sam had asked Tatiana to join us, footing the bill for the two of them. Tatiana had been staying at Sam's place ever since we'd stopped Svetlana's bombing attempt in Spain.

Svetlana had killed Tatiana's mother, and then blackmailed her father to carry out the bombing. He'd gotten caught, and was now spending time in a Spanish prison. We all assumed that Svetlana's enmity extended to Tatiana, and it was no longer safe for her in Russia.

So while I understood Sam inviting Tatiana to stay at her estate, that didn't mean I was happy about it. I was even less happy about her coming along on this trip.

Tatiana had just turned twenty-one. She was uncommunicative, and, when she did speak, she was surly and arrogant, with a breathtaking commitment to negativity for anything other than Russia's cultural superiority. The only time we spoke was when we argued.

She thought most Americans, including me, were stupid and ignorant, with at best a derivative culture that paled in comparison to Russia's, a position she maintained even in the face of the Ukraine invasion.

"Putin is not Russia," she'd said, on one of the few occasions where she deigned me worthy of conversation. "The war is his, not Russian people's."

"Has it occurred to you that the 'Russian people' are the ones who allowed a string of murderous autocrats to run the country for most of the last hundred years? Including the one currently ruining millions of lives?"

"Tchaikovsky, Baryshnikov, Tolstoy, Chagall—" Her fallback to any criticism of Russia was to list the country's great artists and achievements.

Here we go again. "Chagall is from Belarus."

"Dostoevsky, Solzhenitsyn, Pushkin, Chekhov—"

"Beam me up, Scotty," I said, my response every time she brought up Chekhov.

"First man in space. First woman in space. The periodic table of the elements—"

"Jeans. Hearing aids. Chocolate chip cookies."

She'd snorted and walked away. The only time we could stand to be in the same room for any length of time was when we were drinking. As far as I knew she was the sole person on the planet who could drink me under the table. I couldn't figure it out; she was about my size, but could put away vodka like it was water.

She'd been lukewarm about going on this trip, but once she found out that Gideon was going, she was in. She'd had a crush on him since Sam had brought her back to the States. We'd tried, numerous times, to get her to understand that Gideon was gay. But she seemed to believe that his orientation was mutable, and he just hadn't met the right woman yet. Of course this came on the heels of her learning that Gideon and I had dated in college.

I managed to avoid sitting next to her on the flight to Athens, and then when we changed planes from there for the short flight to Crete's Heraklion Airport.

I'd been looking forward to the last leg of the trip, but to my disappointment it was overcast, and what would have been a spectacular view of the Greek islands was blocked by gray clouds.

After we landed we took a taxi from the airport to the Celestial Hotel, then checked into four adjacent rooms on the sixth floor. After dinner Gideon and I did a final run-through of our presentation.

I was excited. An hour in a conference room the next day and then I'd be free to explore.

We were a late addition to the schedule, and our session didn't make it to the official program, meriting only a small paper insert. So it was a little bit of a surprise when we arrived at the designated room and it was packed.

Every seat was taken, and people were standing against the walls. Over a hundred people in a room designed for sixty.

I'd told Sam not to come, and Tatiana wouldn't have thought

of it, likely spending the morning doing several thousand laps in the pool, and then running a marathon around the city. With luck, she'd be out on her own until we flew back.

Our forty-five-minute presentation summarized our work in Spain and Ireland, a combination of Sam's and my work on the ground augmented with Gideon's computer skills. In Spain we'd discovered Svetlana's plot to blow up the liquid natural gas plant in Bilbao; in Ireland Sam and I had gone to help a relative find his missing daughter, and in the process we'd ended up taking down a drug kingpin.

Gideon and I switched the narration easily between the two of us for thirty minutes, then he opened it up to questions. Hands shot up all over the room.

Before he could call on the first person, I stepped forward.

"You know how people say, 'there are no stupid questions'?"

Vigorous head nods were accompanied by a few more hands going up.

"They're wrong. So if you aren't completely, one hundred percent sure that your question isn't stupid, please put your hand down."

A disappointing few of the hands dropped.

"Great. While we're at it, if your question is about something that you missed because you were on your phone, or not paying attention, go ahead and put your hand down, too."

About half of the hands went down.

"Super. Now, if your question isn't really a question, and you just want to talk to show how smart you are, because you want to drum up clients for your own little business, don't even think about it."

I was gratified to see more than half of the remaining hands drop. Mission accomplished.

"Are you done?" Gideon whispered.

"Yep," I said, stepping back. "Go for it."

He pointed to a man in the front row.

"Hello, yes, I am Guillaume LeBlanc, with the Gendarmerie Nationale. Doctor O'Hara, you say that your photographic memory helps you with your investigations, and in particular to note when people are lying. It is frankly quite difficult to believe. Can you say a little more about this so-called ability you claim to have?"

"Sure. Let's start with you. Are you cheating on your wife, with someone at this conference?"

The man reddened. "Uh, no—"

"You're lying. Next?"

He'd been lightly touching the hand of the woman next to him off and on during the entire presentation. She'd smiled each time, and neither of them had looked at each other. He was dressed up, more than most of the attendees, with a silk jacket and shirt open at the collar, and she was wearing a low-cut number more suited for a club than a conference. And they were acting sneaky, probably because there were coworkers in the room who knew his wife.

Hands went up again. Gideon called on one of the few women in the room.

"Doctor O'Hara, can you recommend some exercises to develop a photographic memory?"

"I watch a lot of television."

As far as I could tell I was born with near perfect recall. But I'd been glued to the TV since I was a kid; who knows what benefits that had had on my development?

A man in the back in a black suit and tie was standing, his hand straight up. Gideon called on him.

"John Mitchell." No doubt a fake name, and he'd not mentioned his organization, which meant he was with the CIA. They loved to think of themselves as mysterious, even though everyone knew that by not naming his organization, he was naming his organization.

"We know that there is a symbiotic relationship between human intelligence and technology. You are describing elements of HUMINT and SIGINT, and I'd be interested to know how MASINT, and OSINT fit into your investigatory structure. For example . . ."

I'd stopped listening at "symbiotic." When I couldn't hear him talk anymore, I assumed he'd finished. "That's a great question, John, and a little more involved than what we can get into here. Why don't you meet me in the lobby about a half hour after we're done, and we can go over it?"

He nodded and sat down.

The place had a back door, and it wouldn't be much of a problem for me to avoid the hotel lobby for an hour or so.

A guy in a dark maroon suit and designer sunglasses waved his hand casually. Gideon pointed at him.

"I am Wolfgang Müller from the Bundesnachrichtendienst. Isn't it true that you were reckless, in both cases, taking over for the police? After all, they are trained, and you are an amateur. You interfered with an undercover operation in Ireland, and could have blown up a cruise ship full of tourists in Spain. If you ask me, you are dangerous."

I stared at him for a long moment.

The room was silent. A small cough from the back was quickly covered up.

"No one asked you."

Inside Sunglass Guy didn't take the hint. "You must address the fact that you have been interfering in natural law enforcement. How do you explain yourself?"

Natural law enforcement? "OK. Well, the sting operation in Ireland was being led by a guy who was sacrificing civilians for his own personal glory. And that's not just my opinion, the Irish law enforcement community thought so, too, and as a result he's now doing paperwork in the basement of a farmhouse in Donegal. And did you miss the part where we saved his life, because he was too incompetent to work undercover, and got himself caught? And, by the way, we worked closely with the Sligo gardaí to bring down one of the biggest drug lords in Ireland.

"So I don't know what the hell you're talking about. Did you even pay attention?" His English was good, so he couldn't blame his lack of comprehension on a language barrier.

"That is what you say. But what—"

"As far as the cruise ship in Spain was concerned, people were already dying on that boat. And we were minutes away from the largest liquid natural gas plant in Spain getting blown up. And if you'd been paying attention to *that* part of the presentation, you'd have picked up that we actually did work with the Spanish police."

"Work" was a little euphemistic, as I'd started to date one of them, and we happened to end up solving it together. But no reason to add in that detail.

"Yes, but—"

"You know the saying, 'It's better to have some people think you're an asshole, than to open your mouth and confirm it?'"

"I am not sure that is—"

"Seriously, why are you wasting everyone's time with your data-free opinion? And more importantly, why are you wearing sunglasses indoors? Are you worried about retinal damage from the monitors? Cell phone glare? Pale tourist sheen?"

I stared at him until he looked away, and by now most of the rest of the hands dropped down. The next question was pointedly directed at Gideon, and he used the remaining time to describe his approach to infiltrating server networks.

He loved to talk about the details of his work, which was usually a little dull, but it came in handy now as he spent the rest of the time on that one question, sparing me from having to deal with anyone else.

When it was over we collected our materials to leave the podium, around which a group had gathered, waiting to ask more questions. Or worse, chat.

As I looked in vain for an escape route the crowd abruptly parted, deferentially letting a man through to the front.

He was small, under five eight, and slight, with styled, gelled, black hair, and a perfectly fitting three-piece suit, complete with an actual fucking pocket square.

Next to him was a woman, even smaller than him, with slumped shoulders, a furrowed brow, and wearing large, dark-rimmed eyeglasses. She carried an oversized briefcase, a purse and a phone in one hand, and was balancing a stack of folders in the other. She looked like a tiny Joan Cusack, from her nerdy role as Principal Mullins in *School of Rock*.

"Mr. Spielberg, Doctor O'Hara? May I have a moment of your time?"

I was coming up with a reason to not give up a moment of my time, when the man said, "I am Eleftherios Karadimitropoulos, from the Ministry of Citizen Protection. May I buy you both lunch?"

I was a little curious about this Greek government guy that made everyone else stand aside, and also considered it a good trade: a free lunch with one guy, in place of interacting with lots of others.

The fact that Inside Sunglass Guy was in the group waiting to talk with us sealed the deal. "OK."

We followed Government Guy – dubbed "GG" in my head, given that there was no chance in hell we were reproducing his name – out of the room, accompanied by Tiny Joan and a small team of men arranged around us like a mini Roman phalanx.

He led us out of the conference center and to a restaurant a short walk down the street. I became more intrigued when we walked in and were obsequiously greeted by the host, who escorted us to a reserved table near the window. The men who had flanked GG took up discrete positions on the sidewalk and at a nearby table.

We weren't given menus, but the food started arriving almost immediately. Traditional Greek fare, not fancy, but everything perfect and delicious. A plate of appetizers, "mezze," with grilled octopus, kalamata olives, and various marinated vegetables, was followed by a whole branzino fish. Salads and a plate of large, cooked beans were placed around what was left of the room on the table.

GG was a fastidious eater with impeccable table manners, and spent a large portion of the meal delicately wiping at the corners of his mouth with his napkin.

I wasn't sure why he bothered. I'd never seen anyone eat that carefully in my life. I was curious to see how he would do with spaghetti, or ribs; it was almost worth eating with him again to find out.

Tiny Joan didn't eat, spending most of the lunch trying to find where to put down her folders so they wouldn't slide off the table. It was obvious why she was so tiny.

GG chatted amicably throughout the meal, but waited until we'd made it through most of it before getting to the point. "Thank you for joining me."

I looked at Tiny Joan. So far, he'd acted like she didn't exist.

"Eh, yes, this is Cora Gataki. She is my assistant."

Tiny Joan gave a little wave, which upset her folders and landed them and her phone on the floor. She disappeared under the table to pick them up.

"I very much enjoyed your presentation. And I am impressed by your abilities. We have studied your work in Spain and in Ireland closely."

I wondered who "we" was, and wished he would hurry up and get to the point. I had museums to visit.

"As I said, I am with the government, the Ministry of Citizen Protection. I work directly for the Prime Minister." He puffed up his birdlike chest at the last bit of information.

The Prime Minister? OK, so this explained why the crowd had let him through. This guy was big time.

"I am the Minister for Special Projects. One of my areas of responsibility is terrorism. We have a . . . eh . . . situation that the Prime Minister has tasked me to address. I would like to hire you both to help us."

"What kind of situation?"

"It involves some, eh, investigatory work."

"Why us?" If this guy was who he said he was, he would already have access to every law enforcement agency and officer in Greece.

"Yes, well, eh, you both have very unique skills."

He was keeping something back. "Why don't you—"

He held his hand up. "I would like to continue this discussion at our offices, in Athens."

I looked at Gideon, who shrugged.

"What's involved?" No way was I taking on a job with this little amount of information.

GG looked at Tiny Joan and nodded his head. She set her folders down on the table and moved her briefcase to her lap. She opened it, causing the stack of folders to slide off the table again.

She reached into the briefcase and pulled out a fat envelope, then handed it to GG before bending down to gather her folders.

"We will pay you for giving us a week of your time. This is a down payment. You may keep this even if you decide not to accept our small project." He put the envelope on the table and pushed it towards me with the tips of his fingers, like it was something dirty.

I picked up the envelope and peeked in. It was full of euros.

OK, so maybe I would take on a job with this little amount of information. "Sure, we'll meet with you."

"Wonderful." He exhaled, clearly worried that we'd turn him down.

I doubted he had any idea how destitute I was. Living off of the largess of my best friend was getting old. All of this money to spend a little time in Athens sounded like the best deal I'd be getting for a while.

"We have booked you on the flight to Athens for tomorrow morning, and reserved rooms at the Artemis Towers Hotel. It is walking distance to our office, both are near Syntagma Square."

"Sorry, that's not going to work. I have a day of looking at old stuff planned here." I wasn't giving up the chance to visit Knossos when I was this close. The site contained the remnants of one of the oldest civilizations in the world, predating both *Clash of the Titans* and *Xena* eras.

"The day after?" he asked hopefully.

I looked at Gideon, who nodded.

"OK. We'll need four tickets, and four rooms. We're traveling with friends." I wasn't sure Sam and Tatiana would want to go, but if not, they could stay here until we were done.

He exhaled again. "Yes, that will be no problem." He looked at his watch. "I must leave for another meeting, but please stay and enjoy whatever you want here. We will see you the day after tomorrow. I will have your tickets and itinerary sent to your hotel."

He stood up, at which point Tiny Joan stood up too, dumping all of her folders, the briefcase and her phone back on the floor. I hoped for her sake the phone was in a Kevlar case.

While she scrambled around on the floor GG shook our hands. "I am very glad you were able to come to this conference. And on such short notice. A tragedy, though . . ."

"What tragedy?"

"The original presenters, Jenny and Matt Perkins. They were killed in a car accident on Karpathos two weeks ago. Such a shame. It was their honeymoon."

# THREE

Sam, Tatiana, Gideon and I had reconvened for dinner, and were now sitting outside of a café enjoying drinks.

"How did the presentation go?" asked Sam.

"Great! Our session was packed," said Gideon. "The Q&A was a little rough, though."

"There's a shock," she murmured under her breath, glancing at me.

"I'm a little surprised there weren't more questions."

"What did you expect?" said Gideon. "You hammered the first guy for asking a stupid one."

"It *was* a stupid question. Answering that would have positively reinforced a very dangerous precedent. What did you guys do all day?"

"Shopping," said Sam. No surprise there. "Then we went to the Kotsanas Museum, and the Municipal Art Gallery."

"Greek culture is similar to Russian—" Tatiana started.

"So are you up for joining us in Athens?" I'd told them about GG's offer. And I didn't want to hear any more about the superiority of Russian culture, which she would inevitably tie to their trip to the museum.

"Definitely," said Sam.

"Great, we leave tomorrow at—"

"I will go as well," said Tatiana, which was too bad. I'd been hoping she'd found an exciting, two-hundred-mile loop to run around Crete, and wouldn't be able to join us. "Athens is center of Greek culture, which is like Russian. Very old, and the basis from which all others evolve."

"You just can't help yourself, can you?"

She had a baiting smirk on her face. But at the moment I didn't feel up to an argument.

This place was having a strange effect on me. The sun had just gone down, and the lights strung above us created a festive, happy vibe. And we were in the center of the history of western civilization, not to mention not far from the birthplaces of Xena and Wonder Woman.

"I had time for some shopping, too." I leaned down and grabbed my bag, pulling a box out of it.

"What's that?" Gideon reached for the box.

"It's a *Xena: Warrior Princess* action figure. It turns out the Greeks love that show."

"You're kidding," said Sam. "Isn't it a campy parody of Greek myths?"

"I thought you said you'd never seen it?"

"I watched a few scenes once. I find it hard to believe that they would find it interesting."

"Believe it. While it was running it was one of the most popular in the country, along with *The X Files*, and the more recent incarnations of *Star Trek*. And Lucy Lawless is a criminally underrated actress. You know she did a lot of her own stunts? And she speaks four languages."

"Why on earth would the Greeks like that show?"

"Well, to start with, it's awesome. And it's about a flawed hero with a sketchy past who travels with a sidekick, which is a common theme in Greek stories. It also incorporates Greek mythology, along with concepts that resonate with everybody. You know, good versus evil, revenge stories, unrequited love, requited love, leather outfits . . ."

"Along those lines," I turned back to Tatiana. "Who do you think wins in a fight to the death, between Xena and Wonder Woman?"

She snorted. "It does not matter. They are fictional characters."

"Wonder Woman, obviously," said Gideon. "She was gifted superhuman powers by the Greek gods. Xena's skilled, but she's still completely human." Gideon and I had spent a fair time in college watching *Xena* together.

"Really? What about Xena's chakram? That's a waaay better weapon than Wonder Woman's 'lasso of truth.' The chakram would slice that thing in half. And—"

"I'm a little surprised you're taking the job," interrupted Sam, as uninterested in the Xena versus Wonder Woman debate as Tatiana.

"We haven't taken it yet. He's paying us to go to Athens and hear him out. We can always say no."

"I hope we do it," said Gideon. "An investigation in Greece, for one of the ministries? Sounds exciting."

"That's what you think. Let's see if you still feel that way when you're getting shot at."

"I doubt that's going to happen. And you make it sound like I'm just a sidekick."

"Not at all. We couldn't have done anything without your help. But you don't have a clue about what it's like on the street. It's really dangerous, and people get hurt."

While we were talking, I'd noticed a good-looking man sitting alone, staring at us.

Probably at Sam. I was used to it; she was world-class beautiful, and men would often stop in their tracks when they saw her. The child of a Spanish mother and Jamaican father, she was tall and abjectly stunning, with long wavy hair, high cheekbones, and perfect skin. The slight English lilt to her accent, the product of years of boarding school abroad, was the finishing touch.

Right on schedule, the man got up and walked over to our table. Sam started to offer her standard "thank you, but I'm not available" thing, when he turned his back to her and faced Gideon.

"Yásas."

Gideon looked at him blankly.

"Uh, English?"

"American." Gideon smiled.

The man smiled back. "My name is Nicholas."

"Gideon." They shook hands. Tall, Dark and Handsome held on to Gideon's long enough to make his intentions clear.

"Gideon, may I buy you a drink somewhere else?"

Without looking at any of us, Gideon said, "Sure." He got up and left the table.

Tatiana watched him leave, frowning slightly.

I didn't blame her for being attracted to Gideon. I had been, too, when we'd met in college. We dated steadily for three years before he figured out he was gay. We'd remained close friends, one of two for me, and I loved him dearly. Just no longer in the biblical sense.

"That wasn't very nice," said Sam. "Telling Gideon he doesn't know what it's like on the street. You know he's sensitive about his work."

"What? It was the truth. He has no idea how dangerous these investigations are."

"He was with us every step of the way, in Spain and in Ireland, and available to us at all hours with critical information. There's no way we could have done any of it without his help."

"I know, I know. I'm talking about his cavalier attitude towards dealing with criminals. To him it's a game, or a movie." I watched him and his new friend walk down the street. "He'll be fine, Nick will see to that."

We finished our drinks and went back to the hotel. Before we went upstairs, I checked at the desk. True to his word, GG had left us our tickets to Athens. I wasn't sure what he wanted, but his connections and resources seemed to be the real deal.

And I was intrigued. He'd piqued what Sam referred to as my "terminal curiosity," which as much as anything was responsible for constantly getting me into trouble.

As we were walking to the elevator, a man got up from a seat in the lobby and walked over to me.

"Doctor O'Hara?"

Great, a groupie. "Yeah?"

"I saw your presentation this morning."

Sam waved goodbye; she and Tatiana got into the elevator. I looked on longingly as the door closed.

"I am Loukas Papadopoulos, from the *Patris*." He showed me a press badge. At least, I thought it was a press badge. It was all in Greek.

"I am responsible for the crime section, and I wonder if you are interested in doing an interview for our paper?"

There weren't many things I was interested in less. "No thanks." I hit the elevator button again several times, silently imploring the next one to come quickly.

"I can make it worth your while." His English was accented but perfect.

"Thanks, but no thanks. I don't need the money." This was a complete lie, but I couldn't imagine he would have enough money to pay me for the pain and suffering caused by having to interact with him. And we already had the wad of cash from GG.

He shook his head and smiled. "Not money. Do you like archaeology?"

The elevator arrived and opened. I let it close.

"A friend of mine works at Knossos. I have access to some things there that are normally not available to tourists. I can take you there tomorrow, we can do the interview while we tour the site."

I didn't know what the interview would entail, but it didn't matter.

"You're on."

"Wonderful. May I pick you up tomorrow at three, here in the lobby?"

"Sure."

The next elevator came and I got in and waved goodbye.

When I got to my room the light on my phone was blinking. There was a package for me at the front desk.

Something else from GG? I went back down to the lobby, where the host handed me a familiar, brown-paper-wrapped box.

I pulled out my knife and sliced open the top. Empty eyes stared at me from a glass skull.

*Dammit.* How had she figured out so quickly we were here?

Not only did Svetlana know we were here, but we were out of our element. More vulnerable than ever.

I closed the box back up and took it with me upstairs, then put it in the bathroom and closed the door. I didn't want it watching me while I slept.


The next morning I left the box of vodka on the dresser, with a note for the maid to take it as my gift, then headed to the Heraklion Archaeological Museum. Among other things it contained artifacts from the Knossos Palace I'd be visiting later, which would provide a good backdrop for the tour.

Gideon appeared to be still on his date with Nicholas. I'd invited Sam to join me, but she wasn't interested. She liked archaeology, but was more of an art girl, and was heading out to see the Asmanis Art Center with Tatiana.

Sam and Tatiana had a good relationship. That wasn't surprising, as Sam brought out the best in people, and got along with almost everyone. In addition to being world-class gorgeous, she was

compassionate and kind, generous in her support of Chicago's art
community, well-traveled, multilingual, and loaded, courtesy of
the estate of her extremely wealthy grandparents.

She was the antithesis of the spoiled rich kid, and literally no
one disliked her. It made us a good team, as almost everyone
disliked me.

We'd met accidentally when we were both in graduate school
at Northwestern. I'd come across a group of thugs attempting to
sexually assault her in a campus bathroom. I'd managed to distract
them long enough for her to get out and hit the fire alarm, although
not in time for me to avoid getting the crap beaten out of me. But
the two of us survived, and the shared trauma created a bond
between us, one that had gotten stronger over the years. I touched
the scar on my forehead, my lasting physical souvenir of that
event.

I spent a few hours at the museum and could have spent more.
It was curated in Greek and in English, and laid out chronologi-
cally, making it easy to follow the flow of the various Cretan
civilizations through the millennia. After getting through as much
as I had time for, I grabbed a late lunch and took a shower.

At three on the dot Loukas showed up in the lobby. He escorted
me to his car, a blue Toyota Yaris, and drove us out of the city.

He was about my age, and taller than most men I'd seen here,
at slightly over six feet, with dark curly hair that fell just below
his ears, lively brown eyes, and very white teeth. He was casually
dressed in jeans and a T-shirt that hugged his biceps.

He looked a lot like a young Harry Hamlin. I vaguely wondered
what he'd look like in a loincloth.

He didn't say much on the way over, other than to ask me how
I was finding Greece. It was a bonus that he didn't feel the need
to fill every silence with small talk.

The sky was darkening, and soon after we left the city it started
to rain.

# FOUR

Knossos was only fifteen minutes away, but by the time we got there the rain had become a downpour. Nevertheless the parking lot was distressingly full.

I groaned inwardly as we approached the entrance and the long line to the gate that snaked a hundred feet back. But Loukas walked to the front of the line and spoke to the man taking tickets. He immediately waved us both in.

Well then. This was already worth doing an interview.

The Knossos site was large, over three acres of tan stone building remnants and partial walls. Still, the tourists crowded the site, many in large groups, and like us many were carrying large umbrellas which obscured the view.

We'd bypassed the ticket line, but other lines were formed in front of individual chambers with people waiting to get a glimpse of the palace's smaller rooms. I was pleased to see that Loukas had not only managed to get us past the ticket line, but also to the front of every line at every chamber, as well as into a few that were labeled off limits to tourists.

Defying the "earth is 6,000 years old" crowd by its very existence, artifacts from the earliest civilizations at Knossos had been carbon dated at over 7,000 years old. The site, sitting favorably near ample water sources and easily defended at the top of a hill, had been home to numerous communities over the millennia, most notably the Minoans that resided here for 2,000 years, and who were responsible for building the palace.

It was no surprise that a little rain wouldn't keep people away. Signs in Greek and English described Knossos as the larges Bronze Age archaeological site on Crete, and it was considered by some to be Europe's oldest city. Other than the crowds, the only downer was that the remains of the original site were indistinguishable from the reconstructions, most of which had been done using modern building materials following its excavation in the early 1900s.

Regardless, it was amazing, and I couldn't imagine navigating all of it without Loukas. At this point I didn't care what kind of interview he wanted.

We'd been walking around for about an hour when an announcement came over the intercom, in Greek and then in English.

"The site is now closed for today, please make your way to the exits."

People were murmuring and heading towards the gates. The ticket counters were closed, and new arrivals were being turned away.

"What's happening? Why is it closing?"

"The site is being closed due to weather."

"A little rain is 'weather' here?"

He shook his head. "They are expecting a thunderstorm. Several years ago a group of tourists and a worker were struck by lightning. A few were injured, and one had to go to the hospital. Since then they close it during storms. But not for us." He winked.

That sucked for everyone else, but was great for me. Now we'd have the entire place to ourselves.

Eventually all of the tourists were escorted out, and Loukas and I walked the rest of the site at our leisure. With just the two of us it was a completely different experience; without the throngs of brightly clad people I could easily imagine what it might have been like thousands of years ago.

To his credit Loukas didn't pester me with interview questions while we explored. After another hour we took a break at a little table near the café.

"Would you like something to drink?"

We were in the shade but the rain had stopped and it was hot. "Sure. Beer if you can get it." The café looked closed, but he returned shortly with two brightly colored bottles. He popped the tops and handed one to me.

"Yámas," he said, raising his beer and smiling.

"Cheers to you." I surprised myself by smiling back. The beer was ice cold. "This is tasty. What is it?" Unlike a lot of American beers, this one didn't taste like they were in a competition to see who could cram the most hops into every bottle.

"It is from the Solo brewery, which is nearby. This is their pale ale. The hops are grown on Tinos Island, a little over two hundred kilometers from here."

We sipped for a few minutes before he took out his notebook.

"May I ask you some questions?"

He'd already more than fulfilled his part of the bargain. "Sure, shoot."

"So, Doctor O'Hara—"

"You can call me Jesse, Loukas."

He smiled, shining his perfect teeth at me. "Jesse. You broke up a drug operation that led to the downfall of the most prominent drug criminal in Ireland. Before that, you stopped a terrorist bombing in Bilbao. I am interested to know what you think is the most important ability that you yourself bring to investigations?"

I didn't have to think too hard about this one. "My memory. There's no such thing as a true photographic memory, but I'm about as close as it gets."

"Really?" He raised his eyebrows.

People were always skeptical until they saw it for themselves. I looked down at the table; without looking up, I said, "You're driving a 2017 Toyota Yaris, in the back seat of which is an emergency kit, a T-shirt and a couple of bottles of water. You're wearing some kind of pendant around your neck, a sun, with sixteen points.

"At my presentation yesterday, you were sitting in the back row, on the aisle on the west side of the room. You were wearing a light blue, short-sleeved, button-down shirt and jeans. During the question and answer period you were the one who coughed when the German guy asked his stupid question.

"And you like soccer." His car had a small sticker on the back windshield, and while I couldn't read the lettering, the soccer ball in the middle of it was a dead giveaway.

He chuckled. "You've convinced me." He wrote something in his notebook. "Can you tell me, in your opinion, what stands out to you as the most important traits that lead to successful investigations?"

That was actually a good question. I thought for a moment. "Curiosity, and tenacity. And luck."

He laughed, but I was serious. In Ireland I'd stumbled upon an illegal fuel laundering operation. That had set off a string of events that led to a major drug bust, none of which would have happened if I hadn't decided on the spur of the moment to take a hike in a remote area where the fuel laundering happened to be taking place.

He wrote that down, then asked a few more simple questions about my methods and our process. It was a little weird talking about a "process"; I'd always felt like I was just winging it, doing what felt right, and taking advantage of opportunities. But he seemed to think it was all important, meticulously scribbling everything down.

"Did you have any help solving these crimes?"

"A lot. I couldn't have done anything without my friends."

He shuffled through the pages of his notebook. "You mean, Gideon Spielberg, the man you presented with yesterday? The technologist?"

"Yes. And Sam."

"Sam?"

"Salbatore Hernandez."

"Tell me about them. What do they bring to your work?"

"Gideon's a computer genius. There isn't a system he can't infiltrate, and not a program or network he can't hack. And he can find anything out about anyone.

"Sam, well . . . I'm not particularly good with people" – the understatement of the century – "and when we find ourselves in situations where we need to work with other people, she's the master."

I was relaxed and happy, a rare state for me, and was telling this guy way more than I usually shared with strangers. It must be something about the site, or the surroundings.

Or maybe it was his eyes, or the fact that I hadn't had a date since Brian in Ireland, six months ago. And that wasn't really a date; more of a celebratory booty call. I wasn't exactly swimming in prospects, which was largely my fault. I hated dating.

Loukas closed his book and put away his pen. I was surprised, it hadn't taken that long. Spending an entire day to ask a few questions didn't seem like much bang for his buck, but it was his dime.

"Is there anything else you want to see here?"

"We've pretty much seen it all, haven't we?"

"Yes."

We got up from the table and made our way to the exit.

"Would you like to see a few more sites before we head back into town?"

I was having a great time. He wasn't nearly as obnoxious as most journalists, and great to look at on top of it. "Sure."

We walked to the empty parking lot, then he drove through rolling green hills about a mile away from Knossos to the Spilia Venetian Aqueduct, which I learned was a mere four hundred years old. Thirty minutes from that was the Malia Palace, another Minoan structure built near the coast, essentially a smaller, less crowded version of Knossos. As we walked the sites I noticed for the first time the floral, earthy smell of the countryside.

We took our time, and by the time we got in the car to return to Heraklion the sun was setting.

"Please say you will have dinner with me."

It was late, but Gideon was probably still with Nicholas. Sam was self-sufficient and used to me going off on my own, and I didn't care what Tatiana was doing.

"I'd love to."

He drove us into town, navigating narrow streets lined with shops and restaurants.

"What's with all the blue here?"

"What do you mean?"

"Almost all of the signs are blue and white. And people seem to wear a lot of it."

"Oh. White is good to keep houses cooler. As for the blue, historically people would decorate or trim their houses with what-ever was available. Especially on the islands, blue was the cheapest paint, left over after sailors painted their boats. Now many continue to use blue as it attracts tourists. Also, light blue represents truth, which some people believe repels the Evil Eye."

"The Evil Eye?"

"Yes, the Mati. It is a curse, given from one person to another."

"Does that happen often here? People cursing each other?" I wondered how many times I'd gotten the Evil Eye in my life. Probably a lot.

"No more than any other place, I imagine. It is a very old belief, going back thousands of years."

He stopped the car and parked in front of a taverna that was surrounded on the street by parked motorcycles.

*Peskesi*, Authentic Cretan Cuisine.

The host met us at the door and hugged Loukas, then led us

through several small rooms to a table against an ancient-looking
stone wall, one of many that delineated rooms and alcoves inside
the restaurant. Outside the same walls surrounded a patio with
tables arranged underneath a flower-laden trellis. The aroma of
blossoms joined strong wafts of oregano and thyme, similar to
what we'd experienced in the countryside.

"Do you mind if I order for us?" He didn't bother opening up
the menu.

"No, go for it."

He spoke rapidly in Greek to the host, and they clasped hands
before he left. A waiter returned shortly with a bottle of red wine.

Loukas filled our glasses. "This is a specialty of Crete."

I wasn't a big wine girl, but this was good; very mellow, soft,
even. Shortly after the wine came several plates of appetizers, all
of which I recognized except for some square, lightly browned,
flat pieces of dough.

"What's this?" I said, taking a bite.

"A Cretan specialty, Kalitsounia. This one is made with cheese
and spinach."

I finished it and took another. I hadn't realized how much of
an appetite I'd worked up, and was happy to let him talk while I
stuffed my face.

"This restaurant tells the history of Crete. It is farm to table;
the owners know their food purveyors, everything is sustainable,
and much of what we are going to eat is from their own farm,
only a few kilometers from here."

More food came, this time braised lamb, some kind of vinegared
and smoked pork, and a generous portion of moussaka.

Loukas spoke easily about himself, his history, and the history
of Crete. They appeared intertwined in his mind.

"You really love your country," I said, finishing up the last of
the moussaka.

"It is everything. My family has lived in the same home for
generations."

The waiter cleared the plates, and I thought the meal was over,
but a few moments later he returned with a tray, on which was a
small ceramic carafe and two glasses, alongside a plate of baklava.

Loukas poured a clear liquid from the carafe into our glasses,
then raised it for a toast.

"Yámas."

"Yámas to you."

We drank. The drink was clear and strong, like grappa, but fruitier, and with more of a grape taste. It definitely had a kick.

"Do you like?"

"Yes. What is it?"

"Tsikoudia, Cretan raki. It is our hospitality drink, traditionally served at the end of the meal with baklava, or some other kind of dessert. It is made from the pomace, the grape skins and other things left over after the wine making process."

"I've heard of raki. I thought it was Turkish?"

"Yes, there is Turkish raki. Tsikoudia is Greek."

He refilled my glass and we toasted again.

This might not be an early night, and I was OK with that. I also wondered if we'd be able to postpone our trip to Athens a day or two. It might be worth sticking around to see if Loukas had more free time.

I looked at my watch. It was after eleven, but the owners not only seemed in no hurry to kick us out, they were still seating guests.

"Is this normal, here, for restaurants to stay open this late?"

"Yes, especially this time of year. It—"

*BOOM*

Our table shook, and I heard the tinkling of glassware.

"What the hell was that?"

He shook his head.

Sirens were wailing in the distance, and I pulled out my phone. I felt the blood drain from my face.

"We have to go." I stood up, my napkin falling to the floor.

"What is wrong?"

"Let's go!" I grabbed his arm and ran for the door.

"Where are we going?"

"There's been a bombing at my hotel."

# FIVE

Loukas drove us towards the hotel. We didn't get very far before traffic came to a complete stop.

"Thanks." I leapt out of his car and slammed the door behind me.

I ran several blocks to the hotel, then stopped at a line of red and white police tape that was being set up around the building. One police car sat just outside the tape, along with an ambulance and a firetruck. Distant sirens signaled several more on their way.

Billows of dust and smoke were flowing out the front doors of the hotel, along with people, some by themselves, and some with escorts. Many were wearing pajamas or robes, almost all had dazed looks on their faces.

Two paramedics were leaving the hotel with a stretcher, a sheet completely covering whoever was on it.

I ran around the perimeter of the police tape to the side of the building.

Nothing was left of the walls where our rooms had been, just a gaping hole framed by a few pieces of mangled rebar and crumbling brick.

In Loukas's car on the way over I'd called Sam. It had gone directly to voicemail, as did my calls to Gideon and Tatiana. I tried to tell myself that there was a good chance they weren't in the hotel when the bomb went off, and that they were OK, even though they weren't answering.

Gideon might still be on his date, and Tatiana often didn't answer my calls, the few times that I'd bothered to call her.

But Sam almost always picked up.

I looked back up at the hole where our rooms had been. Nothing in those rooms would be intact, and no way could anyone have survived that blast if they'd been there.

But if they hadn't been in the rooms when the blast went off they could still be in the hotel somewhere. I ran back to the front.

One police officer was standing just outside the tape. When he turned away for a moment I ducked under it and ran to the hotel entrance.

I was a fish going upstream, pushing my way through the mob of people escaping through the lobby. When I managed to get through the door I looked around wildly for signs of my friends.

They weren't in the lobby. But there might be something left of the sixth floor. Maybe they were up there.

I covered my nose and mouth and fought through the crowded space toward the stairwell. I was halfway across when—

*BOOM*

A chunk of ceiling gave way and crashed to the floor in the center of the lobby, just where I had been a moment ago. A woman's leg was caught underneath the piece of ceiling, and she was laying on the ground, trapped and screaming. A cloud of dust curled into the air.

I turned back to the stairwell. A firefighter stood at the opening, helping people out, and preventing others from going up.

*BOOM*

Another piece of the ceiling came down, a few feet away from the first one, narrowly missing a firefighter carrying out a man who looked unconscious. There was more screaming, and the crowd pushed harder to get outside. People were now trampling over each other to get to safety.

The first responders were doing what they could to hurry people through the lobby and outside without killing each other. I used the distraction to push past the firefighter at the door to the stairwell.

I navigated my way through the throng flooding down the stairs, and climbed until I got to the sixth floor.

Unlike the other floors I'd passed, on this one nobody was escaping out to the stairwell.

When I opened it I understood why.

The door to every room in the hallway had been blown off. I took a few steps around the corner to where our set of rooms was.

Most of the section was simply gone. I could see the hotel across the street through the space where the walls had been. Mounds of rubble and glass were strewn around the area. Dust, or maybe smoke, was wafting up from the floor.

No one could have survived this.

Still, I walked down the hallway as far as I could, until I was stopped by a wall of wreckage.

"Sam! Sam! Gideon! *Sam!*" I could barely hear myself over the sirens and the noise from the rescue operation, directly below me on the street.

There wouldn't be much left of anyone in these rooms when the bomb went off. Still, someone might have gotten lucky, and if there was a chance, I had to look. I started to climb over chunks of concrete, pulling aside the ones that looked like they could be covering a person, but were still small enough for me to move.

I heard yelling, and turned around, hopeful.

A firefighter was at the door to the stairwell, gesturing to me. I ignored him, and continued to scramble around the rubble, moving chunks of debris. As I was climbing over a large piece in the center of what had been Sam's room, he came up beside me and grabbed my arm.

"Let me go! My friends are up here."

I unsuccessfully tried to twist out of his grip, and he dragged me to the door and down the stairs, then out of the lobby to the street, the entire time talking to me in a reassuring voice.

He led me to one of the ambulances where a masked paramedic was wrapping a thick piece of gauze around a woman's arm.

"Borís na tin kitáxis, nomízo óti éhi pligothí?"

The paramedic looked up briefly from the wounded woman he was tending to and nodded.

The firefighter let me go, and as soon as he did I ran back towards the hotel entrance. I got past the police tape and was almost to the door before he caught up to me. He grabbed me around the waist and spun me back away from the hotel.

This time he walked me past the ambulance with a firm grip on my upper arm, and handed me over to one of the policemen who was standing next to a patrol car. They had a short conversation, and the fireman's hold on my arm was replaced by the cop's.

"Miss, you must not go into the hotel. It is not safe."

"My friends are in there."

"You must let the firefighters work. They are bringing the people out. Are you injured?" he asked, looking me over.

"No. Look, I saw one of my friends in there. She's unconscious, on the sixth floor, and no one is helping her," I lied, putting on my best innocent face. I wanted someone to get up there and look for them.

"OK. I will notify the firefighters."

While he was looking around for a spare firefighter he got a call on his radio. He flicked the switch on his shoulder and listened.

After a few moments the expression on his face went from helpful to dark. The conversation continued, and as it did his fingers tightened on my arm.

He turned off his radio and started to lead me further away from the hotel.

"Please come with me."

"What the hell are you doing?" I said, standing my ground.

He called to one of his buddies and another uniform joined us. They each took an arm, roughly escorting me to one of their cars. He opened the door and started to push me into the back seat.

I'd been in the back of enough police cars to know that once I got in, I wasn't getting out any time soon.

"No way, buddy." I twisted free and burst past the surprised cops, then ran back towards the hotel.

The first cop yelled something, and the next thing I knew I was tackled around the legs by another one. I slammed into the ground.

The cop that tackled me was joined by another, and they held me while I struggled, wriggling around and swinging my arms. I caught one of them in the side of the face and knocked him back.

Eventually one of them got my hands behind my back and the other one slapped on handcuffs. They pulled me up and dragged me back to the police car, pushing me into the back. The original officer I'd been taken to spoke to them rapidly, and then one of them got in the car and started it.

The cop who'd tackled me got in the passenger seat, and as we drove off he turned around and started yelling in my face. I had no idea what he was saying, but there was no mistaking the rage behind his words.

We hadn't been here three days and already I'd been picked up by the police. A new record for me.

I didn't care. I couldn't help but think that everyone who mattered to me was dead.

\* \* \*

They drove me to the police station, then turned me over to a cop who shoved me into a cell with three other women.

Two of them looked like working girls. The third was big and burly, sporting good-sized biceps replete with tattoos, accessorized with a unibrow and a prominent scar that started below one eye and ran down her cheek to just above her mouth.

"Hey, what about these?" I said to the cop who was closing the door. He growled something and slammed it hard behind him before he left the room.

What the hell. I was the only person in the cell in cuffs.

The burly chick walked over to me and said something. She was my height, but outweighed me by at least fifty pounds.

"I don't speak Greek, Spanky Ham."

She smirked, then roughly ran her hands over and into my pockets, then rooted through my jacket.

Fortunately, or not, the police had taken my wallet and phone. All I had left on me was my lighter, and my Datu knife and lock-picks, the latter two discretely nestled in my boot. But they were no good to me now with my hands cuffed.

After finding nothing of use, she leaned close and started spitting a string of what sounded like insults. She was an inch away from me, putting me in her splash zone.

I'd seen *Caged Heat*, and *Orange is the New Black*, and I knew it was important to establish dominance early. I tilted my head back slightly, and then brought it forward as hard as I could.

Direct hit. There was a crunch, and she yelled and staggered back, blood pouring out of her nose.

"Don't you have a big, fat wedding to go to?" I was not in the mood for screwing around. I needed to get out of here and find out what happened to my friends.

I walked to a corner of the cell and sat down on the floor, glowering while the working girls tended to Spanky Ham's bleeding nose. She was staring daggers at me, and I wondered if she was giving me the Evil Eye. But for now she was keeping her distance. Even with my hands cuffed I wouldn't be an easy mark.

It was late and I was exhausted, but I didn't dare fall asleep. As soon as I did they'd be all over me.

Good luck, ladies. These three would be no match for me. I

leaned back against the wall and gave them my own Evil Eye. I was committed to staying awake.

I woke up several hours later. I was alone in the cell, and bootless.

It could have been worse. I was still intact, as far as I could tell. But goddammit . . . I'd had that boot knife for years. I felt naked without it and my lockpicks. And for some reason, they'd taken my socks, too.

I couldn't tell what time it was, but the sun was coming through the slit of a window that was high above my head. I started to drift off back to sleep when the door to the room opened and an officer walked in. He opened the door to my cell and gestured me out, then led me down a hallway to another room.

An interrogation room by the looks of it. Not my first time in one of those.

I took a seat across from a bald guy in a suit. The uniform closed the door and stood in the corner with his hands behind his back.

The suit started talking to me in Greek, and I shook my head.

"Why the hell are you keeping me here? I need to find out about my friends."

"You are Jesse O'Hara?" He was looking at my driver's license that he'd pulled from my wallet.

I'd left my passport locked in the hopefully fireproof room safe at the hotel.

"Doctor O'Hara."

"Doctor O'Hara. There was a bombing at your hotel tonight."

"No shit, Kojak. Let me go. I need to find my friends. And I need my phone back."

"Your friends?"

"I'm here for the law enforcement conference. I was a presenter, with a friend of mine, and we're traveling with two others. They may have been in the hotel when it was bombed, and I haven't seen them since. I need to call them.

"Do you have my phone? Do you know how many casualties there were? Do you have a list? Where are they taking everyone who—"

He shook his head, cutting me off. "I am not the one answering questions. You are in serious trouble. We have information that someone matching your description was seen running away from the hotel just before the blast."

# SIX

"Hang on . . . you think *I* did this?"

"Someone matching your description was seen running from the hotel shortly before the explosion."

"Yeah, I heard you the first time. It wasn't me. Let me out of here."

He leaned back. "It was late when the bomb went off. Almost everyone at the hotel was in their rooms. If you weren't at the hotel, where were you this evening?"

"I'm not answering any more questions until you take off these handcuffs." I leaned forward in the chair.

He stared at me a moment, then nodded to the uniform in the corner, who walked over and unlocked my cuffs. I rubbed my wrists, raw after having the damn things on all night.

"If you try anything, the handcuffs go back on. Do you understand?"

I nodded.

"So, where were you this evening?"

"I was out seeing the sites, and having dinner."

"Can anyone confirm that?"

"Of course," I realized I didn't have Loukas's number. I'd left him so abruptly that we hadn't had time to exchange information.

"I was with a man. A Greek man, Loukas Papadopoulos. We went to Knossos and some other sites. Then we had dinner at a little restaurant called *Peskesi*."

"Loukas Papadopoulos?" He shook his head at me, like I was a child. "Papadopoulos is the most common surname in Greece."

"He's a journalist, with the *Patris*. He was doing an interview with me."

"Which paper did you say it was?"

"The *Patris*."

He raised one eyebrow, in a "do you think I'm stupid" way.

"Look, he was also at the conference. Just check the registration, and let me out of here."

Kojak got up and left the room, leaving the bailiff from *Night Court* standing in the corner.

An hour later he came back.

"There was a Loukas Papadopoulos at the conference. However he does not work at the *Patris*. They have never heard of him."

"What?"

My mind raced. Loukas had lied about being a reporter. *Dammit.* Why hadn't I checked him out? And why had he lied to me?

Not only that, but somebody had reported that someone looking like me was seen running away from the hotel just before the bomb went off.

I'd only been here three days. No way could anyone have recognized me. Whoever had done it must have been lying, too.

Something strange was going on. And whatever it was, Loukas was in on it. Had he taken me out for the day to get me away from the hotel? And if so, why?

It didn't matter. At the moment my first priority was to get out of here and find Sam and Gideon.

"Call the restaurant. I was there at the time of the bombing, and for at least two hours before that."

"With this non-existent Loukas person?"

It was clear he wasn't going to believe anything I said, nor was he going to check out my story. I stood up to leave.

Bailiff Bull took a few quick steps and grabbed my arm as I reached for the door handle.

"Let go of me."

I twisted my arm away, silently thanking the Krav Maga training I'd been doing for years. I wasn't a black belt, but I at least knew a few solid moves.

"Miss, you are not free to leave."

"It's Doctor, and you can't hold me here. Get out of my way."

Bull tried to grab me again, and I kicked him between the legs. He doubled over, and I brushed past him and pushed through the door.

Kojak was yelling as I ran around the desks and toward the exit. I almost made it to the front door when I was tackled by someone in a suit. He took me to the ground and held me there, while two others came over, one holding me down and the other twisting my arms behind my back and clicking on handcuffs. More tightly this time.

They lifted me up to my feet. Kojak barked something at them, and they frog-marched me back to the cells.

They shoved me back into the cell, locked the door and left the room.

I awoke with a start to voices. The guy I'd racked was standing over me, another uniform next to him.

He said something that I guessed meant "get up." I stood up awkwardly in the cuffs, and each of them grabbed an arm and dragged me out of the cell and back to the interrogation room. I guess breakfast wasn't on the agenda.

Racked guy pushed me into the room and then into a chair. He unlocked one of the cuffs and brought my hands in front of me, then locked them via a chain to an eyebolt on the table. He took another pair of cuffs from his belt and put one around my ankle, and the other around a fixture on the floor.

Happy Fun Time must be over. He took his position in the corner, keeping his distance, never taking his eyes off of me.

I couldn't blame him; I'd nailed him pretty good. His girlfriend would be out of luck for a while.

After a few minutes Kojak joined us. He sat down across from me and stared, without blinking, for several minutes. His eyes were red, he looked like he hadn't slept in a while.

*Fuck you, asshat.* I could stare with the best of them. I matched his glare.

"Miss O'Hara—"

"Doctor O'Hara."

"We now have you not only as a suspect in the bombing of the Celestial Hotel, but you have also assaulted a member of the police force. That alone carries a sentence of eight years.

"I ask you again, where were you at the time of the bombing?"

"I told you, I was at a restaurant. Ask the people at *Peskesi.*"

"They are not open yet, as I suspect you already know. Why did you bomb the hotel?"

*Jesus H.,* this guy was convinced I was the bomber. This was not only highly irritating, but it meant that they were not investigating any other leads.

"I told you, I had nothing to do with the bombing. My friends were in that hotel, why would I want to hurt them? Let me out of here."

He shook his head. "This will not be happening any time soon."

The door opened, and a young uniform walked in and spoke haltingly to Kojak, who turned from me and started yelling at him.

I'd seen enough TV cop shows to know that detectives hated when someone interrupted their interrogations. Leroy Jethro Gibbs would go nuclear. Whoever did the interrupting better have a damn good reason, or face the music.

The young officer stood stoically and withstood Kojak's verbal beating, then patiently spoke again. Kojak stood up, throwing his pen to the floor, and left the room, slamming the door behind him.

I could hear him screaming in the hallway, and then a woman's voice, speaking calmly but firmly.

He came back a few minutes later, his face bright red. He growled something to Racked Guy, who frowned, and then reluctantly unlocked my cuffs.

"Thanks, Princess," I said, rubbing my wrists.

"You are free to go," Kojak said through gritted teeth. He tossed my phone and wallet on the table and left the room.

I didn't know what had happened, but I wasn't going to look a gift centaur in the mouth. I grabbed my stuff and rushed out of the room.

I tried not to run through the lobby and out the front door.

GG was standing on the sidewalk, just outside of the building; Tiny Joan was next to him, both loosely surrounded by his protection squad. He saw me and waved.

"Thanks," I said, pulling out my phone and calling Sam's number. "Look, I need to find my friends. They were at the hotel when the bomb went off, and I haven't—"

"It is OK, Doctor O'Hara. They are all fine."

I started to exhale. "Are you sure?"

"Yes, I am sure. Miss Hernandez, Mr. Spielberg and Miss Alekseeva were not in the hotel when the bomb went off. It was a very lucky thing; the investigators have determined that the epicenter of the bomb was on the sixth floor. Two people were killed, and a number of others were badly injured. We were fortunate it was not worse."

I didn't entirely trust him, and scrolled through my phone.

Yep, over thirty messages from Sam and Gideon since the bombing.

I breathed an enormous sigh of relief. "Just two?" It had looked like a large blast.

"Yes. There was damage all over the hotel, and several rooms were demolished. Thankfully few people were in them at the time."

He gestured towards a black Mercedes on the curb. A man in a suit was waiting next to the open back door.

"Thanks. Uh . . . how did you know I was here?"

"As I mentioned before, my remit includes terrorism. I was informed you had been . . . detained. We have looked at the security footage, and have identified the potential bomber as a man."

"Do you know who it was?"

"We will talk about that later." He nudged Tiny Joan, who balanced a large briefcase on her thigh while she reached into it, and handed me my passport and laptop. "I've collected your effects from the hotel. Most of your things were incinerated, other than what was in the safe. Are you ready to go? Our flight leaves in an hour."

I marveled at the pull of this guy, who could get hotel staff to open a personal safe in the aftermath of a bombing.

Tiny Joan sat in the front, and GG and I got in the back, joining a plump, well-dressed woman. As we were adjusting ourselves to the tight fit, GG said, "Doctor O'Hara, this is Sophia Drakou. She also works for me."

Sophia held out her hand and offered a firm shake. I wasn't sure how old she was; her face looked unlined, like a twenty-year-old's. But her conservative suit and demeanor indicated someone older. "It is very nice to meet you, Doctor O'Hara."

"Likewise." I settled back in the seat, rubbing my wrists as the car pulled out onto the road. "Do we have time to make a stop on the way?"

GG looked down at his watch. "I do not think so, why?"

"I need some boots. And another pair of socks."

He pulled out his phone and spoke into it for a few minutes before hanging up. "It will be taken care of."

Apparently government employees didn't have to observe speed limits, and we made it to the airport quickly. Another black Mercedes met us at the departure doors, where a large man in a suit got out of it with a shopping bag. He handed it to GG, who handed it to me.

Boots and socks, in my size.

*Wow.* I could get used to working for someone who had instant access to anything I needed.

We met Sam, Gideon and Tatiana at the gate. Even though GG had told me they were safe, I felt a wave of relief in seeing them. Sam and Gideon rushed over and we shared a tight group hug.

Tatiana waved at me, and I waved back, the most extreme show of positive emotion between us to date.

"How come you guys weren't in the hotel?" I extricated myself from the group hug. "And," I raised my voice, "why didn't you answer your damn phones?"

Now that I knew they were safe, I was free to be mad about the fact that they'd worried the shit out of me.

"Tatiana and I had a spa appointment," said Sam.

"A spa appointment? At midnight?"

"I have a friend here, she owns a salon."

*Of course she does.*

"She's booked up months in advance, but took care of us after hours. We had our phones turned off. I tried to call you when we were done, but you didn't answer. We were worried, too, you know. Why didn't you call us?"

"The police took my phone."

"The police." She didn't even bother saying it like a question.

"And what about you? What's your excuse for not answering your phone and worrying the hell out of me?" I turned my glare to Gideon, who at least had the decency to blush.

"Never mind." I knew what he was doing. Or, rather, who.

As I was learning with all things related to GG, we had priority boarding. The flight to Athens took less than an hour, giving me enough time to wolf down some snacks and several tiny bottle drinks, both courtesy of Sam, and check my other phone messages.

Three more from my dad. I deleted all three without listening to them.

# SEVEN

We landed at Eleftherios Venizelos Airport and were greeted outside of the controlled area by a driver, who led us to another black Mercedes parked in the no parking zone.

He drove us into Athens via a four-lane divided highway that soon gave way to two-lane roads, then to even narrower roads once we entered the city.

Thirty minutes later the car stopped in front of the Artemis Towers Hotel. It was one of many buildings that bordered a multi-block, well-developed pedestrian area, with planters, trees, stairs and a fountain, all surrounded by hotels, restaurants, cafés, shops, office buildings, and one large, palace-looking structure.

The driver got out and opened the back door near the curb.

"We have booked you all rooms here," said GG. "However, Doctor O'Hara and Mr. Spielberg, would you mind if we go to the office right away?"

"Fine, but Sam's coming, too."

"We do not need anyone but you and Mr. Spielberg."

I wasn't sure we'd be taking this on, but if we did, I wanted Sam in on it from the beginning.

"No dice, GG. She comes or we're done."

He sighed, "As you wish."

"What about Tatiana?" whispered Sam.

"I'm sure she'll be fine on her own."

She stared at me. "Really?"

I never won when she gave me that look. "Tatiana's coming too."

GG said something to the driver, who closed the door and got back in. He drove a few hundred feet to a nondescript, nine-story office building and let us out in front.

Just inside the door was a serious security set-up that filled most of the lobby. We were instructed to empty our pockets, take off our belts and place everything on a slowly moving conveyor that ran underneath a scanner. We each walked through a metal detector, including GG, and then were thoroughly wanded.

Once convinced we weren't there to *Die Hard*, we were allowed to collect our things and took the elevator to the top floor, with a smaller lobby that was dominated by a large desk manned by another security guard.

GG walked briskly past the desk and into a large room filled with cubicles, ringed by doored offices and a few larger conference rooms. In one corner was an entrance to a narrow hallway. Only five other people were visible in the entire space.

"Not much of a group, eh?"

"There are other members of the department on other floors. We keep our staff here small, to minimize the chance for leaks. I can assure you, Doctor O'Hara, each person here is an expert in their field."

He motioned to the group with a small wave of his hand and they ambled over.

"You've met my assistant, and Sophia. This," he said, pointing to a round, balding man with glasses, and a woman who could be his twin except for the balding part, "is Ioannis and Lydia, our communications experts."

"Communications? You mean, like public relations?"

"No . . . eh, they are in charge of internal and, eh, discovered communications. They receive all of the intelligence we collect and disseminate it to the team.

"This –" he pointed to a thin guy with glasses – "is Ilias, he is our technical expert." Ilias stared at us, frowning. "He will be working with Mr. Spielberg."

"And these two –" he pointed to two very large, fit-looking men – "are Dimitrios and Konstantinos. They are our, eh, tactical responders."

Beefcake headbusters. Got it.

Ioannis and Lydia smiled; the muscle hamsters gave barely perceptible head nods, and Ilias continued to scowl at us.

I wondered what his problem was. Maybe he didn't like the fact that GG had felt the need to call in someone else.

GG led us into one of the conference rooms. One wall was all windows, providing a view of the sprawling city, punctuated by the Parthenon on the Acropolis, and the lesser known, but taller

Lycabettus Hill, the highest peak among the seven hills of Athens.

A large table surrounded by cushioned chairs took up the center of the room, and in place of pictures, the walls were covered in computer monitors.

GG closed the door and sat down at the table near a console, where he flipped a switch that lowered the blinds on the glass wall facing the rest of the office. On either side of him sat Sophia and Tiny Joan, the latter setting down her precarious stack of folders with her phone on top of them. I made a mental bet with myself that the phone would be on the floor within five minutes.

He gestured for us to take seats around the table. "I would like to start by thanking you for considering this project. As I mentioned before, what we are asking you to do is to help us address a terrorism issue.

"Before we start, you must know this work is highly confidential. You must agree to not speak of it to anyone, or repeat anything you hear here outside of this building."

Sophia pulled out some papers and pens from her briefcase and placed a set in front of each of us.

"As I said, whether or not you decide to take on this project, you may keep the money. But you must sign these forms before we can proceed, indicating that you will not repeat anything you hear. And please, do not think that because you are from America that you will be able to escape the repercussions of breaking this agreement."

The forms were all in Greek, so I waited for Sam to look them over. She read through them quickly, then nodded, and the four of us signed and handed them back to Sophia.

"Good." GG pushed a few more buttons on the console, and blinds now covered the windows facing outside. The room wasn't dark for long, as the large monitor on the front wall came to life. On it was a map of Greece and surrounding countries. He pulled a small pen out of his pocket and clicked it, shining a point of red light onto the map.

"This is Greece, today."

He ran the laser pointer around the border, then changed the picture. "This was Greece in the thirteenth century. Greater Greece, as it is known, containing large parts of what are now Albania, Bulgaria and Turkey."

He waved his laser around a different region on the map, partially on Greece and then north and east of it. "This is what was previously known as the Ottoman Empire, essentially Greater Turkey. The current administration of Turkey, led by their president, Recep Tayyip Erdoğan, has made it clear its goal is to regain Turkey's influence in the region, and has taken steps toward that end."

"You want us to help you fight the Turks?" This was already starting to sound like way more of a project than I was willing to take on.

"No, no, nothing like that. We have another division that is dealing with the Turkish issue. What we have for you is a little more complicated.

"Have any of you heard of the Golden Dawn?"

We all shook our heads.

"They are a Greek nationalist group, a far-right political party that grew to some prominence a few years ago. They were neo-Nazis, and responsible for a number of murders and hate crimes. They are now defunct, and their leader, Nikolaos Michaloliakos, is in jail. However, we are seeing signs that there is a new group operating, one that is similar."

"Signs?" I asked. "Can you be more specific?"

"I will get to that in a moment. As far as we can tell, this new group has been working for at least five years." He looked to Sophia, who handed him a manila folder.

"This is their leader."

He opened up the folder and pulled out a photograph, pushing it across the table to us. "The man in the center. He calls himself 'Platon.' You would know him as Plato."

I picked up the picture and looked at it closely. Four men, standing on a sidewalk outside of a café. One was taller than the rest, and the only blonde, his wavy hair flowing to his shoulders. He looked like a beefier version of Colin Farrell's Alexander the Great.

"I've seen this guy." The photograph was grainy, but I recognized the face.

"You've seen Platon? I find that highly unlikely. This is the only known photograph of him."

"No, the guy standing next to him. He was at the presentation we gave in Heraklion."

"You recognize him? The room was very crowded. I know because I was there."

"I know. You arrived just after the presentation ended. You came in the south door, with five of your guys, and her." I pointed to Tiny Joan. "The sixth member of your team entered a minute later, carrying a document that he handed to you. She dropped her folders on the floor four times while we were talking."

He smiled. "Yes, yes, of course. I have heard about your amazing memory. It is just . . . eh, a little hard to believe. But it is exactly the kind of thing that will help us. And it makes sense that this man would be at the conference."

"What? Why?"

"Platon's group is amassing money, building contacts in the criminal underworld here and abroad, and starting to commit escalating acts of violence, including possibly the bomb at your hotel. He is also working to develop contacts and friends in law enforcement."

I perked up at the "bomb at your hotel" part. Now that I was over my fear of Sam and Gideon's safety, I was angry. Anything that would get us closer to who set that bomb off would be a good thing. "You think his group bombed the hotel? How do you know that? Did they claim responsibility?"

"Eh . . . no, but we have video of a man fleeing the hotel shortly before the bomb went off."

Sam leaned over, whispering, "If the police mistook you for a man, maybe it's time to update your wardrobe."

"And maybe it's time for you to—"

"Platon's group appears to be more well organized, and more sophisticated, than the Golden Dawn. We believe this is because Platon is much smarter than the previous leader. His network is extensive, and growing; our intelligence has found his name mentioned in greater frequency in our monitored criminal networks, and it appears to be correlated with violent acts that are also increasing in frequency.

"Most importantly, his message is reaching many people in Greece." He turned to Sophia, who handed him another folder, from which he pulled out a stack of papers.

"We conduct national polls every few years. The latest ones show increased feelings of hostility towards the Turks, and more Greeks are embracing extreme nationalistic views."

He handed me the stack and I skimmed through the reports.

"Why would the message from a domestic terrorist resonate with the Greek people?"

"Times are hard here. The EU sanctions, and tighter economic restrictions such as increased age of retirement are, eh, causing stress for the people. Also, Erdoğan is increasingly speaking of Neo-Ottomanism."

"Neo what?"

"Neo-Ottomanism. President Erdoğan is conducting his own parallel efforts to return Turkey to its previous, more influential state, and has been taking an increasingly aggressive stance. Their fighter jets fly over our country regularly, particularly over the island of Chios, which is vulnerable due to its proximity to the Turkish border.

"We in the government are pursuing diplomatic channels to keep Erdoğan contained, and not be reactive to his provocations. Historically we know that most of the people of Greece, and of Turkey, have little enmity for each other, that it has been the governments to stir up trouble."

No shock there, wasn't that always the case?

"However, Platon is activating the Greek people, not waiting for the government to respond to Erdoğan. Some of Platon's actions can be interpreted as to incite both sides to war."

He stared at me darkly. "All-out war, Doctor O'Hara. Do you know what that means?"

# EIGHT

"All-out war? Seriously?" Given the relative sizes of Turkey and Greece, it didn't take a genius to know that Greece would be a massive underdog. "Why would Platon do that? Wouldn't Greece get creamed?"

"Both sides would 'get creamed,' as you say. Our military planners forecast that any weaponized hostilities between our two countries would result in enormous destruction to life and property, but very little changing of borders. However, there is one element that will be far more important than borders.

"The most important, single thing in any war between Greece and Turkey, will be who started it."

"That's a bit childish, isn't it? The 'he started it' argument?"

He shook his head. "No. Who is deemed the aggressor in any war between us will have severe repercussions. Both countries are members of NATO, and the UN. And while Turkey is not yet a member of the European Union, it is a strategic partner to the EU with regards to several elements, such as security, and counter-terrorism. If war happens, the member countries will take the side of whoever they determine is not the aggressor, and be obligated by treaty to actively help the other."

This was starting to make sense. "OK. So if Turkey is seen to attack Greece, Greece gets the help of the other nations. But what does it matter? You know this, so Turkey must know it, too. And presumably you don't have any intention of attacking them."

"I will get to that in a moment."

He'd said this was complicated.

"If there is war between Greece and Turkey, not only will the NATO and EU nations be forced to participate, other, non-EU or NATO nations, will also become involved, leading to a World War One situation in which many countries take sides. History tells us that no one wins a war on that scale. However, if the treaty countries support Greece, it is possible that a war of this nature would result in shrinking Turkish territory.

"This is where Platon comes in. The increased frequency of violent incidents at the border coincides with his organization's growth. They make it appear as if Turkey is setting off bombs, destroying monuments, things of that nature. We have tied his group definitively to several of these incidents that were designed to fan the flames of Greek anger. This, combined with his communications, has been effective: as you can see from the reports, his message is increasingly resonating with people, particularly as Erdoğan is ramping up his own talk of Greater Turkey.

"In short, Platon appears to be committed to making it appear that Turkey has initiated hostilities. For example, one month ago there was a bombing at the Holy Cathedral of Saint Athanasius, in Eastern Macedonia, near the border. The police found evidence leading them to the Turks as the perpetrators. We believe it was not the Turks, but Platon's group who set the bomb. We know the Turks would never bomb a holy site, but to many people it looks as though they did."

"Is smart," said Tatiana. The first words she'd uttered since we'd gotten off of the plane. "False flag operation."

"Exactly." GG smiled at her. "Designed to inflame passions. And it was largely successful. The Holy Cathedral of Saint Athanasius is one of our most beloved churches." His eyes lingered on her.

"What is Platon's 'message,' exactly?" I asked, eager to break up the creepy stare he was giving Tatiana.

"Simply, 'A Greater Greece.' It is what is known as the Megali Idea."

"Megali?"

"The Megali Idea is similar to Neo-Ottomanism. It is an irredentist – eh, looking to past geographic spheres of influence – concept that aims to remake Greece into the larger state it was in ancient times."

"Sounds a lot like the Germans in the forties. Or Putin with Ukraine," Gideon said.

"Yes, but unlike those groups, and Greece's Golden Dawn, Platon's rhetoric is not the hate-filled, racist, misogynist rantings of the undereducated. In fact it is quite all-encompassing, and in stark contrast to Erdoğan's religious purity and homophobia. Platon's brand of nationalism is wholly focused on bringing Greece back to its ancient glory. It is an . . . inclusive kind of nationalism, for lack of a better word, and therefore far more dangerous."

"Greece's 'ancient glory'? What does that mean?"

He clicked back to the current map of Greece, and stood up in front of the monitor.

"It means, among other things, restoring the ancient Greek lands to modern Greece."

He pointed to the northeast corner of Greece again, moving his hand in a small circle between Greece, Turkey and Bulgaria. "This region here, known as Thrace, was once part of ancient Greece."

He moved his hand up to the left. "Greater Greece also included what we now know as Albania. And, obviously, the island of Cyprus. As I am sure you are aware, the island is currently split into Greek and Turkish territory. It is a constant source of conflict.

"To make this happen, this Greater Greece, Platon is growing a network of criminals to carry out his operations. And he has amassed considerable wealth in a short time; we know this as we have identified some of his money-laundering operations. He is also involved in smuggling guns and other weapons into Greece."

"So if you know all of this, why don't you just pick him up?"

He sat down heavily. "We cannot find him. We do not know where he lives, or from where he operates. It is possible he moves from place to place. We would like you and Mr. Spielberg to help us track him down. Once we have his location we will arrest him."

"How are we supposed to do that? Do you have any leads?"

"We know he is on an island."

"That doesn't sound too tough," said Gideon.

"Greece has over six thousand islands," I said. "What else do you know?"

"Platon is moving a large quantity of money around. As I said, we have found a few of his money-laundering operations, but although these involved considerable sums, we believe it is just 'scratching the surface,' as you say. And we have exhausted our own ability to track his finances. His information technology is advanced, too much for us."

He turned to Gideon. "We are hoping you can help us to unravel his financial trail. Finding his laundering operations and closing down his accounts would be a big start to shutting him down, or at least rendering him, eh, less effective."

This was a good call on their part. Gideon was a world-class computer hacker. He worked for the Chicago PD in their Special Investigations Unit, where he tracked down pedophile rings, many of which were global in scope. He had access to a myriad of national and international databases, was a darknet expert, and one of the smartest people I'd ever met. If anyone could follow this guy's finances, it was Gideon.

And it wasn't surprising that a government entity would be lacking in IT acumen. If Greece was anything like the US, lots of their agencies, like our IRS, were still operating via paper.

GG looked worried that Gideon might turn him down, and added hurriedly, "Of course, in addition to the advance I provided, we will pay you for your work. You will each receive ten thousand euros a week."

"I'm happy to help," said Gideon. He probably would have done it for free.

"Thank you." GG tried to hide an exhale. He turned to me.

"In addition to Platon's financial operations, we are starting to see more frequent violent expressions of his work. And we fear he is gearing up for a larger operation, very soon."

"Why?"

"Greece is unfortunately a transit hub for illegal weapons trafficking. The weapons come from Albania, pass through Greece, and move into Turkey, eventually ending up in other countries, such as Syria. Recently we intercepted an arms smuggler carrying a significant amount of weapons.

"After some, eh, interrogation, we learned that his illegal arms had two delivery destinations. One in Turkey, and one here in Greece. The sheer number of weapons was such that one would expect it was destined for delivery to a country. But it was destined for one man. Platon. The shipment also included explosives."

This got my attention. "So, was Platon's group responsible for the hotel bombing?"

GG frowned. "As I said, we are not sure. While it could have been one of his men we saw running from the hotel, it is not clear how that bombing moves Platon's objectives forward. And his group did not claim responsibility for this act, nor was there any indication that it was of Turkish origin."

It made sense to me that GG wanted Gideon to help him. But he still hadn't told me why or how he needed me. "So what do you want me to do?"

"We want you to help us find Platon. We have a number of . . . eh . . . informants, in Athens, in Thrace, and elsewhere around the country. They keep a low profile, as Platon is very well connected. But they are able to provide us information from time to time. As of this moment they are primarily focused on helping us identify the location of his base of operations.

"I would like you to meet with our informants, take in their most recent information, and bring it to me. You would start with our Athens informant, Christos. Just a quick meeting, at the Varvakios Market. It is not far from here."

This made no sense. "Why don't you meet with him? Or get someone from law enforcement to do it?" This guy had to have a slew of consultants, mercenaries, whoever, at his fingertips.

He looked down, embarrassed. "We, eh . . . we are not sure that we can trust everyone in the government."

"Are you saying you've got a mole?"

"At least one. This is why we have trimmed our staff down here to just a small group, and why the other elements of the overall department, who work in this building and in others, know only what they need to know about our specific operations.

"The notion of a Greater Greece resonates with many people. Law enforcement personnel tend towards conservatism, and it is likely there is at least one Platon supporter in our department. Until we can identify who they are, we need to be absolutely certain that whoever helps with this is not connected to Platon's operation, and is not in any way sympathetic to it."

Normally I wouldn't have hesitated to take on this kind of job. I was in Greece, and would be getting paid a lot to just talk to a few guys. But I was a little spooked from the bombing, and I didn't like the idea of putting my friends in danger.

I looked around the table. Gideon looked eager. Sam nodded to me. Tatiana was staring out the window.

"Does Platon's group have a name?"

"They call themselves the Megali Titans."

"As in the 'release the Kraken' Titans? Seriously?"

"Yes."

I was intrigued, and I liked the idea of getting payback on the guy who might have almost killed my friends.

"OK. Sam's going to join me meeting the informants."

"Yes, of course." He looked at Tatiana. "Eh, if you are, eh, amenable, Miss Alekseeva, we do have some things we could use some help with here, related to translations. I assume you speak Russian? If that is, eh, OK." He gave her another smile, which was apparently only reserved for her.

I expected her to give him her habitual snort of contempt, but she nodded. GG started to get up and Sophia grabbed his arm. He leaned down and she whispered something to him. He pursed his lips, looking out the window.

"Eh . . . I feel I should tell you. Platon is extremely intelligent, and cultured, even. But he is ruthless. He has shown that he will let nothing stand in his way. He has, eh . . . had people killed for less than what we are asking you to do."

That would have been nice to know before we accepted. "Like who?"

"Eh, his rivals, and people from the original Golden Dawn."

"How do you know it was him?"

"He leaves his mark."

"His mark?"

"Yes, the Pi symbol."

"Well, we're not part of any group."

Sophia looked at him sternly and GG looked down at the floor. "Yes, eh . . . also, two of our informants were found dead earlier this year, both with Platon's mark on them."

Now he tells us. Still . . .

"You said his group might be behind the hotel bombing?"

"Possibly, yes."

I looked at Sam. "You don't have to go. I'll be careful."

"I know how careful you are. I'm going with you."

The son of a bitch might have tried to take out my friends. And as Gideon had said, I was two for two in tracking down and stopping dirtbags.

"OK, we're in. But I'm going to need a few things."

# NINE

G G had balked initially at my request for a boot knife and a set of lockpicks, but I'd told them that was non-negotiable, and they arrived in a discrete package at the front desk of our hotel the next morning. He'd also fulfilled our order for some clothes and other things, to replace everything we'd lost when our hotel had been bombed.

Gideon was ensconced in the computer room at GG's office, already hard at work doing his thing to track down Platon's finances. Tatiana had trailed off behind him, ostensibly to help GG with his translation job, but still obviously hoping that Gideon would change his mind and decide he was into girls.

Sam and I were at the hotel, heading out the door to go meet with GG's informant.

"You seem excited," I said.

I knew I was; this was turning out to be a sweet deal. I'd wanted to go to the market anyway, and now we were being paid for it.

"The market will be fun. After we meet with Christos we can do some shopping."

The market was less than a mile from the hotel so we walked, the trip taking us through streets lined with shops, most of which sat below several stories of apartments. Scooters, motorcycles and cars were parked packed together on the curbs.

The Varvakios Central Municipal Market, known as Varva to locals, was centered around a large warehouse that took up an entire block in the middle of Athens' vibrant Psiri neighborhood. Outside of the warehouse and across the street were fresh produce and dried bean vendors, along with coffee and tchotchke shops, many sitting against the walls of the market, most of which were covered in graffiti, as was the arched stone entrance.

The inside of the warehouse was divided into a fish side and a meat side. We were early, and decided to wander around before going to the designated spot to meet with Christos.

It was early afternoon, and the heat of the day had already had its effect. The crowds were starting to thin, those in the know visiting earlier before it got too hot. We were on the fish side of the building, and as we entered the smell hit us like a rogue wave.

Rows of finned fish, some whole and some filleted, lined the aisles, as were squid nestled together like alien families, octopi, prawns, and vast arrays of smaller fish that were displayed as wide, gray-black, shiny waves in overflowing wooden boxes.

We walked each row before making our way to the meat side. Whole lambs, some inside cases and some out in the open, hung from hooks, followed by huge displays of tightly packed chickens and pork products, including pig heads and feet, and – disgustingly – testicles. Other aisles displayed case after case of sausages and deer, rabbit, quail, pheasant, and wild boar products.

I hadn't been too put off by any of the smells, or meat products, other than the testicles, until we reached the metal trays stacked with hundreds of red, glossy livers.

"Looks fresh," noted Sam.

"I'd have to be starving to eat that." I swallowed the bile rising in my throat. Years of being force-fed it as a kid had put me off liver in a big way.

Almost everything, including the sickening livers, was sitting out in the hot air. I'd always wondered how long meat could sit out in places like this and not go bad; it must not be an issue, or everyone would be getting sick.

The floor was surprisingly clean, but still sticky and slippery in some places, and we had to be careful as we walked. Many of the meat vendors were in the process of chopping and separating, and I stopped looking at the cases to pay more attention to where I stepped, carefully avoiding the occasional chunk of unidentified flesh that had made its way to the floor.

It would have all been a little overwhelming if we'd been food shopping, but we weren't. Today was a work day.

We were to meet Christos in the meat section. GG had told us to look for a thirty-something-year-old man, wearing a red baseball cap and carrying a blue shopping bag. We'd talk to him, get his update, and then report back to GG.

At five to two we headed to the designated vendor stall located near one of the intersections. I leaned against the case, in which dangled four, skinned lamb carcasses above a selection of large roasts. Next to us, outside the case, were two entire pigs, hanging from thin ropes attached to hooks on poles.

"Have you see him ye—"

*BANG*

The hanging pig closest to Sam started to move back and forth.

"*Down!*" I grabbed her arm and pulled her around the case to a crouch on the floor next to me.

"What's going on?"

"That was a gunshot." I pointed up to the swinging meat. Visible as it swung by was a ragged exit wound on one side: the pig had been a literal meat shield.

A few more individual shots rang out, then a barrage of gunfire, seemingly coming from every direction.

Greece was not a place where people were used to hearing gunfire, and it took a few moments for everyone to realize there was shooting going on. But once glass started breaking, the screaming started, and people stampeded for the exits. Others took cover, crouching like us behind the cases. A few were lying on the ground, not moving, including someone a few feet away from us.

A man in a red baseball cap. On the floor next to him was a blue shopping bag.

I pointed to his body. "Sam, that's Christos."

"If he was the target, why are they still shooting?"

If anything, the flurry of bullets was getting more dense. I didn't know who was shooting, but it was clear that at least some of them were aimed at us. Bullets were beating a staccato rhythm into the case we were crouched behind, and pinging on the floor around us.

It was only a matter of time before we got hit with a ricochet. Or whoever was shooting would realize we weren't shooting back, and get close enough to where they couldn't miss.

"We need to get out of here," I yelled to make myself heard above the gunfire. "We're sitting ducks."

"How are we going to do that?" she yelled back, her eyes wide.

We were pinned down. The shooting was getting louder, and the frequency of bullet strikes on our case was speeding up. We didn't have time to wait for the police.

I poked my head around the case and took a quick look. Just inside one of the entrances was a group of four men. Two guns were pointed in our direction, and the other two were aimed at the far side of the market, from which another set of gunshots were coming.

This was a clusterfuck of epic proportion. *Who the hell were these guys?*

I leaned back behind the case. "There are two groups of shooters. It's hard to say, but I don't think they're all shooting at us. Some of them are shooting at each other."

"Maybe some of them are GG's men?"

"I doubt it. No way would they open up like this in a crowded market." I took another look around the case. "One of the groups is blocking the north exit. There's another exit, but to get to it we have to go in between the shooters. Once we're out on the street we can get away. Are you ready to run?"

She nodded, reaching down to take off her shoes. Heels wouldn't be an asset in this situation.

"Meet me back at the hotel, in the lobby. OK?"

"Not GG's building?"

"No. One, two, *three*."

We jumped out from behind the case, and raced for the cover of another one across the aisle from us. Bullets pinged off of the second case just after we knelt behind it.

From there I led us behind the row of cases. We ran, crouching low, until we hit a wall.

Shouting now accompanied the heavy sound of boots running on cement.

"Stay here. I'll draw their fire, and you can go through to the fish section. Make your way to the entrance where we came in earlier."

I jumped up and ran across the aisle and down a side row. I ran as fast as I could until I hit a T.

The floor was covered here with something extra slippery I didn't want to identify, and when I hit the T, instead of turning the direction I wanted to go I slid forward, crashing into one of the low tables that was stacked high with the beef livers.

I ended up on my stomach and slid across the livers on the table, landing on the floor on the other side. I stood up quickly, slimy black-red goo covering my pants and shirt, and continued to run down the aisle.

I took a quick look behind me. Two of the men were chasing me, both wearing machine guns swinging from straps. They weren't shooting at me, yet, although I could hear distant bullets on the other side of the market.

I sped up, swerving back and forth, and grabbing whatever I could from the displays to throw on the floor and slow them down. Whole chickens, steaks, anything I could get a hold of at full speed landed on the floor behind me. I paused when I got to a skewered meat table, where I grabbed a handful of the wooden skewers and stopped long enough to hurl them at my pursuers.

When I finally made it to the fish section I was once again foiled by a section of slimy floor. This time I landed face-first in a box filled with squid on ice. I dumped the box on the floor behind me as I ran out of the market.

The footsteps behind me were getting closer. I turned up the sidewalk, and as I did I saw the two men coming out of the market.

I skidded to a stop next to a dried bean vendor, and picked up one of the bins of beans and threw it on the ground. The vendor yelled and came around the stall. As he did I grabbed two more and turned them over.

Thousands of dried beans bounced like ball bearings on the sidewalk behind me. I kept running, and when I got to the next corner I turned around just in time to see the gunmen, and a bunch of tourists, flailing around on the ground.

I turned the corner and ran as fast as I could away from the market.

I ran until I couldn't go anymore, then ducked into a narrow side street. I stood with my hands on my knees, trying to catch my breath.

After a few minutes I poked my head out.

I could hear sirens, finally, coming from the direction of the market. But there was no sign of the gunmen. I stepped back out to the main street, and then walked around for an hour to make sure I'd lost them before I went back to our hotel.

Sam was standing inside by one of the lobby windows. I went to her and she moved to hug me, then backed off, her nose wrinkling.

I was covered in slimy liver goo and fish guts, and whatever else had been on the floor in the market. All of it had had a chance to marinate in the afternoon heat for over an hour.

"Where have you been? Are you OK? I thought you'd been shot."

"I'm fine. You?"

"Fine. What happened?"

"I have no idea. GG's informant is dead, but there were two groups of shooters. It makes sense that Platon's guys would have taken out Christos. But I don't know who the other guys were." I had a guess about that, but wasn't ready to share. "GG said he thought he had a mole inside his organization. I guess we can confirm that. But they were definitely shooting at each other, in addition to shooting at us."

Sam looked down at the ground, and said in a small voice, "I don't think they were trying to kill us. They were shooting at me."

"What?"

"When you ran across the aisle, the bullets stopped. They didn't start up again until I ran out. And at the meat case, that first shot . . . it hit the side of the pig that was just next to me."

She was looking a little shell-shocked. I'd learned from our experience in Ireland that getting shot at was one of the few things that broke her normally unflappable demeanor.

And she was right. The guys chasing me could have mown me down any time they wanted to, but they hadn't fired a single shot while they were chasing me.

"We're done with this. GG can fight these guys on his own," I said, angry.

I pulled out my phone and called Gideon. The call went to voicemail.

*Shit.* He was probably still working. You'd think by now he'd make it a point to answer his phone when one of us called him.

"I'm going back to GG's office to get Gideon and Tatiana. And then we're out of here." I was used to putting myself in danger. It was a whole other matter to worry about Sam.

"Do you, uh, want to take a shower first?"

"No." I didn't give a shit about GG's reaction to rotting fish guts and liver slop. "Can you keep trying to get a hold of Gideon, and let him know what happened, and to be ready to leave when I get there? And can you find us a flight out of here?"

"Where to?"

"Home."

"Home? Why don't we go back to Crete?"

"I don't think it's safe." I hadn't told her yet about the gift from Svetlana that had showed up in our hotel. In addition to whatever was going on with GG's Platon group, Svetlana knew we were here, too, and we were sitting ducks.

Not only that, GG was right about one thing: he definitely had a mole in his office. There was no other explanation for how Platon's guys knew that Christos would be there.

Maybe it was even GG himself. But I wasn't interested in finding that out at this point. It was time to leave.

# TEN

When I made it back to the government building I could barely stand waiting for the security checks in the lobby. Fortunately they didn't take long; I smelled like a restaurant dumpster in a heatwave during a garbage strike, and after they rushed me through the metal detector the pat down was unsurprisingly cursory.

I took the elevator to GG's floor and stormed into the main area, ignoring the waving security guy at the desk and going directly to GG's office. The door was closed but I opened it and stepped in. He'd been sitting at his desk, meeting with Sophia and Tiny Joan, but stood up when I walked in.

"'*Simple*,' you said. '*Quick meet*,' you said." I was furious. "What the fuck?"

He put his hands up in a placating gesture of surrender that looked well-practiced.

The security guard ran into the office and GG waved him out.

"I am sorry. I had no idea this would happen."

"Of course not. Because going after big-time crime lords is always *so* safe."

I moved close to him, enjoying his twitching nose and his obvious attempt to breathe through his mouth.

Part of me was mad at myself. I should have known better. At least some of our problems might be Svetlana. It could have been her guys shooting at us in the market, which had nothing to do with GG.

But none of this stopped me from taking the entirety of my anger out on him.

"How the hell did they know we were meeting your informant there? Are you seriously *that* incompetent? You made us sign all of those papers, and it's your group that's been shooting their mouths off. You were right, you do have a mole, you moron."

He wasn't saying anything, or even taking a step back to put distance between himself and my odor. His head was down and he was nodding. Tiny Joan was standing next to his desk, looking down as well.

This was as satisfying as punching wet tissue paper. I took a deep breath and tried to calm down. Sophia had left the room, then returned with a few towels and handed them to me.

"Thanks." It wasn't her fault her boss was an idiot.

"Did you have a chance to get a report from Christos?" GG asked quietly.

"You want a report? Here's your report: Christos is dead. And we're done. Good luck with your little 'who attacked us first' problem. I hope you can avoid a world war."

Sophia gasped, and GG sat down heavily in his chair. He'd heard about the shooting, but it was news to him that Christos was dead.

I'd seen a lot of liars in my life, and his grief and shock looked real. Unless he was the best actor in the universe, which was hard to believe, as I couldn't imagine him being the best at anything, he wasn't the mole.

But at the moment I didn't care. I needed to get out of here, take a shower, and get a drink, not necessarily in that order. "I'm going back to the hotel. Where are Gideon and Tatiana?"

"They are in the computer room. I will get them," said Sophia.

"Never mind. Just send them back to the hotel. And I want a fucking armed escort for them. And then we're flying out of here. And we're keeping your goddamn money."

"Yes, of course," GG mumbled.

I stormed out, leaving a satisfying waft of rotting fish guts in my wake.

When I got back to the hotel Sam was waiting in the lobby bar with a glass of something bubbly in front of her. "Were you able to get a hold of Gideon?"

"No. He was in the computer room with Tatiana. Sophia's letting them know we're leaving, they should be here soon. I need a shower before I do anything else." I looked at her glass with envy.

I took a hurried shower, packed the few things I had and went to the bar for a couple of drinks while Sam checked us out.

An hour later Gideon and Tatiana still hadn't showed, and calls to both went to voicemail.

"Fuck this," I said, finishing my third shot of Redbreast and putting the glass down on the bar. "We're going to get them."

We left our things with the concierge and walked over to the government building. When we got to GG's floor the security guard didn't try to stop me, and I went directly to the computer room where Gideon had been working.

The room was empty.

I went back to GG's office. When he saw me through the glass wall he called for Sophia. Maybe for protection.

"Doctor O'Hara, please come in. We have some information about the incident at the market."

I was calmer now, courtesy of the Redbreast, but nothing he said could get me to stick around. It was one thing for me to get shot at, but Sam had been a pork chop away from getting a bullet to the head.

"Don't get too excited. We're just here to pick up Gideon and Tatiana, and then we're leaving."

He continued as if I hadn't spoken. "Cameras at the scene indicate that Christos was killed by one of Platon's men."

No big surprise there. "Do you know who the other group was?" I was done with this guy, but my curiosity was piqued.

"What other group?"

"There were two groups at the market, and at least one of them was shooting at us."

"It is unlikely that anyone was shooting at you."

*Jesus*, this guy. "Look, I know when people are shooting at me. Your man was already on the ground, dead, and there were still plenty of bullets flying our way. And they chased us out of the damn building."

He stared at me blankly.

*Whatever.* "I don't care one way or the other. I told you, we're done. Getting shot at wasn't part of the deal. I'm only here to pick up Gideon and Tatiana, and then we're out of here."

GG looked puzzled. "Tatiana is with Ioannis. But I thought Gideon was with you."

I was starting to get a bad feeling. I pulled my phone out again to call him. It went to voicemail. "When was the last time you saw him?"

"This morning. He was here early, then he left at lunch. I assumed he was going to join you."

This wasn't like Gideon. He was usually very responsible, and would at least answer his phone, especially after something like the bombing incident.

"He could be on a date," offered Sam.

Given the speed with which he'd hooked up in Heraklion that wasn't outside the realm of possibility.

But I didn't think so.

"Sophia, what was Gideon working on this morning?"

"He was tracing financial transactions. I am not sure of the details."

"Can you unlock his workstation?"

She nodded, and walked us out of GG's office and down to the computer room. On the desk at Gideon's station were several computer monitors. She typed in some passwords and the monitors lit up.

I quickly scanned each one.

"This one is about financial operations in Thrace. But these –" I pointed to the two other monitors – "these are something different. What's 'elaiotriveío'?"

Sophia looked puzzled. "That is an olive oil mill."

"Maybe he was planning our next excursion?" asked Sam.

"No. When Gideon's working, he's working. And he likes to multitask. If he was looking at an olive oil mill, it means something." I peered again at the screen.

"Kladas. Where's that?"

"That is in the Peloponnese, not far from Sparti," said GG. "But it is unlikely that it is anything related to Platon. Kladas is a small village.

"I will ask Ilias to take a look at our video surveillance. We will be able to tell when Gideon left the building." He'd followed us down to the computer room and was standing quietly at the door.

*Fucks sake.* "Why didn't you tell us that in the first place?"

"I did not want to interrupt you."

Sophia rolled her eyes. It took every bit of energy I had not to punch GG in the face.

We went to Ilias' desk and GG asked him to pull up the video surveillance of the front of the building.

He brought it up and fast forwarded.

"Stop. That's him," I said, looking at the time stamp. One thirty.

"Who's that?" I pointed to a man walking next to Gideon.

"I do not know," said GG.

I stared at him. If looks could kill this guy would be lying cold on the ground.

"I know everyone who works here. That man he is with does not work for us."

Gideon was walking next to a guy about his age. The man had short dark hair, jeans and a black T-shirt straining at the start of a paunch.

"A nooner?" asked Sam.

I peered at the monitor. "That guy's not in Gideon's league. Besides, do they look to you like they're on a date?"

"No. But Gideon doesn't look like he's under duress."

"We can't know that. One of the guy's hands is hidden from the camera. He could be holding a gun to him.

"GG, do you have any of that facial recognition shit here?"

"Yes. I can put one of our people on it right away. But it can take some time."

"Bullshit. You're stalling. You want us to stick around and help you. I told you, we're done. As soon as we find Gideon we're leaving."

"Yes, yes, of course. We will do it as fast as possible."

"How long is that?"

"It depends on how quickly the match is found, which is somewhat random, and whether or not the man is in our database. It can range from a few minutes to a few hours."

I didn't like the idea of sitting around while we waited for a result that may or may not be forthcoming. I had to do something.

"If he's really out on a date, where would he go?" I didn't believe Gideon was on a date, but it was possible. He didn't get to travel much, maybe he was taking advantage of it.

"There are men's bars all over Athens, the highest concentration of them is in the Gazi district," said Sophia.

"OK. You guys do your facial recognition shit. In the meantime, Sam and I will check out the bars." After getting shot at and chased, the idea of bar hopping didn't suck.

"I come also," said Tatiana. She'd quietly joined us while we were looking at the video.

"No. Someone needs to stay here with them. To keep them on it." GG looked up and gave another small smile to Tatiana. It disappeared quickly when he saw the look I was giving him.

"You're going to call us as soon as you get a hit on this guy that went with Gideon, won't you?" I said, my voice low.

"Yes, of course."

"All right. C'mon." Sam and I started towards the elevator.

On our way down I felt my phone vibrate in my pocket.

My sister. "Hey Shannon. Everything OK?" She knew I was in Greece, and she never called when I traveled unless something was wrong.

"Hi, yes, everything is fine. Uh, have you heard from Dad lately?"

"No. I mean, yeah. He's called me, like a thousand times."

"And you're not answering him?"

"No, why should I?"

Dad had gotten out of jail two years earlier than he should have, for a sentence that I already thought was at least ten years too light.

I'd run into him briefly at the house months ago when I'd gotten back from Ireland, and since then had steered clear. The son of a bitch had killed my mother, and I wanted nothing to do with him.

"Look, Jesse, I've been spending a lot of time with him lately. He's really changed. And he needs to talk to you. Can't you just give him a chance?"

"I couldn't give fewer fucks about what he needs." There wasn't anything he needed to talk about that would be important to me. "And I'm busy at the moment."

"Could you, at least, give him a call when you have a minute?"

"Did he put you up to this?" Shannon was always trying to help him. She hadn't figured out yet that he was a lost cause.

"He asked me if I could do something. And I'm asking you, as a favor to me, would you just give him a call?"

"If I have a minute." At the very least it might stop his constant nagging me by phone. At this point I'd deleted over fifty messages from him. Whatever it was must be really important to him.

"OK, thanks. How's Greece?"

"Dangerous. Our hotel was bombed, I spent a night in Greek jail, one of my friends is missing, and someone's been shooting at us."

She laughed. "Very funny. Bye Jesse."

# ELEVEN

S am and I took a taxi to the Gazi district. We weren't sure where to go, so had the driver drop us off in the center of the neighborhood near one of the bars.

The Gazi neighborhood was centered near the Technopolis cultural center. Developed around an old gas plant, the industrial steel and brick structure framed contemporary cafés, art installations and outdoor gathering spaces.

We went into the first bar we saw, *Andras*, and took seats at the counter. I showed the bartender a picture of Gideon, one of the three of us I carried around in my wallet. He shook his head, he hadn't seen him.

We went to several more bars, showing the picture at each one, and getting the same answer. No one recognized Gideon. Or, at least, no one admitted they did.

"Is it because they're super careful about potentially outing gay men?" I asked Sam, after the fifth bartender claimed he hadn't seen him.

"It's possible. Maybe we should pretend to be together?"

"OK." We went into three more bars, this time holding hands, and trying our best to look like a couple.

The result was the same. No one remembered seeing Gideon.

"This is hopeless," I said as we came out of the eighth bar.

I was tired, and I'd never been so bummed to be bar hopping in my life.

"And I don't know if you've noticed, but we're being followed."

Sam was smart enough not to look around when I said that. "Who?" she said quietly.

"There's a guy across the street. He looks like he's in his thirties, wearing a dark button-down shirt. He's pretending to look into a sex shop. You can see him through the reflection in this window."

"What should we do?"

"I don't know." I didn't mention that I'd seen him before. He'd been outside of GG's office building when we'd been there earlier.

My phone vibrated, and I was briefly buoyed when I saw it was a call from GG. Maybe he'd found Gideon.

"Yeah? Did you find him?"

"No, eh, but we have a match for the man that left with Gideon from our building today. His name is George Makris. He is a low-level criminal, he has been arrested for various small crimes, nothing serious. He is not a member of Platon's group as far as we know."

"'As far as you know'?" At this point I didn't have a lot of confidence in what he knew. "So he may be with Platon's group? You said they're expanding all the time."

"Yes, it is possible. We do not know everyone in his organization."

I looked at my watch. It was ten p.m. I'd left Gideon ten messages; no matter what he was doing, he would have at least texted me back, especially after the verbal beating I'd given him for not calling me after the bombing.

We had a code. Bye, Sheila meant "Send signs of life." I'd texted that to him hours ago.

I had a very bad feeling now. Gideon wouldn't just walk off with some random dude. He'd been kidnapped. Or worse.

But by who, and why? I hoped to God it wasn't Svetlana.

"Do you know anything else?"

"No, I am sorry. But we are investigating Makris' known associates. I will call you as soon as I know anything else."

"You'd better." *Goddammit.* I hung up on him, and as soon as I did my phone rang. I looked at the number.

My dad again. I started to dismiss the call out of reflex, but stopped. Today had been a complete shitshow, at least I could get this out of the way.

"Hello, Dad. Did you like my card?"

"The anniversary card?" he said, sounding puzzled.

"Yeah. It's the anniversary of the day you killed my mother, you piece of shit. Stop calling me."

"I will. I just need one thing."

"I'm trying to think of a reason why I should care what you need, and I'm struggling to come up with even one."

"Uh, I had a duffle bag in the house. You didn't happen to run across that, did you?"

"Can you describe it?" I knew exactly what it was, but I wanted him to squirm.

"Yes. It was black, with a blue stripe."

"Oh, that. Yeah, I found it."

When he'd gone to prison I'd moved into the house. The first thing I'd done was a general house cleaning, which basically amounted to throwing out everything that belonged to him. I'd found the duffle bag in the garage, in a locked trunk.

I heard him exhale. Then I waited. I wanted him to work for this.

He lasted two seconds. "Where is it?"

"It's under the bed in the guest bedroom."

"Thanks, Jesse. Uh, I hope you're enjoying Greece."

"Whatever, Dad. Bye." I hung up.

I kept the phone in my hand and waited. Two minutes later it rang.

"Hey, did you miss me?"

"The bag's empty."

"Oh yeah?"

"Cut the crap, Jesse, where's the money?"

"Oh, you want to know what happened to what was *in* the bag?" This was fun.

"I mean it. Stop screwing around. This is important."

"You'll be happy to know it's in a safe place."

"Where, goddammit?" He was starting to lose it. I hadn't enjoyed myself this much in a long time.

"I made a very generous donation to Marlena's Place. You know, the women's shelter?"

"Seriously. What did you do with the money?"

"No, really. I have a receipt, and everything."

I waited, hearing him breathe. After several long seconds, he said, "You don't know what you've done."

I hadn't spoken to him in years, other than for the brief interaction we'd had when I'd gotten home from Ireland and found him in my kitchen. I had nothing to say to him.

Long before he'd killed my mother, our house was a dark, anxious place. Night after night the three of us, my mom, Shannon and me, would sit at a dinner table set for four, waiting. Eventually Mom would tell us to start eating, that Dad wasn't coming home tonight.

I remember cold dinners and my sister's relentless questions. When is Dad coming home, where is Dad, ad nauseum, until I wanted to scream. Mom would look at her, doing her best to hide her own pain, and explain that Daddy was working. On the days he did come home he was sullen and uncommunicative.

My mom did everything she could, a herculean effort, really, to raise two girls in the presence of a high-functioning alcoholic. Not to mention the financial problems she had to cope with. We were able to pay the mortgage, as far as I knew, and Mom put food on the table. But we never seemed to have any money for anything other than the basics, even though Dad had a high-paying job.

As a child I'd been sad, as a teenager, depressed. Then I got angry. Which, as it turned out, was a good thing, as it was the impetus behind my drive to get out of the house and go to college as soon as possible. Shortly before I was to leave my dad had decided to take my mom on a trip with him, some kind of celebration.

He was loaded when they left, and more loaded on the way home from the bar when he crashed the car, killing the occupant of the other car, and my mother. He'd walked away without a scratch.

I'd testified against him at his trial, voluntarily offering my testimony to the prosecution about his heavy drinking and his numerous close calls with the police. He'd been driving drunk for years, often with us in the car, and got pulled over on a regular basis. But he was handsome, well dressed and well spoken, so they'd let him go. Every damn time.

It had been marginally gratifying to see him get the maximum sentence, eighteen years for vehicular manslaughter, even though it was probably less about killing my mom, and more for killing the daughter of a state senator who was in the other car.

Since his incarceration I'd gone to every one of his parole hearings, arguing against early release. They'd finally let him out last year. My sister was eager to help him, she thought he was rehabilitated, and held out hope that now he was ready to be a father. But for me, no amount of time in jail was enough to make up for what he'd done to our family.

"Why don't you enlighten me? Is it something that's going to make your life difficult? If so I'd love to hear the details."

He hung up.

My work here was done. At least one thing had gone well today.

"All good?" asked Sam.

"Yeah. Dad stuff."

She knew what "Dad stuff" meant. "You know, all of the anger you're harboring against your dad, it's hurting you more than it is him."

"I'm enjoying my anger right now, if you don't mind. He finally figured out that I found his money, and that I gave it away. Apparently it's going to cause him some big problems. That was worth the wait."

I had no idea where he'd gotten a bag full of money. I speculated he'd been pulling it out of the family savings; that would explain why we always seemed strapped for things like clothes, or food. Regardless, I didn't care. The fact that it was his, and I'd made it go away, was enough.

I let myself savor the moment before looking around surreptitiously. "I think he's gone."

"The guy who was following us?"

"Yeah. Let's go back to the hotel."

She didn't argue with that. At this point neither one of us believed that Gideon was in a bar having a great time.

We took a cab back. When we walked into the lobby the concierge stopped us.

"Doctor O'Hara?"

"Yes?"

He pulled a cream-colored envelope from under his podium and handed it to me.

"This came for you."

"From whom?"

He shrugged. "A messenger."

I opened it. It was a fancy-looking card, covered in Greek writing. I gave it to Sam.

"It says you're invited to an olive oil tasting. At Spartopoulos."

"Let me guess, it's owned by your brother," I said to the concierge, crumpling up the paper and handing it back to him. "Thanks, but no thanks."

He took the invitation and uncrumpled it, then gave it back to me. "Eh, excuse me. This is an invitation. For tomorrow, to a private tasting at Spartopoulos."

"Yeah, so?"

"That is a, eh . . . very exclusive experience. Not many are afforded the opportunity; Spartopoulos Mill is not one of the, eh, oleotourism sites. They do not normally offer tastings. I assure you, it is not run by my brother. He owns a restaurant in the city. Which is also quite nice, if you are looking for an authentic—"

"We're not, thanks," I said, taking the invitation back from him.

If this was a scam, whoever was doing it had spent a fair amount on card stock and printing.

Spartopoulos. "Where is this place?" I asked.

"Outside the village of Kladas. In the Peloponnese."

# TWELVE

"Do you think this is a coincidence?" asked Sam. "That the invitation's from a place near the town that Gideon was looking into?"

She and I were in GG's Mercedes, on Highway 8, driving out of Athens. I'd asked to borrow his car with no explanation of why we needed it, and he'd fallen over himself to give it to me. At this point he'd have been our personal chauffeur if I'd asked him to.

Over my objection Sam had asked Tatiana to join us. Fortunately she'd turned us down.

"I stay here. I help look for Gideon."

I didn't care what she did, as long as she didn't tell GG where we were going. Even though I was pretty sure he wasn't the mole, I didn't trust him, or anyone else in his group, to keep a secret. And I didn't want Svetlana or Platon knowing where we were going, even though it was very possible that one of them was responsible for the invitation.

I wasn't the only one who was happy Tatiana was sticking around Athens. GG was smitten, regularly finding excuses to stand next to her, and to touch her arm, or shoulder. I felt a perverse pleasure knowing that at some point she'd lose it and let him have it.

I hoped I'd be there to see it. I was furious with him for losing Gideon, and for leading us into a "quick and simple" operation that had almost gotten my best friend killed.

"You know how I feel about coincidences. Gideon was looking into something that had to do with Kladas. And now this invitation shows up? No. No way it's a coincidence."

"If he did find something over there, that means this could be some kind of trap."

"I know. But we don't have a choice, do we? We don't have any other leads, and I'm not counting on GG to find anything."

There was no real argument to that, and we drove in silence for almost an hour until she asked me to pull off the road.

"Why?"

"The invitation is for three o'clock, and we're a little early. There's something I want to see. It will only take a few minutes."

Per her directions I pulled the car off into a parking strip next to the road, then I followed her to a small building, the Isthmus Tourist Center.

"We stopped for a tourist center?"

"No." She kept walking past the building to an overlook platform. I joined her at the railing.

"Holy shit," I said, looking down.

The platform was on the edge of a cliff that led almost straight down several hundred feet.

Below us was a narrow channel, running between the side we were on, and a similarly sheer rockface on the other. A suspension bridge nearby spanned the width of the chasm, barely a hundred feet across. The wind whipped at us as we leaned against the railing.

"This is the Corinth Canal. It separates the Peloponnese from the Greek mainland. It's an artificial canal they built in the nineteenth century, that's still used for shipping traffic. It's hard to believe they had the technology for this over a hundred years ago."

The fact that the canal was built over a century ago was not a plus in my book. I looked at the unassuming suspension bridge over which we would be driving. It was just wide enough for two cars and a pedestrian walkway.

"Do you think it's safe?" I wasn't a fan of heights, and forced myself to stop looking down.

"Of course. They closed it for a while a few years ago, because of landslides. This is an active seismic zone." She saw the alarmed look on my face, and added quickly, "But it's been shored up, and they reopened it last year."

I looked to the left and right, and then across the channel. "It doesn't look like they do a whole lot to prevent people from going over the side." There were a few barriers along the edge of the cliffs, but in many places open grassy meadows led right up to the chasm.

"No. That might be why it's a popular suicide spot. There's a few every year."

This was getting better and better. I stepped back from the

railing and went to the car. A few minutes later Sam joined me. I held my breath as I drove over the bridge.

We continued along windy roads, through small hills dotted with low shrubs and gnarled olive trees, broken up every now and then by small towns. Ninety minutes later we drove into Kladas, which was little more than a few blocks with houses. After another few miles I turned on to a small, one-lane road. In a couple of hundred yards we found the entrance to Spartopoulos Mill.

A "Welcome to Spartopoulos" sign in Greek and in English stood at the edge of a long dirt road. Underneath the sign was a handwritten placard: "Closed Today for a Private Party."

"You think we're the 'Private Party'?" asked Sam.

"Only one way to find out." I drove down the dirt road to where it ended in a small gravel parking lot.

The lot was empty. A small house with a sign on it and two large warehouses were the only structures, other than a covered patio next to the parking lot that was adorned with an array of fresh flowers.

"Hello?" I yelled.

It was silent, other than a variety of birdsongs, and the high-pitched drone of cicadas.

Sam looked at her phone. "We're a few minutes early. Try the office?"

We walked across the parking lot to the house. I knocked on the door.

I waited a moment, then tried again.

There was no answer. "I've got a bad feeling about this." I walked to the warehouse and tried the door.

It was unlocked. I opened the door and peeked in.

The warehouse was full of large pieces of machinery, some stretching to the high ceiling. Scattered on and around the equipment closest to the door were piles of tree branches, most with leaves and olives intact. In the center of the building was some kind of electrical switchboard. Empty pallets were stacked against the walls near the door. Lining the walls were a number of large metal vats.

Across from us on the other side was a small door.

"Let's try the other door. Maybe someone is out back."

As we walked across the space I heard a car engine. I went back to the front door and cracked it open.

A black SUV was rolling down the drive. It came to a stop behind our car. On purpose or by accident, it was blocking our exit.

"We've got company."

The doors in the SUV opened up, and four men emptied out at once, all with guns in their hands.

"Something tells me they're not here for the tasting."

One of them yelled something out in Greek.

"What did he say?"

"He wants us to come out."

"I'm not in the mood to take orders from strangers. What about you?"

"No. But what option do we have? Maybe we should talk to them. They might have Gideon."

"I don't think so. That guy in the front? He was in the Athens Market. He's one of the guys who was shooting at us."

I peeked out the door again, and saw the men striding to the warehouse.

"C'mon. Let's try the other door."

We ran back to the far side of the building. On the way I stopped next to the switchboard.

I turned every switch and button I could to the "on" positions, and immediately heard the low hum of machinery.

Near the front door a pile of branches with leaves and olives was pulled through a large, square opening on a metal box structure. Shortly thereafter a less twiggy version of the olives came out of the other side, and then traveled up a conveyor belt to another machine that separated the leaves from the branches. From there the branches were moved by conveyor to a few more separators, and eventually to a square metal platform with holes.

Each step removed more and more of the non-olive elements, until the olives themselves, sans twigs or leaves, were fed into an open vat that mashed them up, apparently pits and all, into a gray paste, that ran out of the machine in a thin ribbon, and flowed into another one. From that machine emerged a stream of translucent green liquid, which was fed into tubes that emptied into one of the large vats.

"You didn't by any chance bring your gun with you, did you?"

Sam opened her purse and took it out.

"I threw it in after our experience in the market. But I don't know what you think I'm going to be able to do with this against four men with submachine guns."

We knelt down behind one of the separators and waited. It didn't take long before the door to the parking lot opened. Three of the men walked in, their guns in a ready position.

"See those big vats?" I whispered. "Think you can hit the one on the far end?"

She fired one shot from the Beretta and it pinged off of the vat. The men ducked down at the gunshot.

"Try it again. Hit it a few times, in the same place."

She fired at the vat, emptying her clip. We were rewarded with a stream of green flowing from the vat onto the floor.

"Can you get the others?"

She put in a fresh clip and proceeded to poke holes in each of the four vats. Soon green oil covered the floor.

"Nice. Let's go."

I leaned over and opened the back door. We ran through it into a narrow walkway. Yelling and a barrage of gunshots followed us out.

The short walkway led to a door to the other warehouse. *Locked.*

I pulled out my lockpicks and opened it quickly, mentally thanking the younger me for her intolerance of locked doors, and the hundreds of hours of practice breaking into rooms that my parents had deemed off limits.

Pipes from the first warehouse ran across the ceiling, branching into smaller ones that led into more vats, under each of which were conveyors with green glass bottles placed below filling spouts.

Against the walls were tables with lab equipment and buckets, some half filled with oil. The whole place smelled like freshly mowed grass.

On the far side of the building was another door. We ran to it and I threw it open. I took one step before I slammed into the fourth guy from the SUV.

I immediately turned around and pushed Sam back into the building, half expecting a bullet in the back. I closed the door behind us.

"Why didn't he shoot us?"

"I don't know," I said. "I ran into him hard. I think he was surprised."

"Now what?"

Just then the door to the walkway opened, and the three other men, scowling and covered in oil, walked into our warehouse.

# THIRTEEN

We were kneeling down behind one of the tables, listening to the men yelling at us.

"What're they saying?"

"For us to come out, for me to throw my gun down, and they won't hurt us."

"Do you believe them?"

"I don't know, maybe. That other guy, the one who's by himself outside of this door? He didn't shoot at us."

"To be more accurate, he didn't shoot at me," I said.

"What?"

"The bullets, in the main warehouse? They were all on your side of the machine. Nothing even came close to me. These guys, whoever they are, are shooting at you. Just like the ones in the market. They've been shooting at you all along."

She paled. "Why would anyone shoot at me? At you I can understand. And by the way, when we get out of this, I'm going to kill you."

I looked around the warehouse. "I have an idea."

"Does it involve something impractical and dangerous?"

"Yes." I explained what I wanted to do.

"If you're wrong, we're both dead."

"If that's the case, we're both dead, anyway. Do you have a better idea?"

She frowned, then shook her head.

"Once we're clear of the guy outside, stay in front of me, and run as fast as you can to the car."

She nodded.

I took a deep breath. "Ready?"

"As ready as I'll ever be."

I reached up to the table above us and grabbed one of the buckets of olive oil. I turned it upside down, dumping the oil on my head, then grabbed another bucket and did it again.

A few bullets rang out from the other side of the warehouse, pinging the walls near Sam.

"Let's go," I said, standing up. I kept my body between Sam and the three men. The bullets stopped.

I unlocked the door and opened it a sliver. "Tell him that we're giving up and coming out, and not to shoot us."

She leaned forward and repeated what I'd said in Greek. I pushed the door completely open and ran through it, ramming into the guy on the other side.

I took him by surprise, again, and we both fell to the ground. He recovered quickly, and stood up and grabbed my arm.

"Sam, go!"

She ran out of the building, then around me toward the car. I pulled away from the guy, who was trying to hold onto me and his gun at the same time. My well-oiled arm easily slipped out of his grasp and I followed Sam to the car, making a point to keep myself between him and her. As I ran I waited for a bullet to come that would slam into my back.

It never came. Sam jumped in and started the car, drove it forward into the patio, then backed up into the field. When she got back on the gravel in front of the SUV she slowed down long enough for me to open one of the back doors and throw myself inside. Once I was in she hit the gas and peeled out.

Gravel kicked up behind us as we sped to the main road that went back to the town. The tires squealed as Sam hit the turn at full speed.

I could hear the sound of the SUV starting up behind us. I looked out the back to see it pop out from the gravel and join us on the main road.

Two of the men were leaning out of the windows with their guns. Bullets were pinging into the back of our car.

"I thought you said they wouldn't shoot at you?"

"They're not. The shots are all coming in low. They're shooting at the tires."

It was smart. If they blew out one of our tires it would all be over.

I didn't need to tell Sam that. She floored it and we sped away.

We drove through Kladas as fast as practical, the SUV close behind us. They stopped shooting while we were in the town, but once we were back among olive groves, the bullets started up again.

Fortunately GG's car was a good one, and Sam was a great driver. Several times I thought we'd lost them. But each time we hit a straightaway I could see them behind us. They weren't gaining, but we weren't losing them, either.

I pulled out my phone and called GG.

"It's Jesse. Listen, we're, uh, in a little bit of trouble. We need your help."

"What kind of trouble? Where are you?"

"I'm not sure. Somewhere between Kladas and the canal."

Bullets whizzed by, some pinging against the back of the car.

"Are those bullets? Is someone shooting at you?"

"Yes. Can you send someone to help us? Are there any local police nearby?"

There was a long pause. Finally he said, "There is a police station in Tripoli."

"Hang on." I scrolled through my phone. Tripoli was less than twenty miles away. "That's great!"

"Eh, Doctor O'Hara, I am not sure that it is a good idea, to go to the police there."

"What do you mean?"

"It is possible that it is Platon's men who are shooting at you. And as I mentioned before, we, eh . . . we know that there are members of the law enforcement community who are sympathetic to his cause. I am not sure that you can be safe there. I recommend that you come back to Athens to our office."

"I don't know if we can make it that far. Can't you send a helicopter, or something?"

"I do not have one that can be in the Peloponnese soon enough."

*Shit.* I hung up on him.

"What's the matter?" asked Sam.

"He's no help, and he doesn't think we can trust the police out here, in case the guys who are shooting at us are Platon's guys."

"Do you think they're Platon's guys?"

"I don't know." I didn't want to bring up Svetlana. "Who knows? Maybe GG's in on it too."

"You don't really believe that, do you?"

"No. But in any case, he can't send anyone for us who would get here in time to help. He recommends we drive to Athens."

She nodded grimly, her eyes focused on the road.

"Here are our options," I said, climbing into the front seat and securing my seat belt, no small feat as I was covered in oil, and everything I touched slipped out of my hands. I tried to grab the hand rest to no effect while Sam careened around a curve. "One: give up."

"Never an option."

"Agreed. Two: try to outrun them, and not get our tires shot out before we make it to Athens." As if on cue, a flurry of bullets banged into the back of the car.

"I'm not feeling particularly optimistic about that one, either."

I scrolled through my phone. "In about a mile there's going to be a long straightaway. When we hit that, drive as fast as you can, and try to get as much distance from them as possible. Then we're going to turn off."

"OK."

For some reason she still trusted my judgment, at least in life-threatening situations. Even though I was usually responsible for getting us into them.

When we hit the straightaway she floored it, and soon the speedometer read over 160 kilometers per hour. A hundred miles an hour, and she was still speeding up. I tightened my seat belt.

"OK. Tripoli's in ten miles. Turn off into the city, and find the first side street you can that blocks the view of our car from the main road. You know, something between buildings."

She continued to speed down the road, weaving around other cars that seemed to be standing still, trees, fields and the occasional small town passing by in a blur. We saw signs for Tripoli, and when we came to the exit she hit the brakes just hard enough to make the turn, tires skidding. I wondered how much rubber was left on them at this point.

She tapped the brakes and we slowed, then drove down the main street until she turned at a side street with buildings that hid us from the main road.

We waited, the car idling.

"Did we lose them?" she asked.

"I don't know. Can I have your scarf?"

"Why do you need my scarf?"

"Can you just give it to me?"

"It's a strange time to make a new fashion statement, but, OK."

She unwound the brightly colored scarf from around her neck and handed it to me.

"Thanks. Now you need to get out."

"What? No," she said, realizing what I was planning. "I'm not getting out."

"It's you they're shooting at. Not me."

She turned away from me and looked out the window.

"Please, just trust me. Get out. Find a restaurant or hotel, go inside, and call GG to send you transportation back to Athens. I'll meet you back at his office."

"What are you going to do?"

"What I always do." In reality I only had a vague idea of what I wanted to do. But I needed to get her out of harm's way.

"I'm not leaving." She crossed her arms and sat back in the seat. "We can both get out here and find help. They're not going to shoot at us in broad daylight."

"They've already done that."

She had her "I'm going to get my way," face on. Rarely used, and never defeated.

"Fine. I'll join you." I leaned over and turned off the car.

She nodded and opened the door. As she put her foot on the ground I leaned over and shoved her out, then grabbed her door and shut it. I hit the locks and turned the car back on.

She tried to open the door, and when she couldn't get it open, pounded on the window. I mouthed, "I'm sorry" at her as I slid over behind the wheel and took off back toward the main road. As I drove I wrapped her scarf around my neck.

When I got back onto the main road to Athens I drove for another ten minutes, not at Sam's speed, but at a good clip. There was no sign of the black SUV.

Maybe I was in the clear. I started to relax.

Too soon. Up ahead a car was pulled over on the shoulder. A black SUV.

I passed it, then watched through the rear-view mirror as it pulled back out onto the road behind me.

I hit the gas and drove as fast as I could, but I wasn't the driver that Sam was. They caught up quickly, and once again bullets were slamming into the car.

It was only a matter of time before they'd hit one of my tires.

I'd spin out, or crash, and if I was alive they'd either finish it, or take me to . . . I didn't know where, but I knew I didn't want to go there.

If I could make it to the canal and closer to Athens, they'd have to stop shooting. But if they were Svetlana's guys, it wouldn't matter. Even if they didn't manage to stop me before I got back to civilization, as long as we were alive they were never going to stop coming after us.

*As long as we were alive . . .*

I sped up, going as fast as I dared, until I saw what I was looking for. Signs for the canal. Seventy kilometers away.

The next twenty minutes seemed to take forever, every bullet the one that could blow one of my tires. I took the curves as fast as I dared, every now and then passing another car that was going half my speed.

As I approached the canal I slowed down just enough to turn off the main highway and head north. I hit a T and turned right, going a few hundred feet on the smaller road Sam and I had taken earlier.

I took the last turn-off before the chasm as fast as I dared, then slowed, driving past a few shops and houses as the road wound towards the canal and eventually parallel to it. The only thing separating me and the edge of the cliff now was a hundred feet of grassy meadow.

I veered off the road into the meadow, over a small hill and behind a copse of trees. Once the trees were between me and the road I stopped and turned off the car.

It was quiet, the only sound my own breathing. A minute later I heard the SUV. Peering through the trees I saw it idling on the road near where I'd turned off.

I started up the car and pushed the gas pedal to the floor, driving diagonally towards the canal in the direction of the bridge that Sam and I had crossed earlier.

I drove crazily, the car weaving back and forth, and when I was twenty feet or so away from the cliff and next to a set of bushes I opened the door.

I flung myself out, rolling behind the bushes. The empty car slowed as it approached the edge, but made it there with more than enough momentum for it to fly over the cliff. I watched it glide down into the chasm underneath the suspension bridge. A few seconds later there was a splash.

The black SUV slowed, and then stopped in the middle of the meadow.

It sat there, idling, for a long moment. Then it backed up and returned to the road. The sound of its engine faded, and eventually disappeared.

# FOURTEEN

I lay in the grass for a long time before I felt safe enough to get up.

My phone was gone. I searched for it in the tall grass but gave up after a few minutes. Walking around in the meadow was viewable from the road, and I felt conspicuous being out here. Small crowds of people were gathering on the bridge and on both sides of the chasm, looking down at where the car had crashed.

I walked back to the side street and up to the door of a café that was next to the main road. It was closed.

There were a few other restaurants and shops across the street that looked open, but I couldn't be sure that the bad guys in the SUV wouldn't go there. My best bet was to get across the bridge, to the tourist center and the larger crowds.

I wasn't thrilled about going over the bridge on foot, recalling how it had swayed underneath us when we'd driven over it before. But it wasn't like I had much choice.

It took me thirty seconds to get across, during which I studiously stared straight ahead. The tourist center parking lot was full, crowds of people were on or near the platform, looking down to the crashed car.

I walked into the center, a soft chime above the door announcing my arrival.

The place was empty, except for a skinny, short-haired man behind the counter who was sorting through some papers.

He looked up as I approached. "Can I help you?"

"Thanks, yeah," I said, pulling a leaf out of my hair. "Do you have a phone?"

"Yes, we do," he said, smiling.

I waited for what felt like minutes.

"Well, may I use it, please?"

"Oh, no. I am sorry, we do not have phones here for public use. However there is a very good signal, you may use your own phone."

"If I could use my own phone, I wouldn't need to be asking to use yours now, would I?" I said, grimacing back at him in the best semblance of a smile I could muster.

I wished Sam were here. She'd be able to get this guy's phone. And probably his car, too.

"Look, it's a little bit of an emergency." I looked behind me out the window.

"Would you like me to call a doctor?"

"No, it's not that kind of emergency."

"Oh. Well then." He went back to shuffling through his papers.

I put my hand down on his papers, smacking the counter a little harder than I'd intended. "I really need to use a phone. Yours would work," I said, noting the phone sticking out of his pocket.

I was doing everything I could to keep from going nuclear on this guy, but he was trying my nerves, which were already shot from almost being gunned down, not to mention being forced to cross a damn suicide bridge.

"I am sorry, miss. My phone is not for public use." He slipped his now oil- and dirt-smeared papers from underneath my hand.

"Look, Zorba, I've been chased, shot at, and forced to jump out of a moving car. Guys with guns are after me, and if I don't get to a phone they may find me in here. I don't think you want that."

The door chime went off again as a family of three walked in. They took one look at me and went back out.

"This sounds like a matter for the authorities." He reached under the counter and came up with a phone, on which he punched in a few numbers. He made a point of dramatically putting the phone up to his ear.

"Fine." I crossed my arms across my chest. If he thought I was going to leave because he was threatening to call the police he had another thing coming. "What do you think other tourists are going to do when they see police cars roll up in front of this place?"

He'd finished his call and put the phone away. "They will think this is an exciting tourist attraction, and have great stories to tell their friends."

*Arghhh.* I didn't know if it would be a good idea to wait for the police, or not. If what GG had said was true, about there being some people in law enforcement who were sympathetic to Platon, they might turn me over to whoever had been shooting at us.

On the other hand, if it had been Svetlana's guys who set the ambush at the olive oil place, police would be helpful.

This was driving me nuts. At this point all I wanted to do was shut myself in a bar for eight hours and drink myself into oblivion.

I decided to try my luck with the police. After all, there was no way I was going to walk back to Athens. I leaned against the counter.

"Would you mind waiting outside?"

"I told you, there are guys after me with guns. I'm not going outside." I waited, looking out onto the parking lot.

It was an hour before a police car showed up. A uniformed officer got out and walked into the center. He spoke to Officious Counter Guy for a few minutes, occasionally looking over his shoulder at me. When they were done talking he turned to me and said, "Would you follow me please, miss," opening the front door and gesturing at me to go through.

I crossed my arms. "I'm not going anywhere until I get a phone."

He sighed, then reached for his handcuffs.

"All right, all right," I said, walking through the door. I'd had enough handcuffs for one trip.

When we got outside I expected him to drive away, but he escorted me to his car and opened the back door, gesturing me in.

The last thing I needed was to go to a police station, GG's warning about law enforcement in the forefront of my brain.

"Look, officer, I just need to make a phone call."

"You will be afforded a phone call at the station. Please, get in the car."

"I'm working with your government. If you just call my contact you can confirm that."

"Who are you working with?"

*Shit.* What was GG's name? He'd said it once, and I hadn't caught all of it. I would have remembered it if I'd seen it written down, but my near perfect memory didn't include auditory recall.

Sophia. Sophia . . . Her name had fewer than a hundred letters. "He works in the Ministry of Citizen Protection. He's high up. He works with Sophia Drakou."

"If I can confirm your story you can leave. But in the meantime, you must get into the car."

I looked down at myself then back at him. "Do you really want me in your car?"

All of the dirt I'd collected from rolling around in the meadow was still clinging to me, courtesy of the olive oil I'd covered myself with at the mill. A lot of the dirt was in oily clumps, some of which were falling off of me as I walked.

He looked down at my clothes, and then past me to the tourist center, the path in between delineated by a trail of brown clods.

"Eh . . . you may stay out of the car if you sit there, and don't move." He pointed to the curb.

I sat down and waited for what seemed like an eternity, while he sat in the front seat of his car with the door open, listening to his radio.

Finally he stood up and walked over to me.

"I am told you are working with the government. So I will not arrest you. Please do not go back to the tourist center." He got back in his car and started to close the door.

"Hey, wait a minute! Is anyone coming to get me?"

"They know you are here," he said non-committedly. He closed the door and drove away.

I sat on the curb for another two hours before a black Mercedes pulled up. I recognized GG's driver and got in. I was starting to see a pattern here: Mercedes for the good guys, SUVs for the bad guys. Nice to know.

The sun was setting by the time I made it back to Athens. I had the driver drop me off at GG's building.

Even though I was filthy, angry, and tired, I could still appreciate the nighttime view of Athens from GG's office, which was even more spectacular than during the day. Lights across the vast metropolis were punctuated at a higher level by those from the Parthenon, lit up from the inside, like a live thing watching over the city. Lycabettus Hill was remarkable in its own right; while lacking a Parthenon at the top, the hill displayed bursts of light at the base that were separated from smaller ones at the top by a mysterious band of dark space.

I wasn't surprised GG was in his office at this hour; he didn't seem like a guy with much of a social life. With him were Tatiana, Sophia, Tiny Joan, and Sam, who was staring daggers at me.

GG looked me up and down, maybe thinking that at least this time I didn't smell like rotting fish. Tiny Joan mirrored him, her glasses bobbing on her face.

"Are you OK?" he asked.

"I'm fine. Have you found out anything about Gideon?"

"No. There is nothing."

I turned to Sophia, and she looked at me sadly. "I am sorry, Doctor O'Hara. We cannot find any trace of him. If he is with Platon, well, as you know, we have not been able to find him on our own. We are continuing to look."

I held out zero hope that would amount to anything. "We're going to need to find a new hotel," I said to GG.

He put his hands up in a placating gesture. I doubted anyone would ever make a statue of the guy, but if they did, he would be in that pose. Apologetic and surrendering.

"Doctor O'Hara, I assure you, the Artemis Towers is the safest hotel you will find in Athens. It is one our own people use, and it has many security features. Besides, you will be unable to find anything else at this time. It is June, everything will be booked."

Sophia was nodding in agreement. *Damn.*

"Whatever. We're leaving."

"Yes, of course. Eh . . . where is my car?"

"In the canal." I ignored his wide eyes and the three of us walked out of his office.

Once we were on the sidewalk, I said, "I don't care what GG says. We need to check out of that hotel. Someone knows we're here, and they're trying to kill us. Or, at least you," I said to Sam. "Let's find a different place."

"I'm not talking to you." She sped up, moving ahead of me.

I fast-walked to get beside her. "I'm sorry I pushed you out of the car. I didn't know what else to do. And I bought us some time. Right now they think we're dead."

"I don't even want to know what you mean by that."

"It means we have some time to think. That is, at least until GG's mole lets whoever's trying to kill us know that we're still alive."

Think about what, I didn't know. We were out of options. All of a sudden I was exhausted.

Sam had been really angry, but now looked at my face and softened. That was one of the things I appreciated about her. No matter what I did, she never stayed mad for long.

"We all need a break." She scrolled through her phone. "C'mon.

He's right, it's not the time to try to change hotels. Let's stop back there so you can take a shower. Taking your mind off of Gideon for a little while might help you come up with something."

I wasn't in the mood to argue so went to the hotel and took a quick shower.

Sam called a taxi, and when the three of us got in she exchanged a few words with the driver. After a short ride he let us out in front of *Low Distiller*.

A whiskey bar. Just what the doctor ordered.

It was standing room only at the counter, but we managed to get three seats together in the middle that were suddenly vacated.

I was used to that. Traveling with Sam meant that we usually received great and attentive service, and guys would fall over themselves to give her their seats, buy her drinks, or give her their phone numbers. On top of that, *Low Distiller* carried the full line of my favorite Redbreast whiskeys: twelve-year-old, fifteen-year-old, Cask Strength, Lustau, PX, twenty-one and twenty-seven-year-old. I intended to drink my way through as many of them as I could.

Sam ordered a glass of very good red wine, and as usual Tatiana got vodka, straight. I started on the Lustau, chased with a glass of lager.

It wasn't until I was on my third shot, Redbreast Cask Strength, before Sam broke the silence.

"Are we going to talk about what's been happening?" She was used to me debriefing with her during investigations, and it was unusual for me to go very long without streams of conversation. But at the moment I didn't want to talk, or think. I finished my shot and gestured to the bartender for another. Redbreast fifteen-year-old this time.

"Sure, OK. Let's summarize," I said, finishing half of the shot in one gulp. "Gideon's gone, maybe dead. Someone's trying to kill you. We can't trust anyone, and the only person that we know in this country with any clout is a moron. We have no leads, and no idea what to do next. Oh, and there's a strange guy following us around. That about sums it up, doesn't it?"

Gideon had no experience in the field, and was completely unequipped for whatever was happening to him. Why couldn't they have taken Tatiana? We still would have looked for her, but I wouldn't be so wrecked and desperate about it.

I was frustrated. And, really, really sad.

I hated sad. Anger was a much more comfortable place for me. Especially alongside heavily inebriated. I finished my drink and waved at the bartender for another.

# FIFTEEN

I had a high tolerance for alcohol, and didn't get very drunk very often. In this case, the rapid-fire drinks on my empty stomach were taking effect.

I'd thrown back the rest of my shot and waved for the next one, Redbreast PX. A limited edition, the PX was aged in Pedro Ximenez sherry casks for over a year before release. Among every whiskey or whisky on the planet, it was by far my favorite.

Tatiana was her usual ebullient self, not speaking a word as she matched me drink for drink with vodka shots. Now that I'd successfully moved from sad to angry, she provided a convenient outlet.

"I can't believe you compared Russian culture to Greek. It's not even close," I said, my preemptive strike. "The Russians are like children compared to the Greeks."

Her eyes flashed. "Baryshnikov, Solzhenitsyn—"

"We're all tired," interrupted Sam. She knew what I was doing, and wanted to nip it in the bud. "Let's try to relax tonight, and start fresh in the morning. Maybe by then GG will have found something."

I snorted. "That guy couldn't find his own ass with both hands and a map."

She persisted, no doubt wanting to distract me from goading Tatiana into an argument. "If this Platon character has Gideon, maybe we should keep working with GG? Their main focus is finding him, and that may lead us to Gideon. And GG has his hands on lots of resources."

"GG's an idiot. Sophia's the one who does all the work, and the only one in the group who appears to be halfway competent. And he's got a mole in his organization. Maybe more than one. No wonder his informant is dead. And, in case you haven't noticed, someone's trying to kill you. And they almost succeeded, twice." I shook my head. "No. Nope. No way. It's time for you to go back home. I'll stay and look for Gideon on my own."

I'd made up my mind on the way out of GG's office. I wasn't

leaving Greece until I found Gideon. But Sam needed to leave, to get home to the relative safety of her house.

I turned back to Tatiana. "The Olympics, the Pythagorean Theorem, cheesecake, the word 'idiot,' democracy—"

"Mikhail Lomonosov—"

"Jennifer Aniston, Tina Fey, Billy Zane, Elizabeth Perkins—"

"You didn't mention trial by jury," said Sam, giving up, and joining in. "That's kind of a big one."

"You mean, where twelve people who are either retired, or out of work, and who don't know enough to get out of it, are stuck being grilled by lawyers who do their best to eliminate anyone with any knowledge about anything?"

"I know, it's not perfect. But do you have a better alternative?"

"Yeah. Everyone just needs to stop being an asshole." I turned back to Tatiana. "Geometry, algebra—"

She snorted. "Algebra was invented by Arabs."

"Nope. The Arabs disseminated it, but Diophantus, from Athens, is the father of algebra. The Hippocratic oath, modern medicine, anchors—"

"Anchors?" Sam said, frowning.

"Yes. Imagine, all of those boats floating willy-nilly. Alarm clocks, condoms . . ." Condoms by themselves were worth a whole pack of Russian writers.

I was on a roll, and this was just what I needed. I felt the comforting rush of anger-fueled adrenaline. Tatiana had made an artform out of looking bored and unaffected, but I could see I was riling her up. We'd had lots of arguments, and had never come to blows, but right now I was more than ready to take things to the next level.

I stood up, the wooden legs of my stool scraping against the floor as I pushed it back. I leaned into her face until our noses were inches away from each other. All of a sudden the loud voices in the bar stopped.

I could feel the eyes of everyone on us. Nothing got people's attention like a girl fight.

To my surprise, Tatiana waved her hand at me and turned back to the bartender for another drink.

I sat back down, disappointed.

Sam sighed and got up. I watched her head towards the bathroom and turned back to my drink.

Since we'd arrived the place had completely filled up, people now two-deep at the counter trying to get the bartender's attention.

I felt someone bump up hard against me. I turned around, "Hey, watch what you're doing."

The perpetrator behind me smiled and put his hands up apologetically, "Signómi."

I stared at him blankly.

"Uh, I am sorry. May I buy you a drink?"

"No. Fuck off," I grumbled, turning back around.

Sam returned from the bathroom and sat down. She took off the coaster she'd set on top of her glass and brought the wine to her lips.

I knocked the glass from her hand. It fell to the bar and rolled.

"Really?" She pulled out her credit card and waved to the bartender. "I think it's time to get you back to your room."

"Wait." I picked the glass up from the bar and set it right side up. There was a small amount of liquid left in the bottom, and I put my nose in to smell it. "When you went to the bathroom you put your coaster over the glass."

"Yes, I always do that when I leave a drink at a bar. Force of habit."

"The printed side was facing up when you left. It was upside down when you got back."

I looked around for the guy that had bumped into me. He was gone, as was the guy he'd come in with. "I think someone may have put something in your drink."

"Now you're being paranoid," she said, looking down to sign our bill. It had arrived quickly, the bartender possibly eager for me to leave. "You've been like that since you heard about the Evil Eye."

I'd told her about the Mati after my day with Loukas. "I'm not wrong about that. I get it all the time."

"That's because you give it all the time."

I put my nose into the glass, and then leaned it toward her. "Smell that."

Her eyes widened. "Almonds."

"Yep."

Cyanide smells like almonds.

I finished my last shot and stood up. Going after me was one thing. But going after my friends . . . that was a completely different matter.

I was filled with resolve. We could do this. We would find Gideon.

As I slid off the barstool I noticed the guy next to me get a pour of Redbreast. He'd ordered the twenty-seven-year-old, the most exclusive and expensive of the Redbreast line, arguably one of the world's most excellent whiskeys.

I watched with horror as he gestured to the bartender to drop several ice cubes into his glass.

I squeezed in next to him, and put both hands on the bar, leaning into his face. "What the hell is the matter with you? Who puts ice in twenty-seven-year-old Redbreast?"

He looked at me, puzzled. "Ti?"

It was true that adding a bit of water, or ice, to some whiskeys changed them in subtle ways, allowing different flavor and olfactory notes to come out of solution. But not this stuff. Putting ice into Redbreast twenty-seven, without even tasting it first, was the equivalent of smearing grape jelly on Ossetra caviar.

"Seriously, *what the actual fuck*? Why order whiskey like that if you're just going to put ice in it?"

My anger needed an immediate outlet. Tatiana wasn't up for it, but this guy would do nicely.

"Sam," I said, staring at the guy, "what's the Greek word for 'fucking idiot'?"

"Right now, it's 'Jesse O'Hara.'" She put her hand on my elbow and tried to move me away from the bar and the poor slob who was now the sole focus of my alcohol-supported rage. "Let's go."

I shook her hand off and leaned further down, my face inches away from the moron who had put ice in a shot of Redbreast twenty-seven in front of the wrong girl at the wrong time.

"Why bother to order good whiskey if you're not even going to taste it, before throwing a bunch of ice into it?" I grabbed his chin with one hand, and moved my other one across his face to point to the shelves of alcohol behind the bar. "*Look at that. There are plenty of cheap, shitty whiskeys that you can throw ice into." I dipped my fingers into his glass, fishing out the cubes and dropping them into his lap.

He stood up quickly, wiping his pants and yelling at me.

"Maybe we can get you some lemonade, or Coke, to mix with it?" Ice in his Whiskey Guy talked rapidly and angrily to the bartender. After a short conversation the bartender shrugged and reached under the bar.

I couldn't understand a word of what they were saying, but I imagined it was something like this:

*"That American woman insinuated that I was an idiot, and dropped ice in my lap. What are you going to do about it?"*

*"Yes, she most certainly did insinuate that you are an idiot. And the rest of us are thinking it."*

*"Why? And why am I being yelled at?"*

*"She is rightly yelling at you because, like an idiot, you requested ice cubes for a twenty-seven-year-old Redbreast whiskey. I am ashamed that I had to be a part of that abomination. If I wasn't being paid to serve you, I would come across the bar and give you a slap. Maybe you should slap yourself. Everyone here is ashamed. Please leave Greece."*

*"I am sorry, I will never do it again."*

*"Also, perhaps because of you, the two hot women with the crazy one are leaving. Everyone here hates you, even though one of the women is a bitchy Russian."*

*"Please, no . . ."*

*"It is too late. What's done is done. Now the Evil Eye will forever be upon you."*

Sam was pulling on my arm again but I stayed put. "Hey, I know. How about I buy you a juice box to mix with your twenty-seven-year-old fucking whiskey?" I leaned further over the bar and waved my hands. "Bartender! A juice box for my friend here." I threw some euros on the counter. "Do you have anything in the blue flavor?"

I felt Sam's hand on my arm again and tried to jerk it away, but this time it held firm. I looked back to see a uniformed police officer standing next to me. The bartender must have had one of those little "call the police" buttons under his counter.

The officer said something to me in Greek. I ignored him and turned back to the bartender. "Hey! Over here! Where's my juice box?"

There was the clinking of metal and my arms were being twisted behind my back, handcuffs closing around my wrists.

"Are you kidding me?" I whipped around, and tried to push past the officer, knocking over the now empty stool where Ice in his Whiskey Guy had been sitting. Out of the corner of my eye I saw Sam and Tatiana walking out the door. An impartial observer might think they didn't know me.

The officer grabbed my bound hands, and with relative ease escorted me away from the bar and to the door.

I turned back and yelled over my shoulder, "You're going to hell for that ice."

He marched me out of the bar and onto the sidewalk, and then to his car, where he opened up the door to the back and gestured me in. I struggled, swinging my bound arms and kicking, basically doing everything I could to avoid being pushed into the car. Eventually I just sat down on the ground.

He was in the process of trying to pick me up when a man in a suit walked briskly over, stopping in front of us.

He said something to the cop at the same time he opened his wallet, and flashed what looked like a badge. The uniform immediately stiffened and let go of me, then stepped behind me to unlock the cuffs.

He got into his car and drove away without another word.

"Uh, thanks," I said, standing up and rubbing my wrists. Who the hell was this guy?

"Come with me, please, Doctor O'Hara. And you as well." He gestured to Sam and Tatiana, both standing on the sidewalk just outside of the bar. He pointed to a black SUV parked on the curb.

*How did he know my name?* "Thanks for your help, but no." No way was I getting into another car with a guy I didn't know, especially not a black SUV, and especially not after someone had just tried to poison Sam.

"I have information about your friend."

"Gideon?"

He nodded.

I stared at him, waiting for him to elaborate. When it was clear he wasn't going to say anything else I reluctantly got into his car. Sam and Tatiana followed me.

"What do you know about Gideon? Is he in custody?" I asked, once he started driving.

That would be a huge relief. International terrorists were one thing, but police I could deal with.

He shook his head. "No. There is a message for you waiting at your hotel."

"Who the hell are you?"

"I was sent by a friend."

He didn't say another word the rest of the way, ignoring my questions. He pulled up outside of our hotel and drove away immediately after we got out.

When we walked into the lobby I expected the concierge to hand us a note. When he didn't we went to the front desk.

There was no message.

"Dammit." I should have known. Yet another person lying to us.

But how had the guy known about Gideon?

I was really starting to feel messed with. First the phony olive oil party, and now this. I'd be hitting the minibar hard tonight.

We took the elevator up and split up to go to our rooms. I opened the door to mine and stepped on an envelope that had been slipped underneath.

I opened it up. Inside was a stack of euros, and a typewritten letter on light blue paper.

"Sam, take a look at this."

She left her door and looked over my shoulder. "What is it?"

"Money." I flipped through the euros. "And a message. It's from Platon. He's got Gideon."

# SIXTEEN

Your colleague Gideon is a guest and enjoying my hospitality. I have a small favor to ask. Please go to Thessalonica, and meet at the below location at five p.m. on the 22nd. Inquire as to the location of Apollo. The enclosed is for the man who will give you the information. Forward any information you obtain to the email address listed here. I am grateful for your assistance. It would be unfortunate if you share any of this with anyone in law enforcement.

"There's an address, and it's Platon's mark," I said, pointing to the Pi sign at the bottom of the page. "Thessalonica? I thought it was Thessaloniki?"

"It's the old spelling. It was known as Thessalonica, and sometimes, just Salonica, until late in the twentieth century. And I'm surprised you know that. Geography's never been your strong suit," Sam said.

"I know it because it's not far from where Gabrielle was born."

"Who?"

"Gabrielle. You know, Xena's best friend? In any case, I'm guessing the Apollo he's referring to is not the space mission. GG told us that Platon gave his gang members Greek god names." I flipped through the banknotes. "There's like five thousand euros in here."

"Do you think it's really from Platon?"

"We can't be sure, but this is too much money for a hoax. GG did tell us that Platon had a lot of sympathetic people in law enforcement. And it was a cop who told us about the message."

Sam was frowning. "I don't know. For a man who doesn't want to be found, sending a note like this seems risky. Suppose we were to turn this over to GG's group?"

"Suppose we were? All there is on here is an email address, which I'm sure doesn't lead back to Platon in any traceable way. And whoever he wants us to meet with is presumably expecting us. If anyone else shows up, he'll just bolt. And I'm not sure what 'It would be unfortunate' means, but it sounds like a threat."

"Maybe, but don't we have the opportunity now to set some kind of trap? You know, have GG place some of his people in Thessaloniki, to arrest the man we're supposed to meet with, and get information about Platon?"

I shook my head. "Do you trust GG to do something like that, without screwing it up? And if Platon does have Gideon, and we do anything that spooks him, he might just decide to stop 'extending his hospitality,' and we stand a good chance of finding Gideon in a ditch."

Part of me was relieved. Relieved that Gideon was with Platon, and not dead. Or with Svetlana.

"No." I shook my head. "I'm not sharing this with GG."

"You don't trust him, do you?"

"Not entirely. I mean, he's not giving off a liar, or corrupt vibe, but who knows?" Cross-cultural reads of other people were notoriously unreliable. "But I definitely don't trust him or his team to handle anything like this competently. And we know there's at least one mole in their organization."

I read through the note again. "I want to follow this. If it is from Platon, and he has Gideon, this is our chance to get him back."

"What if it's a trap?"

"It could be, but if Platon wanted to set a trap, why didn't he just have his guy outside the whiskey bar kill us, and dump us in an alley? Or just take us straight to him?"

"Good point."

"And it's not like we have any other options. One thing, though. I want to leave Tatiana here. Someone is definitely trying to take us out, and it's better if we weren't all in one place. If I didn't know you'd refuse, I'd leave you here, too."

"You're not just trying to get rid of her, are you?"

The thought had crossed my mind. "No." It was just a side benefit.

"She's going to want to come with us."

"I know. I've got an idea about that."

"OK. When should we leave?"

"The meet is set for tomorrow evening, let's leave in the morning."

I was very drunk, and if we were going to travel across Greece I wanted to do it on a full night of sleep and blowing less than a 0.3. "We need to let Tatiana know what's going on, and come up with a story for GG."

I called GG and left a message that I had news and would meet with him early the next day.

Then I left a message for Tatiana to meet us in the hotel lobby at seven a.m.

"One more thing." I opened up my laptop and searched for a few minutes before I found what I was looking for. "There was a sticker on that cop's car." I grabbed a hotel notepad and recreated the sticker, the letters and the picture, and showed it to Sam. "That's Panathinaikos FC. As in football club."

"Yes? So?"

"I saw a similar sticker on Loukas's car, when we were in Crete. Loukas's was 'OFI Crete FC;' the cop's was 'Panathinaikos FC.' That team used to be based on Santorini."

"Was?"

"Yeah. It was merged with four other teams into the Santorini Football Club in 2020."

"So these guys are football fans. Almost everyone here is. Why does that matter?"

"It might not, but why would an Athens cop support a Santorini team, unless he's from there?" I closed the computer and sat down on the bed. "GG said Platon was on an island. Maybe he's in Santorini. If his base of operations is there, it makes sense that some of his guys would be from there, too." It was thin, but so far the best lead we had.

"Should we tell GG? Or should we be going there first, instead of Thessaloniki?"

"No. It's too risky to tell him. All GG cares about is finding Platon. I doubt he'll care about any collateral damage, definitely not the health and safety of one American hostage. And if we do find Platon there, he'll just send us on his little errand, anyway. The tone of his letter wasn't threatening. Let's play this out, for now."

The next morning we met with Tatiana and shared the plan with her over a quick breakfast, then the three of us met with GG.

He was in his office with Tiny Joan. Apparently he never went anywhere without her.

"Sam and I are going to Thessaloniki to look for Gideon." I'd decided to be honest about where we were going, if not why, in case something happened. If GG knew we were there, and we ran into trouble, there was still a miniscule chance that he'd be able to help us.

"Do you have information that Gideon is there?"

"No, but Gideon's a huge fan of *Xena: Warrior Princess*. Thessaloniki is near Amphipolis and Potidaea, the birthplaces of Xena and Gabrielle. He's always wanted to see them, and if he is free, and is just on his own, that would be the place he would go."

This was ridiculous on many levels, not the least of which was that Gideon knew if he was going to visit any *Xena*-related sites, I'd insist on joining him.

Tiny Joan looked at us skeptically, but GG said, "Ah, that would make sense."

I couldn't believe he was buying this story. Not that I cared too much, it wasn't like he could stop us from going.

"I too, am a fan, and have visited both cities. If he is there he will not be disappointed."

"Really?" It was hard to fathom that GG was a *Xena* fan. "What's your favorite episode?" I asked, expecting to catch him in a lie.

"It is hard to choose," he said, thinking. "Perhaps it is when Aphrodite casts a spell on Joxer that turns him into a brave and attractive man, who women find irresistible. Or perhaps it is the one where Xena makes peace between the centaurs and the Amazons, and Gabrielle gets her leather outfit."

*Huh.* So he was a *Xena* fan. And his episode choices made sense; the Joxer character was a bumbling fool whose self-image greatly exceeded his actuality. I could definitely see GG empathizing with him.

"What is your favorite episode?" he asked.

"That's tough, there're so many. Maybe the one where Gabrielle gets drugged, and then knocked up by Dahak, the One Evil God, and over a few days she gestates a hell baby that will destroy the world."

"Ah, yes, that is a good one. There is also—"

"Tatiana will stay here, to continue to help you with your own efforts to find Gideon," said Sam, not interested in another *Xena* love fest.

GG didn't try to hide his glee that Tatiana would be sticking around. To her credit, she did her best to not look disappointed. She hadn't been happy to be left in Athens, but Sam had convinced her it was the best way for her to help us get to Gideon.

"I go to computer room," she said, walking out of GG's office.

He watched her leave with undisguised admiration. "She is a remarkable woman. I have never met anyone who is like her." He turned to me. "Does she have a . . . eh . . . husband, or boyfriend?"

"No, she's totally single. You should go for it," I said, ignoring the sharp turn of Sam's head.

"We'll contact you if we find anything in Thessaloniki. In the meantime, if anything turns up about Gideon on your end, let us know right away."

He nodded absently, staring at the door.

Sam and I left the office. She waited until we were in the elevator to let me have it.

"You know she's not interested in him, and that if he does try anything, she's going to take him apart, don't you?"

"I do. I just hope I'm there to see it."

# SEVENTEEN

We made it to Thessaloniki in a little over six hours. If we hadn't been going there to possibly be killed in a trap laid by Platon, it would have been epic.

Sam drove us out of the city. To my surprise she headed east.

"Where are you going? Thessaloniki's north."

"It's only a little out of our way to trace the path of the original marathon. I've always wanted to do that."

She drove east towards a small town, Nea Makri, before turning north.

"The marathon everyone runs today is named after the Battle of Marathon. Legend has it that a Greek messenger, Pheidippides, ran from the battle at Marathon to Athens, a little over twenty-six miles, without stopping, to alert the people in the city of the Greek's victory. He believed the defeated Persians would rush to Athens to claim a false victory, and establish their authority over Greek lands, and end Greece's democratic rule. He made it, but once he delivered his message he collapsed and died."

Seemed far-fetched, except for the "collapsed and dying" part.

Marathon was unspectacular, a town of less than ten thousand people, with little more than olive groves and a few monuments. We drove through without stopping before continuing north to Thessaloniki.

Since leaving Athens' urban sprawl, all of Greece's landscape was on display, the road every now and then taking us close enough to the coast for a view of sparkling blue water. Turning inland, the scenery transitioned to rolling hills, olive trees, vineyards and villages, then to mountains, and some surprisingly rugged passes, before we dropped back down to the plains surrounding Thessaloniki.

As we approached the city, I looked up the address of the meet.

"It's near Aristotle University," I said, as Sam was negotiating a roundabout.

"That's near the Ano Poli neighborhood. It's the oldest part of the city, the only section that didn't go up in the big fire. Some consider it the cultural heart of Thessaloniki." Despite the nature of our trip, she was excited.

She became less excited as we approached the meeting point, which was not in the cultural heart of anything. We pulled onto a dead-end street lined on one side with run-down apartments, many covered in sloppy graffiti, and stone walls on the other, also covered in graffiti, and topped with anti-climbing devices and other theft deterrents.

The address was near the end of the street and down a small set of stairs, in front of a semi-underground shuttered storefront. Sam double-parked the car a half block away.

"I've got a bad feeling about this. Do you want to stay in the car?" I asked.

"I'm not sure that would be any safer. Best to stick together. But maybe we should stay here until we see someone?"

"Good idea."

We waited almost an hour after the designated meeting time before a lone man walked down the street.

He was disheveled, wearing shabby clothes, worn shoes, a frayed knit cap, despite the warm weather, and sported a ten o'clock shadow on his face. He walked to the small set of stairs, constantly looking over his shoulder, and down to the cement patio. He stopped and looked around nervously.

"I guess this is it." We both got out of the car and walked over to him.

He looked surprised, likely expecting a man.

"We were told to meet with you." I said. "What can you tell us about Apollo?"

"Money first," he said, in a thick accent, looking toward the street.

I handed him the envelope. He opened it, and flipped through the stack of euros.

Then he turned to leave.

"Hey, wait a damn minute."

He smirked and started up the stairs.

"Sam, a little help here?"

She reached into her purse and pulled out her gun. I knew she hated doing that, but this was for Gideon.

The man stopped and put his hands up.

"You wanna try this again?" I motioned for him to come back. He walked slowly down the stairs, never taking his eye off of Sam's gun.

"Where is Apollo?"

"We . . . uh . . . exchange. Then men come."

"What kind of exchange?"

He looked around, then said quietly, "Guns. Drugs."

"Drugs?"

"Po. Për disfunksionin erektil."

"Sam, what's he saying?"

"I don't know. It's not Greek. Albanian, perhaps?"

The man nodded his head. "Po, Shqip. Drugs, për disfunksionin erektil."

I looked at Sam but she shook her head. "Albanian's not in my repertoire."

"Uh, for men who no . . ." He made a motion with one hand and pointed to his crotch with the other.

"ED drugs? Viagra?"

"Viagra, po." His head bobbed spastically while his eyes darted between me and Sam's gun.

"You're lying. Nobody smuggles those." I took a step towards him and looked pointedly at Sam's gun. "You better start telling the truth, or you're going to end up with an additional orifice."

She'd never shoot at an unarmed person, or even an armed person, unless they were actively trying to kill us. But this guy didn't know that.

"Uh, Jesse, I'm not sure, I think he might be telling the truth."

"You're kidding."

"No. Greece is the most sexually active country in the world, by a large margin. It wouldn't be surprising at all if there's a big market for Viagra here."

"How do you know that?"

"The condom makers put out a report. On average Greeks do it over a hundred and sixty times a year."

Damn. That might be more times than I'd done it in my life, if I didn't count college.

Guns and ED medication. An interesting combination. And not an entirely surprising one. "Whatever. They're smugglers. GG said Platon was getting guns. Apollo was here to make the exchange."

Albanian Guy was sneaking away as we were talking, and I grabbed his arm and motioned for Sam to put her gun back up.

"Keep going," I said, rolling my hands at him.

"We make exchange, men come."

"What men?"

He shook his head. "Not know. Turkish. Take man, money, guns, drugs."

"Anything else?"

He looked at me blankly, and I waved him away. He didn't move until Sam lowered her gun, then he ran up the stairs and down the road.

"What do you think? That didn't seem like much for five thousand euros," she said, after we watched him disappear around the corner.

"I'm not sure, but it's time to get out of here and find a hotel with good Wi-Fi. Keep your gun out."

We drove back to a safer-looking part of town and found a room at a hotel on the water. Once we were in our room I hooked up my laptop and drafted the message to Platon:

Met with Albanian smuggler. He said that Apollo and all of the stuff was taken during the exchange by men who were speaking Turkish. Sorry about your ED drugs. You can probably get a prescription through your local MD.

Sam was looking over my shoulder. "Is that a good idea? To antagonize him?"

"I doubt it's going to make a difference what I say. He's got Gideon, and there's nothing to keep him from killing him as soon as he gets what he wants. He'll either keep his part of the bargain, or he won't. And I don't believe in demonstrating weakness." I hit send.

"What do we do now?"

"I guess we wait."

"Might as well do some sightseeing, while we wait."

I was usually up for sightseeing, especially in old cities, and very especially here, where millennia-old artifacts could apparently turn up anywhere. I'd already seen a number of ancient columns just laying around, next to some of the roads, and piled in empty lots.

But all I could think about was Gideon. We didn't even know if he was still alive.

Nevertheless, I joined her to kill time. We visited a couple of art galleries, stood under a famous arch, and walked around a white tower, that for some reason was crowded with tourists.

Sam could tell I was just going through the motions, and after two hours of listening to my desultory exclamations of interest, she said, "It's getting late. Do you want to go back to the hotel? There are some bars next to the water."

"Sure," I said, checking my phone for the fifteenth time.

We took a cab to the hotel and walked out the back to the broad walkway that ran along the water and out onto a pier, on which was a small outdoor bar. We took seats underneath a canopy.

Normally I would have appreciated the view of the water at sunset, Thessaloniki's long coastline, and mountains in the distance, along with the gentle breeze that was bringing the smell of the sea to our table.

"Nothing. It's been four hours," I said, slamming my phone down.

"He is a criminal, after all. They're not noted for timeliness."

"I can't just sit here and do nothing."

"Well, there is the matter of figuring out who's been trying to kill us," said Sam.

"You don't think it's Platon, do you?"

"Why would he do that? He just asked us to do a job for him. And not just kill us; someone tried to set you up for the bombing at the hotel. Who hates you that much?"

"Well, since we've been to Greece, I'd say the Cretan Police, the uniform guy I racked in the Heraklion police station, his boss, the woman whose nose I broke in the jail, the guy in the bar who put ice in his whiskey, the bartender who called the police on me, and the guy in the tourist center. Then there are the people who hated me before we came to Greece—"

"Let's try to narrow it down to the ones that really hate you, not just the ones who find you off-putting. It must be someone who knew you before we came here. Framing you for the bombing had to be set up ahead of time; even you couldn't have made someone that angry in two days."

I wasn't so sure about that, but I went along. "OK. Let's see . . .

That would be Danny Ryan, Teagan Ryan, every person in his gang, Northern Ireland's National Police Service, anyone who's friends with my dad, my dad's defense lawyer, most of my previous employers, the DA from the Synchronicity case, almost all of my college professors—"

"OK, OK. What about this: who hates you the most? You're missing the most obvious one."

"Svetlana."

Sam raised her eyebrows and nodded. "And it's not clear that whoever is doing all of this is actually trying to kill you, just the people around you."

"Yeah. If she really wanted to hurt me, she'd kill my friends and set me up to rot in jail." Which was exactly what had almost happened.

"You think she's behind all of this? The bombing? The meat market shooting? The ambush at the olive oil mill? All of the men who were shooting at us, they were speaking Greek, not Russian," she said.

"Remember when we were in Spain? She hired local thugs to help her there."

"Yes, but even if she somehow knew we were coming to this conference, we hadn't planned to come to Athens. Are we even sure she knows we're here?"

I looked down.

"What? What haven't you told me?"

"She definitely knows we're here."

"How do you know that?"

"She sent a bottle of her skull vodka to our hotel."

Sam leaned back and stared at me. "Why didn't you tell me?"

"I didn't want you to worry."

In sharp contrast to me, Sam was almost always gracious, and rarely used profanity. It was shocking to hear her now.

"For fuck's sake, Jesse! Are you kidding?"

I hated when she got angry. It made me realize what she went through with me on a regular basis. This sucked. I vowed to try to be more calm in the future.

We sat in silence for a few minutes. Then she said, "We need to look at everything again, putting Svetlana in the picture."

Now that we were talking about Svetlana, something else was

bugging me. I pulled up the law enforcement conference website on my phone and went to the sponsors page.

On it were several corporate logos, including one of a green trident with a drop of oil in the center.

"The law enforcement conference that Gideon and I spoke at. One of the conference sponsors was Janus Oil."

"Yes, so?"

"So, Svetlana bought Janus Oil last year. I think she brought us here."

"What?"

"She used the conference to bring us to Greece."

"How can you be sure?"

"Think about it. A couple who are scheduled to present at the conference have a deadly car accident two weeks before it starts. The organizers contact me and Gideon to fill in their spots on short notice.

"I mean, we've done good work, but how in hell would these guys have heard of us, or if they had, why would they choose us? There've got to be hundreds of other people nearby, or more well-known, or both, that they could have picked. As a major sponsor, Janus Oil would have been able to influence the selection. I'll bet she sent us the invitation to the ambush at the olive oil place, too."

"Why there?"

I was glad Sam wasn't mad at me any more. She knew that whatever I did, my heart was in the right place.

"I don't know. But Gideon knew something, he was looking into that area on his computer just before he was taken. Maybe Svetlana lives over there, in the Peloponnese? Or she owns the mill? Or just wanted to get us out of Athens? I'm guessing that after the shooting at the market, she couldn't afford to do anything that high-profile again, or risk having the authorities come down on her. It's one thing to anonymously blow up a hotel in Heraklion; it's a totally different matter to have gunmen shooting people in Athens. Even she isn't reckless enough to keep risking collateral damage in a major city."

"Do you think she's responsible for the guy that's been following us? The one we saw in Gazi?"

"Yeah. She wants to keep tabs on us. That's how she knew when we went to Athens, and where we were staying."

"OK. So, what do we do?"

"I think this is a situation where GG might actually be useful."

# EIGHTEEN

We got up early the next morning and Sam made the trip back to Athens in four and a half hours.

"So we're going to tell GG about Svetlana?" She pulled in front of our hotel and got out, handing the keys to the valet.

"Yeah. There must be someone in his department whose job it is to go after the hotel bomber, and the government can't be thrilled about all the other chaos she's causing here, either. GG said they recognized the guy who was running from the hotel just before the bombing, and they didn't definitively connect that guy to Platon. If we're right, and he's tied to Svetlana, GG will have to go after her."

Counting on GG to be able to do anything was a long shot. But at least he wouldn't be able to ignore this.

It turned out he was able to ignore this.

When we got off the elevator at his floor Tatiana was slumped in a chair in the small lobby. She got up quickly and walked towards us.

"We go now."

I didn't blame her for wanting to leave. I couldn't stand to be around GG for very long, and he wasn't romantically interested in me.

"How'd it go?" I asked.

"Eto zhe konchenyi mudak! On pytalsia menia lapat'! V sledui-ushchii raz ia emu iaitsa otorvu!"

Sam started to translate, but I waved her off. "I get the gist."

"I go back to hotel now," Tatiana repeated.

She didn't want to spend another minute in GG's orbit, but after I brought her up to speed on Svetlana, she changed her mind. She had as much to gain from Svetlana's capture as I did. Among other things, she couldn't go back to Russia until Svetlana was out of the picture. Even though her dad was still in prison, she had other family there that she missed.

By now the security guard at the desk must have been given the green light by GG to let us through. He barely glanced in our direction as we made our way to his office in the back.

GG was behind his desk, Sophia next to him. Tiny Joan was in a chair in the corner, sorting folders.

"You know where Gideon is? And Platon?" GG asked eagerly.

That answered one question. They'd made zero progress on Gideon's whereabouts since we'd left.

"No. But we have something else for you. I know who's behind the hotel bombing in Crete, and the shootout at the market."

Sophia looked up. Tiny Joan pulled out her notebook and started to take notes.

"We believe it may have been Platon's group behind the bombing," he said. "And we have already identified the shooters at the market. They were Platon's men, there to kill our informant."

"First of all, I already told you there were *two* sets of gunmen at the market. And you haven't definitively identified the bomber. The other group at the market, and the bombing, were both hired by Svetlana Ivashchenko."

"Who?"

"One of the Russian oligarchs. She bought Janus Oil last year. She's been after me, Sam, Tatiana and Gideon since we stopped her trying to blow up a gas plant in Spain. She got away, but she's been threatening us since."

"I am not sure what—"

I held my hand up. "Just listen. She lured us to Greece, under the guise of a conference presentation, to get us somewhere where she could take us out."

"What evidence do you have that this might be true?"

"I know it's true. We just need a few things to confirm it. Things you can help with."

He placed his hands up in front of him.

"Our priority now is to find Platon. Until that happens we cannot be distracted. My team is not large, we cannot devote any resources to finding evidence you claim might exist about this Svetlana person."

He was avoiding making eye contact with me, and looked away, his gaze landing on Tatiana.

She glared at him, forcing him to avert his eyes to a safe blank spot on the wall.

I was looking forward to getting the story about them from her. He'd obviously made his move; I was a little surprised there were no visible injuries to his face.

"It won't take much of your team's time. Just some work by Ilias. He can start by getting some information about that couple who died on Karpathos, the ones who were originally going to present at the conference. Anything that indicates that they didn't die in an accident, that it could have been deliberate."

"I am sorry, Doctor O'Hara. I am afraid this is not in our purview."

"A hotel bombing isn't in your purview? Aren't you the guy responsible for terrorism?" I'd vowed to be more patient with him, but I was already shouting.

Now that I was sure it was Svetlana doing all of this, I was impatient for him to take action. We still needed to find Gideon, but we had our first chance to get her out of the way since she'd escaped on her helicopter in Spain.

Sophia had been quietly looking on, and didn't seem at all fazed that I was yelling at GG. More than likely it wasn't the first time.

"Well, eh, perhaps, eh, we can take a look at the police report," he said weakly.

"Then there are the guys who were shooting at us in the market. There were two groups."

"Yes, we have identified that some of the men that participated in that shooting are associated with Platon's organization, and we—"

"The other guys were hired by Svetlana. They're Greek. That's her MO, to use local thugs to do her dirty work. Find a link."

"I am, eh, not exactly sure—"

"*Jesus*, get your technical guy on it. None of them were wearing masks. So use that CCTV shit you have all over the place, do some facial recognition, and then track their communications. They likely have criminal records, and I guarantee you one of them will lead to Svetlana."

Ilias wouldn't be at Gideon's level, but I hoped he was at least smarter than GG, or all of this would lead to nothing.

"You said you had identified the guy that was running from the hotel just before the bombing?"

"Yes."

"There's going to be a link between him and Svetlana, too. And have Ilias look into Spartopoulos Mill. She either owns it, or controls the people who own it."

I was gaining a new appreciation for Gideon. It sounded like a lot of stuff to do, when I listed it all out loud like this. And it would have taken him minutes to do all of it, with almost no discussion.

"Then there's Janus Oil."

At the mention of Janus, GG's eyes grew wider and he put his hands up again. "No, no. Janus Oil is one of our biggest and most important oil companies. They provide thousands of jobs, and the tax revenue is very important. We cannot interfere in their work."

"I'm not asking you to interfere in anything. Just verify that it was their idea to bring Gideon and I to that conference. They're one of the biggest sponsors, I'm sure they were the ones who suggested we replace the Perkinses."

He looked down, shaking his head. "I cannot do this." Tiny Joan mirrored him, staring at the floor.

"You owe us, you son of a bitch," I spat at him. "Your little, easy project has gotten us almost killed, and my friend kidnapped." Now that we were this close to getting Svetlana I wasn't about to let this jellyfish get in my way. I stepped toward him and leaned into his face. "I'm not above going to the press. I'm sure they'd love to hear about how the government does nothing while a Russian comes in and uses one of your own companies to bomb hotels, and assassinate people."

That would be an easy sell. It wasn't like the Russians were in anyone's good graces.

He'd been looking at the ground, but at the mention of "the press" he turned his face up to me.

"I could make some discreet inquiries with Janus," interjected Sophia. She looked at GG, and added quickly, "We can tell them we are investigating the bombing at the hotel, and that we want to talk to some of their own security people, who may have been at the conference."

She was the only person in the office with anything going for her. "Thanks. And I'll want to talk to someone at Janus who's got access to the financial records. Svetlana's got to be paying for all of this somehow, and I'm guessing it's going through the company."

Going through corporate financial records and finding things that were out of order was my superpower. I could uncover hidden flows of money and other discrepancies in less time than it took most people to turn the pages.

"No," GG said, a little more backbone in his voice this time. "I will not allow this. If we find anything from these other, er, avenues, then perhaps we can revisit it. But the government cannot coerce a company to open up their financial records with no evidence of, er, anything."

"Fine." If Ilias was even marginally competent they'd find ample evidence linking Svetlana to one or more murderous illegal activities. Once we had that I'd try again. "I'll expect to hear from you tomorrow about what you're able to find." I stared at him with as much menace as I could generate.

We left his office and went back to the hotel. Without speaking all three of us turned into the bar. There was nothing to do now but wait for GG's group to find something.

"So, what happened with GG?" I asked Tatiana after we ordered our drinks.

"He is slabak. Chmo. Zasranets. Chertov kusok der'ma . . ."

As she was venting I pulled out my phone and checked my email for the thousandth time. I'd been checking both my inbox and the spam folder just in case.

"Anything?" asked Sam.

I smiled. "Not from Platon."

"What is it?"

"It's an email. From Gideon."

"Gideon?"

"Yeah," I said, chugging my beer and standing up.

"We're going to Santorini."

She pulled the phone from my hand and looked at the message. "What's 'ebay arefulcay'?"

"It's pig Latin. For 'be careful.'"

# NINETEEN

"**W**ait a minute." Sam pulled me back down onto the stool and took my phone out of my hand to look at the message. "Are you sure that's from Gideon? 'Art deals, today only,' looks like spam. And who's 'goblin pedigrees'?"

"That was my nickname for him when we were dating in college," I said, noting Tatiana's frown at the word dating. "'Goblin pedigrees' is an anagram of his name."

"And 'Savings galore, today only at the alderacay!' How do you get 'Santorini' out of that?"

"'Alderacay' is pig Latin for 'caldera.' The dominant feature of Santorini is the caldera."

"Pig Latin?"

"We talked in pig Latin when we went out drinking in college."

"That seems thin."

"Not when you put this together with what I saw earlier. Remember? The Santorini FC sticker on that cop's car? No," I said, shaking my head firmly, "Gideon's there, and he has access to a computer, or phone. But he must have to hide what he's doing."

There were a million daily flights to Santorini from Athens, and even though it was the beginning of high tourist season, the three of us were able to find seats on one that was leaving in a few hours. We took a cab to the airport and easily made the forty-five-minute flight to the island.

Unlike our earlier trip from Athens to Crete, the skies were clear, and we were treated to the magnificent view of the Aegean Sea and one of Greece's most emblematic islands. Beaches, farms and rolling hills lay around and in between Santorini's famous whitewashed buildings and blue-topped churches, all curled around the caldera that defined the island, formed thousands of years ago in a volcanic eruption.

From the airport we took a taxi to the main city, Fira, aka,

Thera, which as far as I could tell was Greek for "mobs of people slowly moving in cow-like herds."

We joined the tourists packed like sardines on the sidewalks and narrow streets, lined by a seemingly infinite number of tchotchke shops, restaurants, and bars, all with signs in Greek and English.

I didn't think Platon would be in a place this populated, but we had to start somewhere.

"You think he's here?" asked Sam. We were on Nomikos, the main drag, being jostled by tourists.

"Yeah. Somewhere."

I ran through Gideon's message in my head. He'd told us where, I just had to figure it out.

Most importantly, it meant he was still alive. I hadn't realized how devastated I'd been at the prospect of him being dead. I hadn't allowed myself to think about it, but it had been there, just under the surface. I was weak with relief.

"Let's get a drink."

Sam pointed to the bar we were standing next to. *Lucky's Grecian Bar*. It was packed with sunburnt vacationers.

"No, not that."

I walked to the first cross street, abandoning the main drag for a less populated one, and went into the first bar that wasn't crowded with tourists. There was no big, gaudy sign out front, and the only one they did have was in Greek.

We sat in the relatively cool interior at the counter and ordered drinks.

"So, now what?" asked Sam.

"I guess we start asking around."

I'd taken a picture with my phone during the first meeting with GG, where he'd shown us the only known picture of Platon. When the bartender served our drinks I showed him pictures of Gideon, and then Platon.

"Have you seen either of these men?" I asked.

"No English."

"Éhete di kápion apó aftús tus ántres?" Sam asked.

"Óhi," he said, shaking his head and walking away.

"Do you think he doesn't recognize either of them because he doesn't recognize them, because he's a Platon supporter, or because we're not local?" I asked.

"No idea."

We finished our drinks and walked to the next bar, also with signs only in Greek, and also not teeming with tourists. This time Sam asked about the pictures, in Greek. We got the same result there, and then in the next four bars we visited.

"This plan is not good," said Tatiana.

"Thanks, Captain Obvious. If you've got a better idea I'd love to hear it."

We'd grabbed some gyros at a small shop and were sitting on a bench at the edge of town, high above the water. I loved gyros, and these were terrific, with the perfect proportion of meat to tzatziki, nestled in a soft pita with fresh tomatoes, slices of red onion and French fries.

I considered gyros to be the second-best hangover food, after Taco Bell. Not that I got hangovers very often. Thanks no doubt to my dad, I seemed genetically predisposed to avoiding them.

The view was spectacular, too, but I just couldn't appreciate it right now.

Unfortunately, Tatiana was right; I didn't know what I'd been thinking. That we'd just wander around Santorini, showing their pictures, and find someone who would tell us exactly where they were? GG had said Platon was reclusive. Anyone who recognized him either worked for him, or was a supporter.

"This isn't getting us anywhere," I muttered.

"Let's go through it again," said Sam. "Let's suppose Platon really is on this island."

"We don't need to suppose. He's here."

"OK, yes. He's here. Gideon's email was short. He told you about the caldera, and left his name. The only other part of the email that we haven't used is 'art deals.' Maybe that's a clue?"

I scrolled through my phone for "art in Santorini."

"There's a ton of art galleries," I said, looking at my search results. "And museums with art in them. And," I said, looking around, "about a million people selling it on the street."

"Let's try to narrow it down. Platon wants to stay in the background. His place would be somewhere off the beaten path."

"Santorini's hardly off the beaten path. It's one of the most popular tourist destinations in Greece."

"During the tourist season. And most of them stick to the city. There are more remote areas on the island."

"So, art spaces that are outside the city. OK." I redid my Google search. "That leaves fewer than ten."

Sam thought for a moment. "Platon's a nationalist, a Greek chauvinist in the true meaning of the word. A man like that would surround himself with all things Greek."

"Yes, this makes sense," said Tatiana. "Greece, like Russia, has rich history and culture, it—"

"Give it a rest," I said, frowning at her.

I turned back to Sam. "All things Greek? You mean like olive oil?"

"Yes. And Greek wine, food, art, architecture . . . Look for some place that is one hundred percent, unequivocally Greek, somewhere that is all about celebrating Greece."

I refined my search and was rewarded. "Here!" I handed my phone to Sam.

"Ελληνικός Χώρος. Loosely translated, it's 'Greek Space.'"

"It looks like an art gallery." I translated the page to English. "Every year the proprietor travels around Greece and chooses the most interesting art made by Greeks."

"Who's the proprietor?"

"Someone named Éllinas Ánthropos."

She laughed. "That literally translates as 'Greek Man.'"

I scrolled through the website. "It says 'Tours by appointment only.' Do you think Platon would be stationed in a compound that allows tourists?"

"Maybe he never makes any appointments?"

"Damn," I murmured.

"What?"

"The place is at the top of a hill, three and half miles from here. About as remote as it gets on Santorini. And it's not just an art gallery. It's an estate, with olive groves. They make their own raki, and have a tasting room.

"Look," I said, handing her my phone again, and showing one of the pictures. "It doesn't look like the owner is catering to tourists; the sign out front is only in Greek."

I had a good feeling about this. "I'm going to see if we can get an appointment."

I called and it went to voicemail. Of course it was in Greek. I called again and had Sam listen to it.

"The message says all of the tours are booked at the moment, but to try to call at least two months ahead for reservations." She handed me my phone. "What do we do now?"

"Let's see how they handle drop-ins."

Santorini, an island home to fewer than 30,000 people, grew to hundreds of thousands in June, and our efforts to get a taxi or a rideshare were fruitless.

We walked to the bus station, and waited a half hour for the bus that shuttled between Fira and Kamari, with a stop not too far from Greek Space.

As the crowded bus left Fira the shops and crush of tourists vanished, giving way to rocky terrain, with low scrub and a few small trees, occasionally sprinkled with white homes, some in clusters, small farms, and the rare gas station.

We got off at the Exo Gonia stop, a quarter mile from the estate, and walked along the road towards Greek Space.

The edge of the estate was delineated by a fenced border that wound up the hill and out of site. Fifty yards from the northern boundary we reached a narrow gravel crossroad. A short way up the road was an imposing metal gate, bounded on either side by square stone pillars. Erected prominently in the center of one of the pillars was a sign: Ελληνικός Χώρος. Επισκέψεις μόνο κατόπιν ραντεβού.

"Let me guess. 'Platon's place. Don't come in.'"

"Close. 'Visits are by appointment only.'"

"No phone number, no call box. They were serious about being appointment-only."

Through the fence we could see the gravel road travel another hundred yards up the hill. In between the gate and where it disappeared near the top were neat rows of olive trees on one side, and grapevines on the other. At the top of the hill I could make out one side of a white house.

The gate itself was painted, the same blue I'd seen on a million other gates in Greece. Unlike the others this one was large, seven or eight feet tall, and topped with pointed metal spikes. The stone gateposts on either side were smooth, painted white, and with flat square tops, about two feet higher than the gate itself.

This thing was not for show; it was for keeping people out.

"I think we can get over these gateposts. Here." I leaned over slightly, weaving my fingers together in a cup.

"You want me to get up on the fence?" asked Sam, looking up.

"Yeah."

"Then what? We just walk up to the estate, and announce that we're here for Gideon?"

"One obstacle at a time. C'mon."

"Shouldn't we let GG know? That we think we've found Platon?"

"We've talked about this. I don't trust GG to go after Platon without getting Gideon hurt, or worse. No," I said, shaking my head. "We have to do it ourselves."

"Do what, exactly? Get ourselves taken hostage, too? If this guy's as dangerous as everyone says he is, we'd be fools to go in there."

"We know Gideon's alive. That means that Platon hasn't killed him. And we did just do a job for him, and he did say he'd get back to us. We're just moving up the timetable."

This had sounded reasonable in my head. Now that I said it out loud, I wasn't so sure.

"I go in," said Tatiana, stepping up to the fence.

"There, see? Even she knows I'm right."

"Fine." Sam stepped into my cupped hand, putting one of her hands on the gate and the other on the face of the gatepost for balance.

I hoisted her high enough for her to get most of her body on the top of the gatepost, and she pulled herself up.

Tatiana went next, easier this time, as she had me hoisting her up at the same time Sam was pulling her. When it was my turn the two of them used themselves as a chain to drop Tatiana's hand down far enough that they could pull me to the top.

The three of us dropped down on the other side.

"What now?" asked Sam.

"Let's wait until it gets dark before we go up to the house and look for Gideon."

There were some bushes and a stray olive tree next to one of the gateposts. I sat on the ground behind the bush and leaned against the stone.

So far this was easier than I'd thought it would be. I'd expected Platon's compound to be crawling with security guys. We'd heard no alarms, and I'd seen no security cameras. It made me wonder if we'd been wrong, that this wasn't his place.

I was just starting to nod off when I heard the crunch of footsteps on gravel.

"Poioi eíste? Ti kánete edó?" A man stood over us, a large one, his biceps straining at the short sleeves of his shirt. In his hands he cradled a gun hanging from a strap across his chest. Behind him were two more men with similar guns, both trained on us.

"Sikothíte!"

Sam and Tatiana immediately stood up. When I didn't move he nudged me in the side with the butt of his gun.

While the other two men trained their guns on us, he zip-tied our hands behind our backs. Once we were tied he frisked us, taking my and Tatiana's phones, and Sam's purse.

"Mbros!"

He poked his gun into my back, and they marched us up the gravel road toward the house at the top of the hill.

# TWENTY

The gravel road ended in a parking lot in between a main house and several outbuildings.

From up here we could see most of the island. In contrast to the crowded, tourist-packed streets of Fira, this felt like we were in the middle of nowhere. A beautiful nowhere; sparkling blue water and green islands, some of them obscured by haze, were visible in every direction.

There was little time to take in the view as the gunmen prodded us past the front door entrance and to the back of the house. Sam gasped when we stepped around the corner.

As far as we could see were olive trees, vast numbers of them, in neat rows behind the house, running up and around the hill. Adjacent to the house was a large stone patio above which a flower- and vine-covered trellis provided shade. Plants hung down in pots at the corners of the pillars that supported the trellis. To one side of the patio, on which sat a few chairs and a small table, was a pond, around and in which were several statues, mostly of naked or scantily clad people. On the other side a gravel path led from the patio to a wild garden.

The idyllic picture was made complete by an accompanying aroma of flowers and herbs, similar to what I'd experienced in Crete, and one I now recognized as uniquely Greek.

Stationed around the garden, next to the house and on the hill, were seven beefy, stone-faced men, and one woman. I recognized two of the men from the shootout at the market.

The beefy guy with the gun in my back pushed me toward the table in the center of the patio.

"Kátse káto."

When I didn't move immediately he nudged me again with his gun, then grabbed my shoulder and pushed me down into one of the chairs.

He stared at Tatiana and Sam, who both sat down.

"Sam, what are they—"

I was shoved in the back with the butt of his gun. "Siopí!"

After a few minutes the sliding glass door to the house opened and a man stepped through. All of the men posted around the back of the house stood up a little taller.

We'd been expecting a monster, and Platon looked like anything but.

He was dressed in a sheer white crew-neck shirt with a few buttons, open at the collar, the sleeves rolled up to just below the elbows. The shirt was untucked, laying over light blue linen pants.

He was young, maybe in his mid-thirties, tall, over six feet, well built, and good-looking.

Extremely good-looking. Sam's league, even, good-looking.

His blonde, slightly wavy hair flowed to his shoulders. Deep blue eyes, piercing and soft at the same time, flanked a straight nose, underneath which he was clean-shaven. Unlike many of the men here there were no signs of stubble.

Sam and Tatiana were both staring appreciatively. But I wasn't about to let his handsomeness get in the way of what we were here to do.

"Where's Gideon?" I demanded.

Platon lifted one of his fingers, and the man who'd marched us up the driveway leaned down and cut the zip ties off of our hands, then returned our phones and Sam's purse to us.

"I am sorry about the unpleasantness, but you were trespassing," Platon said, his voice soft and resonant. "I was preparing to summon you, you arrived a bit earlier than I expected."

"Maybe we didn't feel like waiting around for you to decide to fulfill your end of the bargain. Where's Gideon?"

He smiled. "Just as advertised." His English was perfect. "I am Platon, welcome to my home," he said, gesturing to encompass everything we could see.

"Good for you. Where's Gideon?"

The patio door slid open and a woman with a tray of glasses and a large carafe walked over and set them down on our table. She poured red liquid into each of the glasses and then went back into the house.

Platon reached for a glass on the table and held it up. "Please, join me in a toast."

"We're not toasting, and we're not drinking," I said, vaguely wondering if those words had ever come out of my mouth before. "We're not doing anything until we see Gideon. Where is he?"

Platon's eyes flashed briefly before he resumed his placid expression. He raised a finger slightly and one of the men walked into the house.

A few moments later he returned. Gideon was behind him.

All three of us got up and crowded around him in a group hug.

"Are you OK?" I asked.

"I'm fine. How about you?"

I stepped back and looked him over. He did look fine.

"We're OK. We've been worried."

I turned to Platon. "Thanks for everything. Enjoy your Greek stuff." I turned to the others. "Let's get out of here."

I walked toward the corner of the house where our escorts from the fence were standing. They didn't move.

I turned back to Platon. "We did our part. We went to Thessaloniki and talked to your Albanian blue pill smuggler. I gave you the information. The deal was, find the information about your guy, and we get Gideon. Let us go."

"Yes, thank you for your help. The information you gained in Thessaloniki was indeed useful. With it we were able to locate our colleague. Or, rather, your friend did," he said, looking at Gideon. "He is quite skilled."

"Yes he is. I'm happy for you. C'mon." I turned to the guy with the gun at the side of the house, and made an attempt to push him out of my way. "Move it, Hercules."

He didn't budge, and the other two stepped closer, making clear we weren't going anywhere.

"I am sorry, Ms. O'Hara, but we are not quite finished here yet."

"It's Doctor O'Hara, and yeah, I think we are. We did our part."

"You completed the first part, for which I thank you. However, I still need to get my man back."

I looked around at the men stationed on the patio, in the garden and on the hill. "It looks like you have more than enough people to help you. I'm sure one of them is up to the job."

Platon sighed. "Please, Doctor O'Hara, I promise you, all of you will be free to go. However I would like the opportunity to extend my hospitality to you and your friends for one day, while

I share with you what we are doing. Then, if you like, you may leave."

"Listen, you puffed-up, little Alexander the Great wannabe, I—"

Gideon touched my elbow. "Jesse, I think you should do what he asks."

My head whipped to him. "What are you talking about? We need to get out of here."

"I've been very well treated. It won't hurt to stick around another day, will it?" he said, pleading.

Gideon and I went way back, to the first year of college, and I could count on one hand the number of times he'd asked me for something. If he was doing it now, he had a good reason.

"Fine," I said to Platon. "But we're out of here tomorrow."

"Wonderful! Please, sit down, and enjoy the wine. I have rooms ready for all of you, and then you can be my guests for dinner."

We sat back down around the table. Still standing, Platon raised his glass to us. "Kaló kéfi ke stin iyía mas!" He drank, and gestured the same to us. "It is a traditional toast, it means, 'To good spirit, to the gods, and to your health.'"

I wasn't a wine person, but it tasted good. Sam took a small sip, and then a larger one. Her eyebrows went up.

"This is Xinomavro, yes?" she said, looking at Platon.

He looked at her approvingly. "Yes, you are correct. You have a refined palate, Ms. Hernandez. It is the Mikro Ktima Titos, Goumenissa, Macedonia 2019. It has won a variety of awards, including a gold designation by Decanter."

We finished the carafe, and Platon raised a finger to one of the men on the patio, who left, and returned shortly with another one. As he set it on the table he said something under his breath to Tatiana.

She immediately slammed her glass down on the table and stood up, facing him.

"Chto ty skazal?" she shouted.

He sneered at her. "Ty menia slyshala. Rashka parashka."

She walked towards him aggressively, yelling. He backed up until he was off the patio, on the short gravel walkway in the garden.

"What did he say?" I asked Sam.

"It sounded like 'Rashka parashka.' Loosely translated, it's a phrase that compares Russia to a prison toilet."

I snorted.

"Laugh if you want, but it's about the most insulting thing you can say to a Russian."

I committed the phrase to memory. It might come in handy later.

"It's not exactly Russian. It's Fenya," she added.

"Fenya?"

"Yes. It's a sort of prison slang. A mix of Russian, German, Greek, Georgian, Yiddish and Hebrew."

"You're kidding. How in hell do you know that? Did you spend time in a Russian prison?"

"No. I took a linguistics course in school, we did a unit on slangs. Fenya is one of the most complex slangs in the world. It's used as a secret language in correctional facilities in Russia, and is indecipherable to most people."

"So how does she know it?" I said, looking at Tatiana, who was still yelling.

"Rashka parashka is one of the few Fenya phrases that made it to the mainstream, most Russians know it. It's a popular insult, one you only use when you really want to make someone mad. And for it to come from a foreigner, a non-Russian?" She shook her head. "He might as well have slapped her face and told her he was going to impregnate her mother."

The guy had backed up until he was in the grassy area of the garden, spitting what sounded like insults the whole time. When he got to the center of it he stopped, then stepped towards Tatiana and pushed her in the chest.

She took his hand and turned it back on him.

It was a move I'd seen her do before. Usually it dropped whoever was on the receiving end to the ground. He slipped out easily.

She wasted no time in launching a kick at his stomach, and then it was on.

Tatiana's dad had been with the spetsnaz, the most skilled and dangerous of Russia's military, and he'd taught her everything she knew. The spetsnaz were trained in Systema for hand-to-hand combat, a fighting system analogous to the Israeli's Krav Maga. Like Krav Maga, Systema was an efficient fighting style that borrowed from a variety of other ones, including Judo and Sambo, taking the best from each. Also like Krav Maga, it was brutal. No one practiced Systema for tournaments and belts; it was purely for winning real fights, often to the death.

Tatiana went off on the guy with kicks and punches. Many of them were landing, and he was soon bleeding from the nose.

He was using some kind of mixed martial art himself, also kicking and punching, but at the same time trying to get her in a clinch. He was bigger than her, outweighing her by at least fifty pounds, and a close-in wrestling match would be to his advantage.

He hadn't managed to get her in a real hold yet, but his blows were landing, too, an open cut on her forehead was dripping blood into one of her eyes.

I wasn't worried about her. I'd seen her take down lots of bigger guys, and I also knew she loved a fight. But I was a little surprised that Platon was letting this happen. He'd come across as gracious, refined even, since we'd arrived. And everything about his estate radiated calm beauty.

But rather than stop it, which he could have done with a single word, or one of his little finger waves, he was . . . observing them.

Tatiana's opponent was no slouch, but she was in otherworldly shape. She regularly worked out in Sam's gym, ran long distance almost every day, and where possible, swam several miles.

She wasn't just trained, she was in top physical condition. The guy was about ten years older than her, and while he had a few pounds and lots of muscle on her, it was unlikely he was as fit. The longer it went on, the better it would be for her.

She knew that, too, avoiding any clinching or close-in exchanges where his larger frame and strength would be an advantage.

Sure enough, after a few minutes his breath was coming in gasps.

She kept at it, dancing around him, and aiming selected blows at his stomach, head, back, and legs, that eventually caused him to stumble. As he dropped to the ground she moved in, delivering a barrage of kicks and punches, until he was on his back, where she reigned blows down on his face and kicked him in the head.

Platon said something, and two other men walked over briskly and pulled her off of the guy who was now on his knees, blood pouring from his nose and mouth.

Platon nodded almost imperceptibly to the beaten man. He got up and went into the building.

*What the hell was that?*

"I am sorry about that," Platon said.

He didn't look sorry. "Miss Alekseeva, are you OK?"

She stared at him while she sat back down at the table, a trickle of blood from her nose joining that from the cut above her eye.

Platon said something to the woman, who went inside and returned shortly with a washcloth, a white bottle and a shot glass.

She set the washcloth and glass in front of Tatiana and poured her a clear shot. She drank it quickly and wiped her face with the cloth. Then she poured herself another one, never taking her eyes off of Platon.

He stood up. "Perhaps you would all like a little time to refresh yourselves? And then you can be my guests for dinner." He turned to Tatiana. "Persephone will tend to your injuries."

I didn't know what was going on, but I didn't trust this guy as far as I could throw him, and I didn't want to wait any longer to get the hell out of here.

I stood up to tell him we were leaving but was stopped by the slow shake of Gideon's head.

"Thodore, ta engrafa." Hercules stepped over to the table. Apparently corralling trespassers wasn't enough to warrant one of Platon's cool Greek god names.

"Thodoros will escort you to your rooms. Dinner will be served at eight o'clock."

# TWENTY-ONE

We were each led to a separate room, three of them in a row down one of the hallways.

My room was spacious, adorned with art that I presumed was Greek, and had an adjoining bathroom with a shower.

Despite my eagerness to get out of here, it felt good to get a shower. I reluctantly changed into the clothes that were laid out on the bed, which were all in my size. This guy might be a terrorist, but that was no reason to wear dirty clothes.

Once dressed I left my room, looking down both sides of the hallway, surprised to see no guards.

Sam's door was still closed, so I walked down the hallway to the main room.

The center of the house was the main living space, open to the large kitchen. From the center ran several hallways. No one stopped me as I ventured down the one next to our rooms that ran the length of the house.

Off of the hallway were more sizable, high-ceilinged rooms, all filled with art. Sculptures, paintings, carved wooden figurines and pottery on podiums, all beautiful, and all, no doubt, made in Greece, by Greeks. One entire room was built to feature a series of Giacometti-like iron statues, backlit and standing on one end of a long rectangular space.

The other side of the house seemed primarily devoted to raki production, various doors leading outside to the adjacent olive groves.

I made my way to the front door, and then through it, expecting at any moment to get the "you're not free to leave" treatment by one of Platon's thugs.

A guy was standing in the parking lot, a gun hanging lazily from a strap around his neck. But he only glanced at me before turning back to watch down the driveway.

How far would they let me go? I walked down the driveway as a test.

I kept going until I was out of sight of the house. I looked around again for security cameras, and saw none. If they were installed here, they weren't obvious. But they must be around somewhere, otherwise how else would they have known when we broke in?

I made it all the way down to the gate. If I'd wanted to, I could have gone over the fence.

So we were free to leave.

At least *I* was. I pulled out my phone, a little curious that they'd given it back to me.

I tried to make a call and found out why. No signal.

I walked back up the driveway and into the house, then knocked on Sam's door.

"Come in."

She was dressed, and standing near a large painting that took up almost the entirety of one of the walls.

"What do you think was going on with Tatiana, and that guy? He definitely picked that fight with her," I said.

"Uh-huh." She was staring at the painting. "Do you see this? It's an original. Platon has an amazing eye."

I didn't care about his fucking art. "Doesn't he strike you as the kind of guy that wouldn't tolerate his men fighting with guests? I mean, he's trying to show how cultured he is. But he just sat there, and watched them beat the shit out of each other."

"I don't know," she said, now looking in the mirror. She was wearing a short blue dress that fit perfectly. On the vanity below the mirror was a selection of cosmetics, none of which she'd brought with her, all in her brands and colors.

"We know she's volatile," she added.

"She didn't start it. I think Platon wanted them to fight."

"Why on earth would he do that?" she said, putting the finishing touches on her make-up.

"I don't know. But I don't trust him."

She turned to face me. "You know, everything we know about him is from GG. Has it occurred to you that he might not have been telling us the truth? Maybe Platon's not the villain that GG made him out to be."

Sam was famous for always seeing the best in people. But this time she was way off base.

"You're kidding, right? Even if we don't trust a thing GG has told us, Platon kidnapped Gideon. And it was his guys who opened fire in the Athens Market and killed Christos. *And* he might have been the person who blew up our hotel."

She shook her head. "You have no information, at all, about who bombed the hotel. It could just as easily have been Svetlana. In fact, I'll bet it was her. Gideon said himself, he's fine. It wasn't like they threw a hood over him and forced him into the back of a van. We saw him leaving GG's office on the CCTV. There didn't look to be any coercion."

I rolled my eyes. "I can't believe this. You want Platon to be good because he's Chris Hemsworth, Ryan Reynolds and Brad Pitt all rolled into one."

"All I'm saying is, don't jump to any conclusions. We should at least talk to Gideon before we decide Platon's a violent criminal."

I couldn't believe she was into this guy. There was nothing left to say. I turned around and stalked out the room.

Dinner was on the patio, which had been transformed since we'd arrived. The trellis was lit with a thousand small lights, in and among the foliage. The small drinks table and chairs had been replaced by a linen-covered dining table set for five.

Platon was standing at the head of the table, talking to Gideon. When we stepped onto the patio he walked over to Sam and took her arm, then led her to the seat next to his, pulling the chair out for her.

He tried to do the same to me and I shook him off, taking a seat next to her. Immediately after we were seated, Persephone, who'd been standing discretely next to one of the columns, poured something with bubbles into our glasses.

"Did you enjoy your stroll, Doctor O'Hara?"

"Let me guess. You call this place Olympus. Why don't you call yourself Zeus?"

"Zeus is a god. I am a man. And Platon was known for thinking." He sat down, his glass was immediately filled.

"You mean Plato?"

"Yes, Plato was the Romanized version of Platon. He established the first school in the western world, and was the father of many ideas that laid the foundation for most of western thought, including the tenets upon which most major religions are based. One could ask, where would the world be without Platon, and thus, without Greece?"

This guy made it sound like if it hadn't been for Greece, we'd all still be hanging in trees, throwing our own shit at each other.

While we were talking Tatiana shuffled to the table. She took the last empty seat next to Gideon and immediately emptied the glass of champagne that was poured for her. Persephone quickly poured her another one.

Tatiana would rather die than show weakness, but I could tell she was sore from the fight. Dark bruises were starting to appear underneath both eyes, courtesy of what was likely a broken nose. I had my issues with Tatiana, but I didn't relish seeing her beat up like this. When she emptied the second glass Platon raised a finger at Persephone, who disappeared into the house, returning with the white bottle and pouring Tatiana clear white liquid from it.

Shortly thereafter the food started to arrive. It was served family style, plates of simple but delicious mezze, including figs, feta cheese, olives, marinated vegetables, fresh bread and bowls of fragrant olive oil. Wine, initially white, then shifting to red as we reached the meatier portions of the meal, flowed steadily. No glass was left empty for long.

"You know," Platon said as we were served a platter of herbed meatballs, "the ancient Greeks understood that eating was a social event, something that brought a community together. The Greek historian Plutarch even said, 'We do not sit at the table to eat . . . but to eat together.'

"All of this," he said, waving his hand at the table crowded with platters and wine, "is from Greece. Not a single thing at this table has been imported."

He might be a terrorist, but his food was amazing. It reminded me of a meal I'd had once in Maine. It was a chef's tasting menu, eighteen small courses, where every single ingredient had been sourced from within the state. That meant there had been no oil used in preparing any of the dishes, no wines from France, no chocolate, or coffee. Everything had to be cooked in butter or ghee, and there were lots of local vegetables and fruits, game and seafood, even moss and seaweed. The end result was innovative, and fantastic.

As was this meal. The appetizers were followed by main courses of perfectly grilled lamb chops with tzatziki, a fresh village salad – horiatiki – of cucumbers, tomatoes, feta, olives, oregano and lemon juice, and plates of zucchini stuffed with some kind of minced meat covered in velvety avgolemono sauce.

"Let me guess, all of the lamb is from a special, ancient farm, on a small Greek island," I said, devouring one of the zucchini.

"Yes! How did you know?"

"Lucky guess."

Gideon's head was down. He'd said little during the meal, and had only picked at his food. Earlier he'd said he was fine; and while he wasn't showing any outward signs of abuse, something was bothering him now.

Tatiana was focused on her meal, and on her white bottle: Kástra Elión vodka. Greek, of course. Her bruises didn't seem to affect her appetite, which was always healthy, given that she regularly exercised away tens of thousands of calories daily.

Sam looked comfortable and was clearly enjoying the food. Occasionally Platon leaned down and said something for her ears only. She was smiling, and a few times laughed out loud.

"Quite the place you've got here," I said, breaking up one of their little tête-à-têtes.

"Thank you," he said, slightly bowing his head.

"And lots of room for storage." I looked at the outbuildings scattered on the grounds. "Is that where you keep your smuggled guns?"

Sam gave me a dark look.

"This," he said, gesturing to his property, deftly changing the subject, "entire place was built to honor Greece. Greece as it is now, as well as ancient Greece. Not only the greatest civilization the world has ever known, but also the first."

He was lecturing us, as if he'd done this spiel many times. But it was clear he believed every word of it.

Tatiana bristled at his comment, although she couldn't argue with the Greeks appearing before the Russians. The Egyptians and Chinese might have something to say about that, though.

"I'll give you this," I said, "you have the best set of gods of any culture I know."

"You are familiar with the Greek gods? Have you studied them?"

he asked, eager to engage in something about Greece, and not about his kidnapping and gunrunning. "There are also the twelve Titans. And their precursors, such as Ouranos."

"Oh no," Sam said, lowering her head.

"I'm not as familiar with Uranus." Sam elbowed me in the side.

"It's pronounced, Ouranos, Ore-ah-noss." He leaned forward, energized. "And it is not surprising that you have not heard of him. Most people outside of Greece are only familiar with the most popular Greek gods, the ones who appear in movies, and very few of the original Titans. But they are as much a part of Greek heritage as Hera, Apollo, and Aphrodite.

"Ouranos is the father of all Titans. According to Hesiod, he was the son of Gaia. He had eighteen children, one of whom eventually castrated him. It is said that the blood from that act was the origin of the Furies.

"It is wonderful to hear that the stories of our culture have permeated your lexicon."

"They've permeated, all right. So, what is Uranus the god of?"

"Ore-ah-noss. It means 'heaven.'" He got up from the table and went into the house, returning with a large book. He flipped through the pages and set it down in front of me. "Here, this is a picture of Ouranos, from the frieze at the Pergamonmuseum in Berlin."

He frowned. "Another atrocity on our culture. Much of the art that was stolen from us by the Germans in World War Two has never been returned. It sits in their museums when it is rightfully ours." He continued to flip through, pointing to another page. "This is a fresco of Ouranos' mutilation by Zeus, which currently sits in Italy."

"Are there any paintings of the back of him?" I asked. Sam elbowed me again, harder this time.

"I do not think so," he said, flipping through the book.

While I had him off guard I moved in. "So, tell us, what is this Golden Dawn shit you have going on?"

He closed the book, his lip curled in disgust. "The Golden Dawn were criminals, little more than petty thugs, draping themselves in the Greek flag. They are defunct. The Megali Titans have nothing to do with the Golden Dawn."

I raised my eyebrows.

"The goal of the Megali Titans is a better Greece. That is the reason our message is resonating with so many people. They believe, rightly so, that we will improve their lives, and restore Greek culture."

"Greek lives, yeah? I'm interested to know why those weren't so important to you when you bombed the hotel in Heraklion."

I was expecting to hear him deny it, and was surprised when he said, "I am very sorry about that." He was either the greatest actor on the planet, or he was genuinely remorseful. "We had no idea that would happen."

"So you did bomb the hotel," I said triumphantly, looking at Sam.

"No, no, of course not. I would never do such a thing."

"Wait, what? If you didn't bomb the hotel, what are you sorry for?"

"We were commissioned to take you away from the hotel for the day. That is all."

"By who?" I knew who it was, but wanted to hear him say it.

"I do not know. We were given the job and the funds, through a 'cut out,' I believe you call them."

I snorted.

"I assure you, Doctor O'Hara. We had nothing to do with the bombing. Good Greeks died that day. When I do find out who did that, whoever it is will regret it," he said, his eyes stormy.

I didn't want to believe him. But I did. He actually looked angry.

Maybe Sam was right. This guy wasn't a terrorist, just a political opponent of the current administration.

"OK, what about the guns you're having smuggled over?"

"The current Greek government is ignoring the Turkish threat. We are not. We are preparing our people to take on Erdoğan. Turkey is already taking steps to overrun our country, it is only a matter of time before they strike. It is not a crime to prepare for an attack."

"You really expect them to attack Greece?"

"I do not expect you to understand. Americans do not live with enemies surrounding you. Oceans on both sides, friendly Canada to the north, and Mexico to the south . . . there are no threats at your borders."

"So, you're not a terrorist?"

"Terrorist?" he laughed. "Who told you that?" He raised his

finger, slightly, and the empty platters and plates began to disappear from the table. "If it was someone in our current government, I would take that with a grain of salt, as you say. We have political differences with the approach the government is taking, and we make them known. We are offering something better for Greece. Of course they are trying to censor me. I threaten their power and status."

I couldn't figure this guy out. Was he as bad as GG had said? Were we dealing with a terrorist, or a relatively benign zealot, who'd gotten on the wrong side of the government?

I needed to talk to Gideon. He would know more than we did. Somehow we hadn't had a moment alone since we'd arrived. I didn't think that was an accident.

Once the table was cleared Persephone returned with a carafe and a set of glasses. She poured a small amount into each. Platon gestured for us each to take one.

It was some kind of dessert wine, which I'd always found too sweet. But this was delicious.

"This is Chios Mastiha. It is made from the sap of trees that are found on the island of Chios. The sap is referred to as 'the tears of Chios.' Do you like it?"

"Yeah, it's great."

I couldn't fault this guy for his alcohol. And he was so damn charming. I wasn't usually swayed by that, but his combination of good looks, erudition, apparent humility, and intelligence were all working against me.

They were working against Sam, too. In between their little conversations they were frequently locking eyes. I had to keep reminding myself that even if he hadn't blown up our hotel, he'd kidnapped my friend.

The dessert wine went away, and we were brought yet another tray. Again with a set of small glasses, and a bottle.

"I understand you are a whiskey drinker, Doctor O'Hara."

I nodded.

"Greece is not known for its whiskey, but a friend of mine has been experimenting." He opened the bottle and poured each of us a glass.

"Yámas."

I ignored his toast and sipped.

It wasn't bad. Rich and caramelly, with some flavors I didn't recognize. It wasn't Redbreast, but it was definitely up there.

"What makes it sweet?"

"It is distilled from Xinomavro wine, then aged for three years in Mavrodaphne wine casks. Mavrodaphne grapes grow mainly in the Peloponnese, and account for our sweeter wines."

I now had a good buzz on, and even though he'd thrown some question into whether or not he was really the monster GG had made him out to be, I was done being wined and dined by this guy without getting answers.

"You said you would talk about what it is you're doing. Let's get on with it, because we're leaving right afterwards."

He set his glass down on the table and carefully used his napkin to wipe his hands.

"It is late, let us not ruin a wonderful meal by this kind of talk. I promise you, Doctor O'Hara, I will explain everything tomorrow."

Another delay. Sam might be falling for this guy, but I wasn't fooled. I stood up. "Thanks for dinner. Forget about your explanations, I don't care. We're leaving tomorrow morning." I stared at him. "With Gideon."

"As you wish. In the meantime, please accept my hospitality, and treat this as your home."

"My *home*? I don't kidnap people to get them to my home. I don't put zip ties on people at gunpoint, and I don't insult and then pick fights with my guests. But I guess it's a cultural thing, eh?"

I turned away, hoping Sam would follow me.

She didn't. I went inside the house and to my room. An unopened bottle of his friend's whiskey was sitting on the table next to the bed.

What the hell. I broke the seal and poured myself a glass.

It was many hours later when I heard the door to Sam's room open and close.

# TWENTY-TWO

When I left my room the next morning Sam's door was open and her room was empty. I found her lounging on a chair on the patio, drinking coffee. Despite getting to bed much later than me she was wide awake.

I followed her eyes to the hill behind the house. Tatiana was at the top, running. She came down the hill, ran on the gravel path around the garden, and back up again. Her route took her near the guy she'd fought yesterday, who was at his post by the fountain. Like her, he was sporting a couple of black eyes.

As she went by she said something to him. It didn't take a lip reader to know what she'd said. He scowled and spat on the ground.

"You were up late," I said to Sam.

"We were talking. He's a very interesting man."

"Let me guess . . . you were talking about something else related to Greece that's amazing, that he didn't manage to fit in last night."

"It doesn't hurt to be friendly, and maybe get him on our side."

"I'm not sure it's your side he wants to get on."

She sipped her coffee. "He's an excellent conversationalist."

"I don't doubt it. I guess it's a bonus he's drop-dead goodlooking."

She laughed. "Yes, it is."

"Seriously, we need to get out of here. I'm going to look for Gideon, and then we're leaving." I didn't wait for her response and went back into the house.

I found Gideon at the end of one of the other hallways, in the doorway of a room that had been locked since we'd arrived. He was talking to one of the few men other than Platon who wasn't carrying a gun.

Gideon waved and walked over to me.

"You should see their set-up. Top-of-the-line servers, advanced cooling systems, ergonomic workstations . . . all state of the art."

"Great! All better to start a world war with. C'mon, get your stuff, we're getting out of here."

He shook his head. "We can't go, Jesse. Or, at least, I can't."

"What are you talking about?"

"Platon has a job for us. He's made clear that I'm not free to leave until it's done. Please, listen to what it is he wants us to do. There's a chance that when it's done we can all go."

I didn't like the fact that he'd said "there's a chance" he'd let us go, instead of "he will let us go." But Gideon had been here longer and knew more than me. I'd need to follow his lead for the time being.

As we were talking the guy at the door walked over to us.

"Follow, please."

He led us both down another hallway to a room at the end.

Unlike most of the rest of the rooms in the house, this one was devoid of art. A long table ran down the center, with chairs on either side.

Sam and Tatiana were already there. Gideon took a place at the end of the table near Platon, who was standing in front of a monitor on the wall.

"Good morning, I trust everyone slept well?" he said, his eyes on Sam.

She smiled back. "Yes, thank you."

"Wonderful. Thodore, ta engrafa."

Thodoros handed each of us a small stack of papers. Mine included a Turkish visa and some employment papers. Sam and Tatiana's looked similar, except that Tatiana's also included a passport. An American one.

"What are these for?" I noticed they hadn't given Gideon anything.

"To facilitate crossing the border."

"The border?"

"Thanks to your earlier work, we know that Apollo is in Turkey. We have located him in the Edirne prison. You are going to get him out."

"You want us to break your guy out of a Turkish prison?" All I could think about was *Midnight Express*, the iconic 1978 movie about the young American man who'd been sentenced to thirty years in a Turkish prison for trying to smuggle hash out of the country. Like every other person who'd seen that movie, the images of bleak and torturous incarceration by sadistic Turkish prison guards were seared into my brain. The movie had creamed Turkey's tourist business for a long time.

I stood up. "No way."

"It'll be OK, Jesse," said Gideon softly. "He has a good plan. Please hear him out."

I sat back down. "So what's this big plan?"

"It is actually Gideon's plan." He motioned to Gideon to take over and took his seat.

Gideon opened up a laptop and brought the monitor in the front to life. On it was an image of an aerial view of a large, low structure.

"This is the Edirne prison, in northwest Turkey. It's about six and a half kilometers from the Greek border. This is where Apollo is being held. Since 2013 Turkey has allowed conjugal visits to inmates. We've set up a conjugal visit for Apollo's wife."

I could see where this was going and started shaking my head. "Sam's not doing a booty call in a Turkish prison."

"Not Sam, Jesse."

"What? You're on crack if you think I'm going to f—"

"Please, Doctor O'Hara. No one will be forced into any conjugal activities. Let Gideon finish the explanation."

Gideon looked at Platon, who nodded at him to continue.

"The conjugal rooms are private, and like some of the cells at the prison, they have small courtyards that are open to the sky." He used a laser pointer to highlight a pattern of square breaks in the prison's red roof.

He zoomed out to the wider shot of the area. "This is Kastanies." He pointed to a small town on the Greek side of the border. "You'll go to Kastanies and meet with your contact, who will give you the equipment you need. Primarily this." The image changed to one of a shoebox-sized black container. "Then the three of you will cross the border. Jesse and Sam will go to the prison. On the way you'll drop Tatiana off here." He circled a spot outside of the prison. "There's construction going on outside of the walls." He zoomed in again and we could see a large crane in the center of the construction area.

"Once you are in position, the Kastanies contact will send a drone up from the Greek side of the border, across the Evros river, to the crane. He'll call Tatiana when it's up. Shortly afterwards she'll gain control of the drone herself, and land it next to the crane. At the designated time, she'll activate the drone and send it over the prison walls. It will hone in on the room where Jesse and Apollo's conjugal visit is taking place, and hover above the open courtyard there. It will drop a line down, and Apollo will hook into the line. At that point the drone will leave and take him back across the Greek border."

This was some ridiculous *Mission Impossible* shit. "You can't be serious. Drones can't carry people. And even if they could, how do you expect to get one over a prison without anyone seeing it? I'm assuming Turkish prisons have guards, you know, with eyes."

"There are models big enough to carry a man. And this drone is the quietest one we could find in that size, and it's being painted black. This is why we needed the conjugal visit, they're the only visitations that are allowed in the evening."

"Prisons have lights. Don't you think they're going to notice a drone dragging one of their prisoners away?"

"The drone will be above the prison grounds for less than a minute, most of that directly over the courtyard. It will be up high before it drops down. By the time they figure out what's happening, it will be back outside the prison walls and only a few kilometers from the border.

"And," offered Platon, "We have a little distraction planned. I doubt the prison guards will be worried about a drone at that time," he said mildly.

"You want to tell me what that distraction is?"

"It is better if you do not know."

"How will Apollo get up to the drone?"

Gideon reached into a box sitting on the floor next to him, and pulled out some canvas straps and a shirt, handing both to me. The shirt was a woman's light blue button-down, with long sleeves. The thick canvas straps were some kind of harness.

"You'll wear that," Gideon said, pointing to the harness, "under your clothes when you go to the prison. When you get in the conjugal room Apollo will put it on. The rope that will be sent down from the drone will have a carabiner, he'll attach it to the harness."

"Under my clothes? Don't they search visitors when they come into the prison? What if they find it?"

"They only scan for metal."

"Just tell them it's for your conjugal visit," added Sam. "That Apollo has certain tastes." Of course she would think of that.

Gideon pointed to the shirt I was holding. "The top button on the shirt is a transponder. When you meet with the contact in Kastanies, he'll sync it up with the drone's controller. When you're inside the conjugal room you take off the button, activate it, and put it in the open courtyard, as high up as you can get it. This is how the drone will hone in on your location."

My mind was reeling. They were talking like this was some kind of visit to a petting zoo, not a Turkish prison, where we'd be responsible for some *Papillon* fucking *Shawshank Great Escape* shit.

Still, it was Gideon's plan. I trusted him with this kind of thing more than I trusted anyone else on the planet.

"What if they find the button? You said they search visitors at the prison for metal?"

"All of the buttons on the shirt are metal. Platon tells me it's, uh, unlikely they'll make you take off your shirt," he said, looking at Platon.

"Most of the Turks you meet will be deferential to you, as an American," added Platon. "Their prisons are under much scrutiny, especially now, by humanitarian groups, not just for unlawful incarceration, but also for poor conditions and overcrowding. Apollo is a high-profile prisoner, and they will want to use your visit to show that their reputation is undeserved."

OK. If not easy, they'd at least thought all of this out. It had started out sounding ridiculous and impossible, and was now at least sounding feasible. And so far not that dangerous, at least not for us. We wouldn't be the ones dangling underneath a drone flying over a prison.

"After Apollo is taken away with the drone, you'll leave the room. When you do, you'll bribe the guards to make sure he's undisturbed for ten minutes. That's the most you'll be able to get, and should be more than enough time for Apollo to make it across the border, and for you to get out of the prison."

Again with the "should."

"Turkey is one of the most corrupt places on earth," said Platon. "They will gladly let him sleep for a few minutes if you pay them."

I wondered if his hatred for Turkey and his Greek nationalism were clouding his judgment. "Let's suppose, for the sake of argument, that all this shit works, and we're actually able to get him out of the prison, and they let me leave. Then what? We just drive back across the border?"

"Uh, no . . ." said Gideon, averting his eyes for the first time since they'd started. It was obvious he was least confident in this part of the plan.

"I doubt you will be allowed back across the border," said Platon. "We believe that they will discover that Apollo is missing rather . . . uh . . . quickly after you leave. They will be looking for him at the border, and will search every vehicle they do not recognize. Apollo is a high-value prisoner, and by the time you get back to the crossing, the guards will have been alerted. As the last person to see him, you will be under suspicion, and, eh, detained."

I was pretty sure I wanted nothing to do with the Turkish version of "being detained."

Gideon pulled up the aerial view of the region again, this time showing an area northwest of the prison. A large river marked the border between the two countries. "Here," he said, pointing to a narrow part of the river, "is the shortest crossing point on the Evros river at the border. It's only about a hundred feet wide there."

"The river?"

"Yes. It's used frequently by people who are trying to cross the border from Turkey into Greece. Many of them survive the trip."

"*Many* of them?"

"A lot of people who try to cross in the winter months don't make it. The water's really cold, and some people who try to cross are poor swimmers. It's good it's June, it's much warmer."

"So we're swimming across?"

"No, of course not. That would be dangerous."

I snorted. "Yeah, we wouldn't want anything to be dangerous."

"Your contact in Kastanies will leave a small boat here." He pointed to a spot on the bank on the Turkish side of the river. "After you leave the prison complex, you'll pick up Tatiana near the crane, and then drive here." He pointed to a main road, designated E80 on the map. It ran parallel to the river. On the west, river-side of the road, was a smaller road that went from E80 directly to the river near the boat location.

"This little side road is only a few miles from the prison. You'll just get on the E80, take it until you hit this road, and then it's about a quarter mile to the river and the boat. The river is narrow at that point, it should take less than a minute to get across.

"Here's everything for your trip to Kastanies." Gideon handed me another folder filled with plane tickets, rental car information, and a piece of paper with the address of the Kastanies contact. It also contained an envelope with a wad of euros.

"And if we do this, you'll let Gideon go?" I stared at Platon.

"Of course."

"Why does Sam have to go?"

"She is a polyglot, yes? She will help you in the event that you need someone who speaks Turkish. And, even if not –" he looked at her, his eyes sparkling – "she provides a distraction that you may need."

He was really going all out to get his guy back. "Where did you get a drone?"

He shrugged. "They are expensive, but commercially available."

"This guy must be important to you."

"Apollo is my brother."

I was itching to get out of here, but our flight to Alexandroupolis was leaving at eleven thirty the next morning, and we were forced to stick around another night. We could have taken an earlier flight, but of course Platon would only consider booking us on Aegean Airlines.

I slept fitfully and got up early. When I made it to the patio Sam and Platon were sitting at the small table, on which was laid out a modest buffet.

I grabbed something quickly from the table and left them talking.

It was disturbing and comforting at the same time to see them together. I didn't like the fact that Sam was hot for a terrorist; on the other hand, he seemed into her, too, and I didn't think he'd send her on any kind of mission that would put her in real danger.

I had to kill some time, and while I wandered around the house I found Gideon alone, standing next to the computer room.

"Thanks for the email clue," I said quietly.

"I knew you'd get it. Goblin pedigree." He smiled for the first time since we'd arrived.

"Can you talk?"

"Until Kairos shows up."

"Why didn't you call us?"

"There's a jammer on the property," he whispered. "Cell phone calls can only be made from Platon's room. It's part of their operational security. And the email I sent to you was a one-off; the only reason I was able to do that is because Kairos had to leave for a moment. When he came back he looked over everything I'd done. I told him it was spam. He let it go, but he was suspicious. I won't be able to do it again."

"How confident are you that this plan is going to work?"

I was hoping to hear some words of encouragement. Instead he sighed and looked down, shaking his head. "I don't know. There's a good chance you'll be able to get Apollo out. I'm less sure about what will happen to you afterwards. Platon says he's got something planned as a distraction to help you get out of the prison and to the border, but he hasn't shared the details with me. I do know, if we don't get Apollo out, none of us are going anywhere."

Thodoros walked around the corner, immediately ending our conversation.

"Time to go."

He walked us out to the driveway, where I joined Sam and Platon waiting by the car.

Platon said goodbye to Sam and gave her a hug that no one could mistake for platonic.

Then he turned to me. "I know how you feel about your friends, Doctor O'Hara, and I am confident you will do the right thing. However I suggest you consider Gideon if you are tempted to not do this little job for me."

*Bastard.* How could Sam be into this guy? "I forgot to ask you last night. It was your men, wasn't it, who gunned down Christos in the Athens Market?"

"There is a price to be paid for betrayal. Treason in your own country is punishable by death, is it not?"

"By our government. Last time I checked, you're not the government."

"Not yet. But we are at war, and Christos was a traitor. No one else was hurt by my men."

Gideon stepped in between Platon and me and gave me a big

hug. As he did he put his mouth next to my ear. "You have to get Apollo out. If you don't we're all dead," he whispered before stepping back.

It happened so fast I wondered if I'd imagined him saying it.

We got in the car and Thodoros drove us down the gravel driveway. I turned around and watched Gideon until he disappeared from sight.

# TWENTY-THREE

Our flight included a layover in Athens, and by the time we landed in Alexandroupolis it was ten p.m. Then it took forever to get our rental car.

"What's the hold up?" I asked Sam as we were waiting at the counter.

"Apparently they usually don't allow rental cars into Turkey. Platon must have paid an enormous amount to get us one that would allow that."

"I don't understand why we even need a rental car. Why couldn't he just have his guy pick us up at the airport?"

"They'll check our documents at the border. It looks less suspicious if we have our own car, and that we came from Santorini."

"How do you know that?"

"He told me." During one of their late night discussions, no doubt.

After another thirty minutes of waiting we got our car, and went to the hotel near the airport where Platon had booked us a room for the night.

Our meeting with our Kastanies contact wasn't until three the next day, so we slept in and didn't leave until checkout at eleven. Sam drove and I navigated. Tatiana was in the back, silent as always.

The bruises on her face were in full bloom, dark purple and blue mixed with yellow ringed both of her eyes. I hoped it wouldn't draw scrutiny on us at the border.

Per the map it was an hour and a half trip to Kastanies from the airport. The highway was a mix of four lanes separated by a median, and longer stretches of single-lane road. For most of the trip we were surrounded by flat fields of primarily dirt and rocks. The highlight of the trip was the few times the road came close to the border, and we caught glimpses of the Evros river.

"That's Turkey over there," I said, pointing to the right at some small trees. "We're fewer than five hundred feet from the border here." There were no signs or fences, as far as I could see.

"Looks the same," said Sam.

For most of the trip we didn't speak. I was still a little miffed at her for being so obviously taken with Platon. But now that we were on our own, and I was sure none of his men were eavesdropping on us, I told her what Gideon had said when we'd left Platon's place. If I thought that would break the hold Platon had on her, I was sorely disappointed.

"He actually said that? 'If you don't get Apollo out, we're all dead'?"

"Yep."

"I don't know. You said yourself, Gideon's not a field person. He lives behind a computer screen. Did he tell you anything else? Anything that suggests that Platon is violent?"

"Jesus, Sam, what does this guy have to do to convince you he's bad? Gun one of us down in front of you?" I was beyond frustrated. "And that thing with Tatiana, in the garden? That was a set-up."

"What do you mean?"

"I mean, that guy provoked a fight with her, a really serious one. And it was Platon's idea. He's been testing us, and he wanted to be sure she was up to the job." I jerked my thumb in the direction of the back seat. "Her nose is broken, and it could have been worse."

I wasn't overly concerned with Tatiana's welfare, but I didn't like people messing with my friends, even if I didn't like them very much. Tatiana was an asshole, but she was our asshole.

Sam shook her head. "Why would he do that? You're just looking for reasons to hate him."

"I don't need to look for reasons. He kidnapped our friend. He murdered someone in the market. He was in league with whoever it was that bombed our hotel. And he's making us break someone out of prison. What about all of that screams 'awesome guy' to you?"

"Do we need to have this discussion again? People are complicated. He has a cause he believes in."

That did it, and we drove the rest of the way in silence.

We arrived in Kastanies a few hours before the pre-arranged meet with our contact.

Sam drove through the town, taking the main street all the way to the border to where we'd be crossing.

There wasn't much to see. Gatehouses, fences, a few signs. White one- and two-story buildings with brick roofs, many with shuttered windows, lined largely vacant, not-quite asphalt streets.

We turned around at the border and drove back into the center of town.

It was one o'clock. "What should we do for the next two hours?"

I scrolled through my phone. "This isn't exactly a tourist mecca. The highlight of the place is its proximity to the Turkish border. Let's get something to eat. We might not have the opportunity for a while."

We found a near empty seafood place and went in. Sam ordered for us, grilled calamari, French fries, some small fried fish, tzatziki, red pepper dip, and bread. I limited myself to two beers.

Despite the fact the place was almost empty, service was slow, and the meal took longer than we'd anticipated. By the time we finished and tracked down our waitress to pay our bill it was a little after three o'clock.

Our contact was located about a mile out of town, in a small white house with a brown roof at the end of a one-lane street. Sam parked in front of the house and I got out and knocked on the door.

After a few moments a man opened it. He looked at us suspiciously.

"Doctor O'Hara?"

"Yeah."

"You are late."

"It's not our damn fault everything here takes longer than it should."

Instead of inviting us in he stepped out, and led us around to the back of his house.

The backyard was mostly dirt and tall grass in clumps, with a few trees standing around the edges. In the middle was a barely standing garage, whose large double doors were open.

Inside was a wooden table, next to which sat the drone on a pallet. It looked like an oversized metal insect, arms with propellers coming out of its five-foot-long rectangular body from each corner. Four sturdy legs supported its weight.

He pulled out a folded map from his pocket and spread it out on the table.

"Here is border crossing," he said, pointing. "They will ask for papers and reason for visiting Turkey. Tell them you are there for oil-wrestling tournament."

"Why don't I just tell them I'm there for a conjugal visit with my husband at the prison?"

"They will think is strange there are three of you. Your visit at prison is scheduled for eight o'clock tonight. Go to prison at seven thirty." He traced the path on the map with his finger from the border to the prison. "Do not arrive at prison before then. If there are no lines at border you will arrive in Turkey early, then you must find somewhere to wait."

He handed me a black box with a short antenna coming out of it that had been sitting on the table. It was the same one Gideon had showed an image of in Santorini. "This is controller for drone. At designated time I send drone across border to one of you who are stationed outside prison."

"Tatiana," I said, handing the controller to her.

"We test now, and you learn controls."

He rolled the pallet outside of the shack onto one of the dirt patches.

"Turn on," he said to Tatiana, pointing to a large button on the front. She did, then he walked her through the instructions to get the thing in the air.

She fiddled with the controller for a few moments, then we heard the low hum of the drone as it came to life.

Not completely silent, then. I wondered if Gideon and Platon had actually ever seen one of these in operation.

She brought the drone into the air a few feet, and then set it back down on the pallet.

"Is simple," she said.

He picked up a heavy rope that was coiled next to him, and attached it firmly to a hook on the bottom of the drone. I noticed a thick carabiner on the free end.

"Where is transponder?"

I pointed to my shirt button. He took the controller back from Tatiana, pointed it at my shirt, and fiddled with more settings.

"Transponder now synced with drone. When you are in prison, you must place button outside in courtyard, high. It must be no further than fifty centimeters below roof, or drone will not hear it. You understand?"

I nodded.

"After you cross border, you drop off woman with controller here." He pointed to a circled point on the map. "It is crane, they do construction there." He looked at her. "You can climb, yes?"

She snorted. "Yes."

"Is important to be up high. At eight o'clock I send drone and it land next to crane." He turned to Tatiana. "When it comes you take control. At eight thirty you activate drone, bring into air, and press switch." He pointed to a red button on the controller. "This tells drone to go to transponder. You must not be late. Drone have charge for only thirty minutes."

So I had thirty minutes once in the booty call room to get the harness on Apollo and activate the button.

"How does it know when to come back, from the prison?" I asked.

"She call me when drone hovering over prison." He handed Tatiana a small set of binoculars. "When you see Apollo lifted on drone, you tell me, and I take control and bring back across border. Then you must all leave immediately."

We followed him out of the garage and back around the house to our car.

"Open trunk," he said. I opened it, and he gently wrapped the controller in a blanket and set it down in the back. "Do not let border guards see."

"What if they want to look in the trunk?"

"Then you have trouble." He turned and walked back to the house.

"Wait, what about the boat?"

"Boat?"

"Yeah, the boat. Platon said there would be a boat waiting to take us back across the river."

"Oh, yes," he said, not turning around. "Eh, boat will be at spot on river." He walked into his house and shut the door.

The three of us got in the car and drove back into town, then returned to the main road, where we joined the line of cars waiting to cross the border into Turkey.

The wait at the border wasn't long, and we were at the crossing within a few minutes.

I wasn't too worried about getting across. Gideon would have made sure that our papers were what they needed to be, and Platon was highly motivated to at least get us into Turkey.

The only thing I was worried about was the border guards discovering the controller. That wouldn't be easy to explain. Gideon had given us a story about it, to tell them that it was a sophisticated photography device. But if they knew anything about electronics it wouldn't hold up.

I needn't have worried. They waived us through without so much as a glance. Platon had been right, our American passports were like the golden tickets.

Our quick crossing meant that we were early for the prison visit.

"What do you want to do for the next two hours?" asked Sam.

Platon had said to say we were here for the oil-wrestling tournament. That sounded cool. "Let's go see some oil wrestling."

We drove a little over four miles into the city of Edirne, to the stadium at Sarayiçi, the site of the oil-wrestling tournament.

It was as much a festival as a tournament, with bands, banners and balloons accompanied by the smell of cooking meat outside of the stadium. Crowds of people were walking in the street, stepping aside every now and then to allow important-looking cars to pull up to the front, out of which stepped suited dignitaries.

The entrance to the tournament was underneath a stone archway, sporting larger than life flags of President Erdoğan's face in between Turkish flags.

We went in and took our seats near the top of the covered stands and looked down on a football-sized grass field, on which were small groups of men, many of them shirtless, and most of them hairy. The shirtless guys varied widely in size and shape; some were small, and wiry, others well-muscled, and a few big and soft. All of them were wearing the same kind of leather pants that came to just below their knees.

No one was doing anything yet, as far as I could tell, other than a warm-up that included lots of walking, kneeling, and grass pulling.

After a serenade of drums and some kind of clarinet thing, men started dumping oil on their heads and rubbing it around on themselves and each other. Then they were paired off, roughly according to size. The pairs of men strode into the field, each couple joined by a referee wearing blue pants and a white hat and shirt with a number on it.

Even after it finally started, following another set of ceremonial motions between the paired men, the action was slow, especially with the larger men, whose movements consisted of lots of hand-holding and mild slapping.

"Is dumb," said Tatiana. "Not a real sport."

I couldn't argue with that. As far as I could tell the objective was to get the other guy on his back, which was nearly impossible with everyone covered in oil. The only way to gain leverage was to get a hand inside the other guy's leather pants. I doubted this would catch on in the US any time soon.

There was a little more action with the smaller guys, whose movements were quicker, and occasionally involved throwing an opponent. Every now and then a cheer would go up from one part of the crowd.

We watched men grapple and slip with each other for an hour, then left the stands to check out the food and merch counters.

"Do you think we should get Gideon a pair of those little leather pants?" I asked Sam as we were perusing the vendor tables.

"They're called a 'kisbet,' and they retail for several hundred dollars." She looked at her phone. "We should go. It's almost time."

It took us ten minutes to drive to the prison, the last half mile of which was a one-lane road with nothing but empty grass fields on either side. A few hundred feet before we reached the gate we took the last turn-off, little more than compacted dirt, that wound around to another parking lot. From here we could see the construction site behind the prison, and the crane that would be Tatiana's perch.

We dropped her off on the side of the road. "We'll pick you up here when we leave."

Sam drove back around and to the main entrance to the prison. The gate was up, but we stopped in front of a big red and white "DUR" sign at the front. A bored looking guard came from inside the white gatehouse. He checked our names against a visitor's list, then waved us through.

Sam parked in the lot, and we walked into the front doors of the prison.

# TWENTY-FOUR

E dirne's prison was a designated F-type, housing the most violent and dangerous criminals and political prisoners in Turkey. Even so, it didn't look like much; other than the walls and barbed wire around the perimeter, from the outside it looked like an old academic center.

One of the characteristics of F-type prisons was that they were designed to prevent prisoners from congregating. For this reason, the large, iconic prison courtyard, featured in every prison movie ever made, was replaced by individual courtyards, scattered among the cells and open to the sky.

Critically, this included the conjugal visit rooms. Gideon's plan relied on that.

The lobby immediately dispelled the notion that this could be an academic center. Both the gray walls and dirty floor benefited from the poor lighting, which was barely sufficient to reveal that there were no seats or benches in the small space.

I stepped up to the counter. Behind scratched plexiglass sat a corpulent man in a faded brown uniform.

"Hi, I'm here for a conjugal visit with an inmate. Apollo . . ." I had no idea what his last name was. Maybe Platon's guys were like rockstars, with just one name.

"Ziyaret saatleri bitti."

"He said that visiting hours are over," said Sam.

"Tell him I'm here for a conjugal visit."

Sam and the guard exchanged words, and after showing him our passports, he let out a heavy sigh and pushed a log book and a pen across the counter.

We signed in and he took back the book, then with another heavy sigh got up and left the room. Shortly thereafter he opened the only other door in the lobby and gestured us through.

On the other side of the door was a hallway, where there was another counter with another guard sitting behind more plexiglass. A few feet down the hallway was a metal detector.

"Telefonunuzu sepete koyun. Sepete metal içeren her şeyi koyun."

"We need to give them our phones and anything with metal in it."

We put our phones in the basket and Sam dropped in her keys, and we were gestured through the metal detector, where two more guards, a man and a woman, were stationed.

Sam walked through first. I followed her, and predictably it buzzed.

The female guard ran a wand over me, and when it hit the front of my shirt it went off. She ran the wand up and down the line of buttons.

She pointed at the top one with her wand, then to a door to a small room. "Bluzunu çıkar."

"She wants you to—"

"I got that. No way. I'm not taking off my shirt," I looked at her and shook my head.

"Hiçbir metale izin vermiyoruz," she said, pointing again at my shirt and the small room.

Sam stepped in front of me and spoke to the male guard in Turkish, gently placing her hand on his upper arm. He smirked, and she winked at him. He gestured at us to follow him.

"What did you tell him?"

"I said that you'd gone to a lot of trouble to look nice for your husband. That you hadn't seen each other in months, and that the last thing he'd be thinking about was escaping with metal buttons."

The check-in had taken a long time, and it was already almost eight, which didn't leave us much time to get to the room and get things set up before the drone arrived.

The guard escorted us through the next door and then down a long hallway. I could see metal gates ahead, but before we got to them he turned down another hallway. He walked for thirty feet and then opened a door and led us into a small waiting room.

"What's that?" I pointed to a sign above the only other door in the room.

"It's the warden's office."

I turned to the guard. "I'm not here to see the warden, I'm here for a visit with my husband."

"Sit," he said brusquely.

We sat down on the only two chairs in the room, both faded blue plastic covered in various stains that I didn't want to think about. Then we waited.

After what seemed like an eternity the door opened, and a small, very fat man stood at the doorway.

"Doctor O'Hara, please, may I have a moment of your time?"

Like I had a choice. I walked into his office and he closed the door behind me. He gestured to a chair across a large, ornate wooden desk.

"Welcome to Edirne prison. I am Murat Öztürk, the warden. I understand you are here for a conjugal visit?"

"Yeah."

He leered a greasy smile. "May I offer you some coffee?"

"No thanks."

"I can assure you, it is the best coffee in the world."

"No, that's fine."

"Have you had real Turkish coffee? It is much better than what you had in Greece."

*Jesus.* I guess I wasn't getting out of here until I drank his damn coffee. The minutes were ticking down.

"Uh, OK, sure."

He leaned over his desk and spoke into an intercom. A few moments later the guard walked back into the room, carrying a tray with two tiny cups of coffee and some baklava. He set it on the table and left.

"Please." Öztürk gestured toward the tray.

I reached over and took one of the tiny cups, then downed it in one gulp.

Big mistake. I choked on thick sediment that coated my mouth and throat.

"Oh, I should have warned you, just to sip. The sediment at the bottom is not to be consumed."

I knew that, but was so focused on getting out of here I'd forgotten about their coffee. He handed me a glass and poured from a pitcher of water on his desk. I drank it, getting most of the sediment out of my mouth.

"Please," he said again, picking up the tray of baklava.

I probably wasn't going to get out of here until I tried his damn baklava, too, so I took one, shoving the whole thing in my mouth at once. "Mmm, yeah, really great."

He raised his eyebrows.

"Uh, yeah, waaay better than Greek baklava. This stuff is the bomb." He nodded, as if that was what he was waiting to hear.

"As you can see, rumors of how bad conditions are in Turkish prisons are grossly exaggerated. Mere fantasy. I hope you appreciate our hospitality, and that after today you will tell your American friends how we do things here."

"Sure, yeah." It was well after eight. We would have to move fast, providing this fat loser would ever stop trying to get me to taste Turkish stuff.

I looked up at the clock again.

"Are you in a hurry, Doctor O'Hara?"

"I'm, uh, anxious to see my husband," I said, doing my best to look anxious to see my husband.

He leered at me again. "I am sure that you are. Yes, this is another area where we are more civilized than your American prisons. Even our most dangerous criminals may receive conjugal visits."

He stared at me in a way that made me feel like I needed a shower, then finally pushed a button on his desk. Almost immediately the door was opened by the guard.

"Batuk will take you to the room."

Batuk walked Sam and I out of the waiting room and back to the main hallway, until we were stopped by a heavy metal gate that ran the width of the corridor.

He said something into his radio. The door buzzed and he pushed it open. We stepped through the gate, stopping again a few feet in front of a second gate.

The first gate closed with a loud clang and he moved on.

When he got to the second gate he repeated the procedure. Once we were on the other side of the double gates we walked down another long hallway. We passed several doors before he stopped. He took out his keys and unlocked a door and opened it.

A large man in prison garb stood at the opening.

It was Loukas.

Loukas, the guy who'd lured me away from the hotel in Crete while someone tried to blow up my friends, was Apollo.

He grinned. "Hi, honey."

I stared at him.

Sam elbowed me in the ribs.

I stepped forward. "I missed you," I said loudly, putting my arms around him and hugging him lightly. I put my mouth to his ear and whispered, "You bastard."

He pulled back and started kissing me.

Sam stepped forward, interrupting him before I did something stupid. "I just wanted to see you, Apollo, and tell you that the whole gang sends its love." They hugged, then he stepped back into the room, taking my hand.

He looked at Batuk. "Do you mind?"

Sam stepped back and Batuk moved in to close the door. I heard it lock.

We were alone. The room was small, a single chair against one wall and the rest of the room dominated by a double bed with two pillows. No pictures on the walls, just a small side table next to the bed. A door on the opposite side of the room led to what I hoped was the courtyard.

"It's good to see—" he started, before I punched him in the face. He backed up, holding his nose.

"You son of a bitch." I wanted to kill this guy, and looked around the room for something more useful than my hands to hit him with.

Naturally, there was nothing in the room that could double as a weapon.

He put his hands up in front of him. "No, no, truly, Jesse, we had nothing to do with the bomb."

Platon had already told me that, but I didn't care.

"My friends were in that hotel, you prick." I closed the gap between us and started kicking him.

"Jesse, please stop. And keep your voice down, they think we are having a conjugal visit."

"Listen, Apollo, or Loukas, or whatever the hell your name is. If it wasn't for Gideon I'd leave you here to rot, and tell the prison guards you tried to kill me so they'd extend your sentence. But we need to work fast. We're on a timetable."

I didn't want to help this guy, I hated him. But I loved Gideon more.

It was nearly eight thirty. I started tearing off my clothes.

He raised his eyebrows and grinned.

"Don't get your hopes up." I took off my shirt and pants and then peeled off the harness and handed it to him.

"Put this on."

He started to strip. "What's the plan?" For the first time I noticed the bruising on his face, and deep scratches on his neck.

"No, shit-for-brains, just put it on over your clothes." I put mine back on, tearing off the button at the top of the shirt.

He fitted the heavy canvas straps over his shoulders and around his upper thighs. I pulled the fittings tight.

"Ouch. Hey, I can hardly breathe."

"Tough."

When I was done tightening the harness I opened the door to the small courtyard and stepped outside.

The space was small, maybe a twelve-foot square, the opening to the sky ten feet above us. I wondered why it wasn't screened. But I guessed that none of the other prisoners had brothers who could afford a drone, along with a gang of people to pull something like this off.

No doubt they'd be putting up screens after today.

Our Kastanies contact had said to put the button up as high as we could, that it would only work if it was within fifty centimeters of the top. Even with my arm stretched as far as I could get it I was well below that.

"Give me a hand."

Loukas helped me pull the side table outside to the courtyard. I stood on top of it and held the button over my head. I was still below the top, but close enough. Hopefully.

"What now? What's the plan?"

"Now we wait. Your ride should be coming any minute."

"My ride?"

I ignored him. It would be fun to watch him hook into the drone with no idea what was going to happen.

I looked at my watch. They'd said it would take only a few seconds to get here once it was over the prison walls. I couldn't hear anything, which meant that it hadn't been sent over yet. Despite what Gideon had said about it being quiet, and black, and flying high until the last moment, I couldn't believe they could bring a drone that size over the prison wall without being noticed.

Ten more minutes went by. My arm was getting tired from

holding up the button. I wondered if it was up high enough. Or maybe Tatiana had gotten caught? Or the drone had malfunctioned? There was so much about this that could go wrong.

"It might be a while," Loukas said, looking back towards the bed. "Would you like to—"

"No."

Five long minutes later I heard a faint buzzing.

This was it. "Get ready."

Moments later the drone appeared above our courtyard, hovering. From it dropped the sturdy rope with the carabiner at the end.

Just out of reach.

Shit.

"C'mere, get on my shoulders. Then hook the carabiner onto the harness."

Loukas climbed on the table. He was big, but I was motivated. I leaned against the wall while he stood on my shoulders. Then he reached toward the rope and brought it to him. He clicked the carabiner onto his harness and stepped off of my shoulders, hanging freely and slightly swinging from the drone.

He smiled down at me. "Try messing up your hair before you leave. And make an expression of extreme satisfaction, it must seem realistic that we had a conjugal visit."

The drone rose up, taking him well above the roof, and then it disappeared from sight.

How long would it take for the prison guards to realize what had happened? If they noticed the drone coming in they'd already be on alert. But I hadn't heard anything yet, so maybe they hadn't seen it, or if they had, they hadn't figured out what it was.

In any case I needed to hurry. The thing was quiet, but not silent. Even if they didn't see Loukas flying back out of the prison, anyone around the prison grounds could notice it. We wouldn't be safe until we were out of the prison, and out of the country.

I moved the side table back to its original position, then messed up the bed. I stuffed pillows underneath the blankets in the rough shape of a person, then tousled my hair, and undid another one of my shirt buttons.

I knocked on the door.

Batuk opened it and leaned his head in, looking around the room. His eyes landed on the bulge in the bed.

"Hey, just in time. Isn't it just like a guy to fall asleep after-wards? Listen, uh," I said, pulling out the wad of euros I had in my pocket, "how about you just let him sleep for a little while, yeah?" I handed him the money. "You know, just ten minutes or so? He's exhausted," I said, giving him my best randy grin.

He stared at the bulge in the bed for a long moment, then looked behind him into the hallway.

"Just sleep. Ten minutes." I put my hands up showing ten fingers.

He took one last look around the room, then snatched the money out of my hand and closed the door.

He walked me back down the hallway, taking his time, while I held my breath, waiting for the alarm to sound.

After what seemed like an eternity we were at the first metal gate. He spoke into his radio, and then there was a click and it opened. We stepped through, the gate closing behind us.

I was almost out of here and inwardly started to celebrate. This had been way easier than I'd expected. Now just to get to the parking lot, across the river, and we'd be—

*AWOOGA*

*AWOOGA*

Too soon. They'd seen the drone. Or realized Loukas was gone. Or both.

Batuk stopped and turned, looking at me darkly. The heavy clanking of metal gates slamming shut reverberated in the hallway, almost but not quite drowning out the piercing shriek of the alarm.

# TWENTY-FIVE

Batuk clicked his radio and talked into it rapidly.

"What's going on?" I said, doing my best to adopt an innocent face.

"It is riot."

Was this Platon's "distraction"? A prison riot? I wasn't sure what kind of riot they could have in a prison that never let prisoners congregate in groups of more than ten. But at least it was better than them sounding an alarm because they knew Loukas was gone.

I walked toward the second locked gate and pulled on it.

He shook his head. "No. Lockdown."

The shrill alarm was sounding every few seconds, and was making my head hurt. In between the *AWOOGA*s I could hear yelling. And then shots.

Were they shooting at Loukas? I didn't think so, the drone should have already cleared the prison by now.

The longer I was stuck in here, the greater the chance they'd figure out Loukas had escaped and that I'd helped him do it. And then that would be it; I'd be stuck in a Turkish prison.

What was the penalty for helping someone escape? Probably years. It was small comfort that Turkey didn't have the death penalty, they could still torture me to tell them how we did it.

I had no illusions about how long it would take for me to break under torture; it would be less than the amount of time it took them to walk me to the torture room. And once they knew it was Platon's doing, that would make them even madder, and more determined to make an example out of me.

And if Loukas had made it out, how motivated would Platon be to help us then? He didn't seem all that concerned about our welfare.

Except for Sam. And she was already out. Hopefully still waiting for me in the parking lot.

The American authorities might eventually work to get me released, but I couldn't imagine I'd be high on their priority list.

I had almost no family, or large group of friends, to pressure the government to take action. And I didn't even know how long it would take them to find out I'd been taken. I'd come over the border on a false visa.

These guys could keep me here for weeks, or months, before there'd be any reason for them to let me go.

All of these thoughts went through my head with lightning speed, and it took only seconds to work myself up into near hysteria.

Which was helpful, as I'd learned something early on in my overseas travels. When in trouble, start speaking very fast in English and wave your hands. Nobody wanted to deal with a hysterical tourist.

"Let me out!" I yelled as loud as I could, at the same time grabbing and pulling on Batuk's sleeve.

He jumped, startled. "No. Lockdown." He pointed behind us, towards the cells.

"If you think you're going to keep me in here while there's a fucking *riot* going on, you've got another thing coming. Let me out," I yelled, pointing to the gate.

"No, lockdown."

"Listen you asshat, I've seen *Midnight Express*. I don't care how much sediment coffee and sweet desserts you hand out, I *know* what happens in here." I was leaning into his face, poking my finger millimeters from his nose. He stepped back.

My tirade had come out of nowhere. Up to now I'd been the polite, quiet wife, anticipating sexy fun times with her husband. Now I was screaming like a lunatic. It didn't hurt that I didn't need to fake my own panic.

I kept it up for a solid minute until he reached for his radio.

I knew he'd eventually give in. I didn't blame him; I'd broken the best of them.

He spoke rapidly into the radio. I couldn't understand what he was saying, but guessed it was something like this:

*"Please, I know it is not the protocol, but you must open the gate and let this woman leave."*

*"We cannot. The protocol is clear: when there is a riot, it is a total lockdown."*

*"I know this. But you must understand, my life is in danger. She is nuts."*

*"You would think after a conjugal visit she would be calmer."*

*"Perhaps the visit was disappointing?"*

*"That is entirely possible. But either way, we cannot let her out."*

*"She mentioned* Midnight Express.*"*

*"Midnight Express? This is bad for us. That movie destroyed our reputation. Since that came out, everyone believes our prisons are horrible."*

*"Our prisons* are *horrible."*

*"I know, but we don't want everyone believing that."*

I took off my shirt, wadded it up in my hand and ran the metal buttons back and forth across the metal bars. *"Att-i-ca! Att-i-ca!"*

*"Please, please, I will do anything. You can have my wife's baklava recipe."*

*"Hmmm . . . that will be nice, but it is not enough. You know I could lose my job."*

*"You must help me, I will give you anything you want."*

*"Anything? Hmmm . . . In that case, I would like your leather pants."*

*"My special leather pants? No, I cannot possibly give those to you."*

*"I want your leather pants. They are very nice. And I believe they are in my size."*

*"No, I cannot."*

*"OK. Good luck with the crazy woman."*

*"No! Wait, yes, I will give you the pants."*

The gate clicked open. Batuk rushed out, not waiting for me.

At the end of the hallway the woman who had wanded me earlier was gesturing wildly to me to hurry up.

I ran to her, putting my shirt back on, and she handed me my phone. "You must leave now," she said, stepping back, not wanting to get too close to me.

She didn't need to tell me twice.

I ran out the front door. Sam was in the parking lot with the car, the engine running.

"Let's go," I said, jumping in. "There's some kind of riot going on. They didn't connect us to the drone, but as soon as they realize Loukas's gone, they will."

She drove us out of the parking area and to the main gate, where we had to make a hard left turn, and then came to a stop at the white guardhouse.

The gate pole was down. Probably standard procedure during a riot.

The guard was stepping out of the gatehouse when his radio crackled.

He listened to it, then his face turned hard, and flashing red lights started to rotate at the top of the small building.

Sam didn't need me to tell her what to do next. She gunned it, driving the car into and through the pole.

The other guard ran out of the gatehouse, and both of them were now waving and yelling at us.

Sam took the first turn onto the side road we'd been on earlier, to where we were to pick up Tatiana.

She was already standing in the parking lot. She must have seen the flashing lights, or heard the claxon, which even out here was still unbelievably loud. She ran towards the car, and I reached back to open the door. She dove into the back seat.

Sam spun the car around and we headed back to the main road. She hit the turn at speed and we skidded. Once she righted the car she put her foot to the floor.

"Where to now?"

"Take this to the E80, there should be signs. It runs parallel to the river. From there we'll take that side road to the river bank."

The sound of the claxon was diminishing, now replaced by sirens. Behind us three cars with flashing lights were speeding through the wreckage we'd made of the prison gate.

Sam raced towards Edirne and then turned north on the E80 highway. It was the largest road in this part of the country, consisting of two lanes in each direction. A thin median strip separated the sides.

We drove for less than a minute, scanning the other side of the road for the turn-off to the river.

"There!" I shouted, looking across the median to a small opening between the trees.

"How do I get to it?"

The median strip was thin, but on each side of it were low metal barriers. Easy to climb over, but no way were we getting the car through them.

There were no breaks in the median, as far as I could see. By the time we got to one it would be a long way from our path to the river, and the police would have had a chance to call for support. Not to mention that Gideon had said this was a popular spot to migrate into Greece; the Turkish authorities would know it well, and probably know exactly where we were going.

"Pull over here."

The breaks squealed and we skidded to a stop on the side of the road. All three of us were out and running while it was still rolling.

We waited for a break in traffic and then sprinted across the road. We jumped over the metal barriers and ran for the dirt path that led to the river.

The distance between the E80 and the river on the path was about a thousand feet, a fifth of a mile. It would take us just a couple of minutes to get to the boat.

The sirens grew louder, then they stopped. I looked over my shoulder and saw police cars with flashing lights gathered on the main road. Uniformed men were jumping over the metal barriers and heading toward us.

"Go! Hurry!" I yelled.

I needn't have bothered, Tatiana was outpacing both of us. And while I didn't consider Sam an athlete, she was in decent shape, and had wisely chosen not to wear heels on this trip.

We made it to the river bank and looked around, out of breath.

The sun had set, but there was enough light to illuminate the beach that was littered with debris, both natural and man-made. An open suitcase lay near the water, covered in mud. Next to it lay a few shirts, along with bits of plastic, rope, and heartbreakingly, a few toys.

But no boats.

"Son of a bitch!"

The boat had seemed like an afterthought to our Kastanies contact when I'd asked him about it; I wondered if it had ever been part of the plan. Maybe Platon intended for us to get stuck over here.

"What do we do?" asked Sam.

The yelling behind us was getting closer. Then I heard a gunshot.

Evros to the Greeks, Meriç to the Turks, the river made up much of the boundary between the two countries, and was a major route for migrants trying to get into the EU. Hundreds of bodies were found in and around it every year, and thousands more were never found, believed to have died trying to cross it. Drowning was the leading cause of death, followed by hypothermia suffered by people attempting to swim across during the winter.

I was well aware of all of this, but it wasn't like we had options.

"We don't have a choice." I ran to the left towards what looked like the narrowest part of the river, pushed my way through some bushes, and jumped into the dark water.

Even though it was June the water was icy cold, and I gasped. I forced myself to move my arms and started swimming for the other side.

Two splashes followed me, and a moment later Tatiana swam by. No surprise there, she was a champion swimmer, and never seemed affected by the cold. I was only halfway across when she made it to the thin beach on the far side and scrambled up the bank and out of sight.

Saving herself. *Bitch.*

I heard more gunshots and looked around. Five uniformed cops were on the beach, all yelling, one shining a flashlight. Two of them were firing at us.

Bullets were whizzing over my head. Every now and then one would splash into the water next to me.

Sam was about ten feet behind me, and making little progress. She wasn't in bad shape, but the water was cold, and while the current wasn't extremely strong, it took an effort to move forward rather than downstream.

I looked back to the Greek side.

I was close enough, I'd be able to make it. But I couldn't leave Sam behind.

I stopped swimming and treaded water, doing my best to maintain my relative position to her against the flow of the current.

"You go," she said weakly. "I'll make it."

Little splashes were kicking up the water around her. Then she yelled, and stopped swimming.

I swam back to her. She was no longer moving her legs or arms, and was floating downstream. "Are you shot?"

"No," she said through chattering teeth. "It's a cramp. Go on."

I put my arms around her and treaded water while the current carried us down the river.

# TWENTY-SIX

The bullets stopped. We'd floated far enough downstream and around a bend so the police no longer had a line of sight on us.

That was small relief. Sam was getting weaker, and heavier, as we drifted.

I was having a harder time myself, my arms and legs taking longer to respond to my brain's instructions. If we were in this water much longer we'd be joining the scores of others who hadn't made it across.

The bank wasn't that far away, fifty feet or so. But it might as well have been a mile.

"Hey!"

Tatiana was on the Greek side, running along the river, outpacing the current.

When she was downstream of us she dove into the water.

She swam with strong strokes to join us in the middle of the river.

"Go," she said to me.

"No. I'm not leaving her."

"I will take her. Go."

I used my remaining strength to swim across the rest of the river until my feet touched ground. I collapsed on the small strip of sand next to the water and lay on my back, chest heaving.

Tatiana was making her way across, holding Sam with one arm and swimming with the other. I stood up and followed them down the river as they drifted. When Tatiana finally reached the bank I helped pull Sam onto solid ground. Her lips were blue.

"We need to get her out of these clothes." I took out my phone.

It was soaked, as was Tatiana's. Sam had lost everything when she'd left her purse in the car.

There was nothing to do but walk. I helped Sam stand up, then Tatiana and I each took one of her arms and we climbed up the low bank.

We pushed through bushes and walked slowly across a grass field until we hit a road, Tatiana and I supporting Sam between us. Kastanies was south, so we turned left, and walked alongside the road.

A few cars drove past, headlights illuminating the landscape. Eventually one pulled over and stopped.

A man leaned out his open window. "Chreiázeste voitheia?"

"Kastanies?"

He nodded and opened the door, gesturing for us to get in the car.

The next sign indicated we were three kilometers from town. I gave the guy the address of our contact, and after a short trip he stopped in front of the house.

"Thank you," I said as we got out of his car. I pulled my sodden wallet out of my back pocket and fished out some euros.

"Óchi. Óchi," he said, shaking his head and putting up his hands.

The famous Greek hospitality was no joke. "Uh, efharistó."

He waved and drove off. We walked up to the stoop and I knocked on the door.

When there was no answer I banged on it with my fist.

A few moments later our contact opened it. "What are you doing here?" He frowned, looking down both sides of the street.

I pushed past him into the house. Tatiana followed with Sam, laying her gently on the couch.

"We need dry clothes," I said, with barely controlled fury.

"You should not be here. You must go."

I stepped forward and kicked him as hard as I could between the legs. I'd caught him by surprise, and he dropped to his knees.

"If anything happens to her, you piece of shit, getting discovered will be the least of your worries. Get us some dry clothes, and she needs a blanket. Now."

He disappeared into a back room, slightly bent over, returning shortly with a stack of pants, socks, shirts, and blankets. We stripped Sam first, then took off our own clothes and put on dry ones. I wrapped the blanket around Sam.

"Need doctor?" he asked. "We have doctor. He is, uh, special doctor, for us."

I assumed "us" meant Platon's group, and "special" meant he wouldn't contact the authorities. Like some kind of mob physician.

"No. How about something hot to drink?"

He went into the kitchen, coming back a little while later with steaming mugs of coffee.

We drank, saying nothing, while I stared daggers at him. Thirty minutes later Sam's lips were returning to their normal color.

Now that we were warm and dry, and I knew Sam wasn't going to die, I let him have it.

"Where the *hell* was our boat?"

"There were, eh, complications."

"Complications? We got shot at, and almost drowned in that fucking river while we were swimming across it."

He shrugged. "You did not drown." He looked toward the door. "I have helped you. Now you must leave. Is not safe for any of us while you here."

"Fine. You need to get us back to Santorini."

He shook his head. "I do my part."

"Then give me your phone."

He tossed his phone on the couch, keeping his distance from me.

Sam sat up on the couch. "It's OK, I'm good to go."

"How do you feel?"

"My leg is sore, but I think I can walk."

There was nothing left to do here. I grabbed his phone and we walked outside without saying goodbye.

"What now?"

"Let's get a room for the night. I'm exhausted."

"And then what?"

"Then we're going back for Gideon."


Once we'd gotten a hotel room I called GG, and told him we needed money, phones and a passport for Sam.

I considered bringing him in on what was going on, but Platon's warning was still fresh in my mind. I had no doubt that he would kill Gideon if it looked like we were working with the government. So I didn't give GG any details, and to his credit, he didn't ask.

It took us two days to get back to Platon's compound on Santorini. We had to wait for the passport, and then getting a car out of Kastanies back to the Alexandroupolis airport was no easy feat. Flights were booked solid, and we waited around on standby for an entire day until we got on a flight with last-minute cancellations. There was a five-hour layover in Athens, during which we bought some clothes and then spent the rest of the time sleeping in airport chairs.

When we landed in Santorini we rented another car and drove straight to Platon's place.

His guards met us at the front gate and waved us through, as though they were expecting us. I parked in front of the house and we walked around to the back patio.

Platon was sitting at the small table. Next to him was Loukas.

"There she is!" Platon stood up, a warm smile on his face. He took a step forward, his arms extended for a hug.

I pushed his arms away and took a step back.

"It is good to see you," he said warmly. "All of you," he added, looking at Sam. "Please, join us." He rattled off something in Greek to Persephone, who moved three additional chairs to the table and then went inside the house.

"What the fuck," I spat at him. "There was supposed to be a boat to cross that river. We had to swim, you son of a bitch."

"Oh." He frowned. "I am sorry." His concern looked genuine. "Are you OK?"

"We're fine. But we were shot at, and Sam almost drowned."

"Shot?" Clearly the guy in Kastanies hadn't filled him in on our trip. Platon's eyes were dark. "I assure you, Nikolaidis will hear about this."

So the Kastanies guy did have a name, although he also didn't rate one of the cool, Greek god names.

"Please, sit, let me take care of you for tonight." Platon looked again at Sam, and I was pretty sure what he meant by "take care of."

The three of us remained standing. Persephone returned with three more place settings, and a tray that included bottles of Platon's Greek whiskey, the Kástra Elión vodka, and two bottles of red wine.

Sam and Tatiana sat down. I didn't join them, but I wouldn't say no to a drink. Platon waited until we each had a drink in our hand and then raised his glass. "A toast, to all of you, for a very successful operation, and the return of Apollo." He pointed his drink towards Loukas, and then at Sam before drinking.

"Thank you, all," said Loukas, "for helping me out of Turkey. I hope you will let me return the favor one day."

Fat chance. I ignored him and worked on my drink.

"Apollo tells me the operation went very well. Although I have to say, I am not surprised."

"Whatever. Now it's your turn. We held up our end of the bargain. Where's Gideon?"

"He is inside," said Platon, still smiling. "He is doing a little job for me."

"Get him out here. We're leaving."

Platon sat back down. "What is the hurry? Stay and have some food with us."

"We're not hungry." That was a complete lie, but I didn't want to sit through another one of his meals. "We kept up our part of the bargain. We're not here for dinner, and we don't want to stay the night. Where's Gideon?"

"As I said, he is doing a small job for me. He will be out shortly. Please, sit down," he said, his smile starting to look a little less genuine.

I didn't need to make him mad so I sat down. Shortly after that waves of food started arriving, similar to what we'd had before. A variety of mezze, salads, and meats.

The smell of the food was enticing; we hadn't eaten real food since before we'd crossed the border. I decided my pride wasn't worth passing over a great meal and dug in, keeping one eye on the house.

Finally, when the meal was over and they were serving the Tsipouro, Gideon came through the patio door.

"Hey, Jesse." He looked relieved, but wasn't smiling. He sat down heavily in the remaining chair.

Platon motioned to Persephone, who brought Gideon a plate and filled up his glass.

"Just water, please."

"Are you OK?" I asked. His eyes were red, and there were dark circles under them.

"Fine. Just a little tired." He drank the water and then started to pick at his food.

"Gideon has been helping us with some, eh, financial matters," said Platon.

"Are you packed?" I said to him.

He didn't look up, and started moving food around on his plate.

"What is the rush? Please, stay the night. It is late, and your rooms are ready for you."

"No, thanks. We've got a plane to catch."

"I insist. It is the least I can do, after all of your hard work."

I looked at Sam, who shrugged. I guess she wouldn't mind another night with her crush. And Gideon looked like he could use some sleep. I knew I could.

"Fine. First thing tomorrow we're out of here."

I finished my drink and got up from the table. I went to my room and took a long shower, then went looking for Gideon. I wanted to talk to him, but I needed to catch him alone.

I wandered through the house, at one point passing Platon and Sam sitting close together in the living room, looking at some art book. She was laughing, and they were both smiling. She was really enjoying herself.

While I was a one-guy-at-a-time kind of girl, and those far and few between, Sam had a healthy omnisexual approach. She welcomed a variety of men and women, sometimes together, into her bed.

But I'd never seen her with anyone who was in her league, someone with the combination of beauty, intelligence, and grace that Platon displayed. She might never want to leave.

I walked past them and outside. Gideon was sitting by himself on the back patio, looking blankly up the hill at the olive trees. I sat down next to him.

"He's never going to let me go, you know," he said quietly.

"What? Why? We did what he asked."

He looked up at me, his eyes sad. "You know what I've been working on?"

I shook my head.

"I've been refining his financial operations."

"Great, I'm sure he appreciates it. He can send you a thank-you card."

"You don't get it," he said, shaking his head slowly. "His *financial* operations. His entire financial structure. Where and how he launders his money, who's on his payroll, his contacts with other organizations, his smuggling operations. You know he's actively building up his war chest?"

GG had told us as much. "Do you know what he's planning to do with all of that?"

"No, but it doesn't matter. There's no way he can let me go now. I know too much. And if you stick around, he's going to assume you know too much, too. You and Sam and Tatiana, you need to get out of here, first thing in the morning." He looked back over his shoulder. "If he thinks I've shared information with you, you're going to be stuck here, too. Go back inside. He can't see us talking together."

"I'm not leaving without you."

"You don't have a choice." He stood up, and hugged me. "You have to leave. Goodbye, Jesse."

He left me on the patio under the stars and walked into the house.

# TWENTY-SEVEN

Despite my misgivings about our situation, I slept hard until after ten the next morning. I woke up groggy, but dressed quickly and walked out to the patio.

Sam and Platon were already sitting at the table, drinking coffee and eating. Tatiana was back up on the hill, running.

"Good morning," said Platon brightly. "I trust you slept well."

I nodded noncommittally and sat down. A cup of coffee appeared in front of me.

"I'd like to suggest that all of you stay another day with us here. One more day of hospitality at least is called for, after all you have done for us."

"I don't think so."

"We shall talk about it later. But first I have a little matter I must take care of."

He disappeared into the house. I finished my coffee and stood up.

"C'mon," I said, grabbing Sam's arm.

"Where are we going?"

"For a walk."

We walked around the corner of the house and into the driveway. Once we were out of earshot of any of Platon's goons, I said, "Gideon doesn't think Platon is going to let him leave. He thinks the three of us should get out of here as soon as possible."

"What? Of course he's going to let him leave."

"No. Gideon knows too much."

"What are you saying?"

"I'm saying, Platon might never let Gideon go, and I'm not sure he's going to let us out, either."

"I don't know. He made a deal, and he strikes me as a man of his word."

"He's a man of something," I said bitterly.

"What's that supposed to mean?"

"It means that you look like you'd be happy sticking around if it means you could get into his pants. That is, if you haven't already."

I'd seen them laughing, and staring into each other's eyes, and Sam had been giving him the look, usually reserved for romantic partners, and only when she found someone very interesting, in the biblical sense.

"No, I'm not, and I haven't. And I do believe he'll let us all go. I'll prove it to you."

"Fine. I hope you're right."

We walked back to the house and around the corner to the patio.

Sitting on one of the chairs at the small table was Nikolaidis. Standing over him was Platon, loosely surrounded by several of his men.

"Yatí to skáfos den ítan stin thési tu?" Platon said, his eyes blazing.

"What's he saying?"

"He asked him what happened to our boat."

Nikolaidis shook his head. "Den bóresa na to páro."

"He says he couldn't get it."

Nikolaidis squirmed in his seat as Platon stared at him. "Ímaste xénoi. Den písteve óti ítan polí simantikó."

"We're foreigners, and he didn't think it was important."

Platon folded his arms. "Ítan ámesi diatayí. Apó eména. Nomízete óti den kséro ti eínai simantikó?"

He didn't raise his voice, continuing to speak in a calm manner. For some reason it was even more terrifying than if he'd been yelling. I wondered how he'd gotten Nikolaidis here so fast.

"Platon says he disobeyed a direct order."

"Signómi. Den tha ksanayíni." Nikolaidis looked around, he was starting to look scared.

"To kséro óti den tha ksanayínei. Den eísai pia Titánas."

"Wow," said Sam. "Platon's kicking him out of the group."

I knew Platon didn't give a shit about me, but putting Sam in danger had pushed him over the edge.

"Óhi, parakaló, orkízomai, den tha káno állo láthos." Nikolaidis was almost crying now. I waved Sam's translation off. I didn't need it to recognize the pleading tone in his voice.

Platon turned away, leaving Nikolaidis slumped in the chair, his shoulders shaking.

"Pár'ton," Platon said to the two goons standing next to the patio.

"Ti na ton kánoome?"

"Káne aftó pu prépi na gíni." He went into the house, closing the door behind him.

At that Nikolaidis started sobbing. They reached to pull him out of the chair and he grabbed on tightly to both armrests. They picked both him and the chair up, and marched him around the side of the house.

"What did he say? Where are they taking him?"

Sam looked queasy.

"C'mon, what did he say? What's going to happen to him?"

"I'm not sure . . . I don't know."

"What?"

"I think they're going to kill him."

This sucked for Nikolaidis, but he had almost gotten us all killed. And I felt vindicated. "Do you believe me, now? That Platon is a murderous scumbag? I can't believe you've been into that guy."

She turned to me, her eyes blazing. "Oh, for Christ's sake, Jesse!" she whispered fiercely. "I was *never* into him. I just wanted him to think so. I thought if things got bad, if at some point we needed something extra, that it would give us a better chance of getting away. If a connection with me made him pause, even for a *second*, to consider our safety, I wanted to make him believe we had one."

*Oh.* I felt my face redden. "Why didn't you tell me?"

"Because you're not exactly a woman of mystery. You're terrible at keeping secrets. I didn't want you to give it away. He's a smart man; if you weren't uncomfortable with it, he would have known I was faking." She frowned, shaking her head. "I can't believe you thought I was into him. He's a terrorist, for God's sake."

She was right. How could I doubt her?

She'd been my best friend for years. She'd never let me down, and always, always, did the right thing.

God, I was an asshole.

And scum. Asshole scum.

Lower than asshole scum. Swamp scum. Moldy swamp asshole scum, that sits around for years, getting more scummy.

No. I was scummier than that. I hung my head.

"I know you have trust issues. This is your ACOA flaring up. I'm sorry I had to keep this from you."

She wouldn't even let me feel bad about myself. But she was right, I was the poster child for adult children of alcoholics, with all of the attendant personality traits, including an extreme lack of trust, feelings of existential separation from other people, and an unfortunate tendency to take action without considering the consequences.

Sam was my saving grace, the person who kept me within shouting distance of the rest of humanity. I couldn't believe I'd doubted her.

We couldn't stay here any longer. I walked into the house, Sam trailing me, and found Platon in the kitchen, drinking a glass of water.

"We're leaving. Can you call us a cab, or a Lyft, or whatever it is that will get us to the airport the quickest?"

"I would like to thank you with another day of hospitality. There will be flights tomorrow."

"Thanks, but no thanks. We're leaving today."

"I am sorry to hear that," he said, looking at Sam. "Are you sure I can't change your mind?"

"Nope."

"As you wish." He motioned out the door to the patio. "Thodoros will drive you to the airport."

*Huh.* So he was letting us go.

That was a relief. Sam looked at me with her "I told you so" face. This was one instance where I was glad to be wrong.

We turned to go, when Platon added, "Gideon will stay with us for an extra day or two, he's in the middle of a project for me."

I whipped around.

Platon put his hand up. "Don't worry, it will only take him a few days. And he is being well compensated."

"I'm not worried about his compensation. I'm worried about his safety."

He looked at me, unblinking. "He is as safe as I am, Doctor O'Hara."


"Do you think we should stay here, for a few days, with Gideon? While he finishes his project?" Sam, Tatiana and I were in my room.

"No. The longer we stay here, the less likely it is that Platon will let any of us leave. And we can't do anything for Gideon while we're here. We need to get away, maintain our freedom, and regroup. We can't help him if we're prisoners, too."

"If he's letting us leave, I still believe he'll let Gideon go, once he's done with the project."

"Didn't you hear him? 'An extra day or two' turned into 'a few days' in the same sentence. Gideon's right. Platon's not going to let him go. Ever. Gideon knows too much. And Platon knows that once Gideon's out of here, there's nothing to keep us from going to the authorities and telling them about this place. Gideon's his insurance."

"Maybe I should stay, too," Sam said.

"No. No way."

"Platon's not going to hurt me. And besides, with Svetlana running around, I'm probably safer here."

I couldn't argue with that. But that wasn't the only consideration. "No. We have to figure out how to get Gideon out of here. I can't do that without you."

I relied heavily on Sam's insight when we were involved in investigations. Especially when I got stuck.

And I was stuck. I'd need her to help me work through our next moves.

She knew it too, and let it go.

"I will stay," said Tatiana. "If it will help Gideon."

I looked at her, considering. A week ago I would have jumped at the chance to get her out of my hair.

"No. Whatever it is we decide to do, it will be easier to get just one of us out of here. And if GG does manage to find this place on his own, the chances that one of us gets killed in a raid are doubled with you here. Thanks for offering, but no."

I tracked down Gideon in the house and gave him a long hug. I hoped not for the last time.

"I'll be back for you," I whispered in his ear.

It took us a little over three hours to drive to the airport, board the flight and make it back to Athens. GG had reserved our rooms in the same hotel we'd been in before, and we were sitting in my room, making liberal use of the minibar.

"What happens now? We go to GG?" Tatiana asked.

I shook my head. "No. Even if his organization didn't have leaks, I don't trust him or his people to take down Platon without killing Gideon. Their priority is Platon, and they're not going to care about any collateral damage.

"And we can't just hang around Athens." I'd been thinking about this since we left Santorini. "Svetlana knows we're here, it's only a matter of time before she gets to us."

"Not if I get her first," said Tatiana, frowning.

I was really glad Sam was here. We needed to figure things out, and talking to Tatiana was like trying to work things out with an angrier version of myself. "Svetlana knew we were here because she brought us here, using the conference, by making sure the scheduled presenters had an accident."

Tatiana nodded. "Svetlana makes many accidents."

"But it doesn't explain how she knew we left Crete and came to Athens," Sam said.

"She is very wealthy, she can hire whoever she wants to follow us."

"Tatiana's right," I said. "It must have been someone at our presentation. Whoever it was saw us walk out with GG. He's kind of a big shot, and it wouldn't be much of a leap to know we'd left Crete to join him here."

I mentally ran through the faces of the people in the room at our presentation. "Yeah, there were a bunch of people that looked like they could have been working for her."

"OK. And someone at the hotel knows when we checked in," said Sam. "Maybe the manager? The concierge? One of the baggage handlers?"

"I'm not sure it matters."

Suddenly I was done with all of this. Sitting in this shitty hotel room, responding to what everyone else was doing. "We're being led around by our noses by the both of them. I'm tired of being everyone else's damn puppet."

It was time to make them do what I wanted. And time to end all of this shit once and for all.

"We need to come up with a way to take care of both of them. Platon and Svetlana."

"I don't see how we can do that. Platon is safe at his compound, which he rarely leaves. And we can't tell GG where he is, there's no guarantee that they're not going to get Gideon killed. And we can't possibly take him on our own."

"I know. That's why we need to get rid of Svetlana first. Platon's bad, but he's not actively trying to kill any of us, at least at the moment." I shook my head. "Nope. She's the priority."

I stood up. "C'mon. We're going to GG."

The three of us finished our drinks and went to GG's building. When we walked into his office he looked surprised.

"Have you found Mr. Spielberg?"

"No, uh, not yet. But we have something else. Remember our discussion about Svetlana? About how she's the one who bombed the Celestial Hotel? We know how to get to her."

He frowned. "I have told you, she is not our priority right now. What news do you have of Platon?"

"I don't get how she can not be your priority. Aren't you responsible for terrorism?"

"Yes, I—"

"I told you before, she's the one who brought my team to Greece. It was her people who killed Jenny and Matt Perkins, to get us here. She's trying to take us out, and causing a lot of casualties while she does it. You said Ilias would be able to look into the accident. Do you have anything yet?"

He looked at me blankly. It was clear he hadn't done anything. I wondered if he'd even mentioned it to Ilias.

I turned to Sophia, who was at her usual post by the window.

"I am sorry, I did contact Janus. But they have no information about the conference program."

At least she'd made an effort. "Whatever. Look, I just need to get into Janus. All I need is a quick look at their financials."

"No, no, I have already said, we cannot interfere with Janus unless we have proof of wrongdoing." Tiny Joan was sitting next to GG, fulfilling her role as GG's mini-me, shaking her head in time with him.

"I'm sure I'll be able to get proof." If I had the chance to look at their books, I was sure I'd be able to find payouts and other things that would definitely link Janus to the bombing. And even if I didn't find anything on that, I'd find something they could nail her with. No corporation was ever squeaky clean.

They'd taken down Al Capone on tax evasion; I could at least get Svetlana out of commission for some time, while she responded to fraud, embezzlement, or similar charges.

"No, no, Doctor O'Hara, this is not a good idea. And our priority is Platon. I ask you again, have you found anything out about his whereabouts?"

"No, but we're uh, getting close. Listen, I just need your help right now getting into Janus. Can you do some government thing, make them open their books for me?"

Tiny Joan shook her head and rolled her eyes. I was really starting to dislike her, despite her unconscious comedic relief.

He sighed. "I have told you, I cannot do that. Even if you had some kind of evidence, we must tread very lightly with the oil companies. They provide many jobs, and are critical to our economy."

"OK. What if I did have a lead on Platon? I might be willing to share it with you, if you help us get into Janus."

He stared at me, lips pursed. "You know I can have you arrested for withholding information about a terrorist threat."

Wow. The first sign of a backbone with this guy, and it has to come now.

Unsurprisingly, it crumbled quickly under my glare. "Of course I would not do that. And, eh, in any case, I believe we are getting close ourselves in determining Platon's location. But we cannot force the company to open their books to you, unless there is proof of wrongdoing."

*Arghhh.* I needed to see the documents to get the proof. "Can you at least get me in contact with someone there?"

I sat down and we stared at each other.

"I have one, eh, contact at Janus," he said, realizing I wasn't going anywhere until he helped us. "His name is Petros. He is an accountant, he used to work in our office. I will see if he can talk to you."

"Great, thanks. Tell him I'll be there tomorrow morning."

"Yes. But, please, tread lightly, Doctor O'Hara."

"Of course, no problem."

Sam rolled her eyes. She knew all about me treading lightly.

# TWENTY-EIGHT

The three of us were back in my room, reconvening before we split up for the night. Tatiana was making drinks for us out of the minibar, and Sam was pulling the tags off of some clothes she'd picked up from a small boutique near the hotel.

"What time do you want to leave?" Sam asked.

"You're not going. It's just me and Tatiana this time."

They both looked up, surprised.

"What? Why? I always go."

"I know. But I need someone here in case Platon or Gideon try to contact us at the hotel."

"You and Tatiana, eh?"

Up to now I'd avoided spending alone time with Tatiana at all costs.

"She really came through in Turkey. Besides, if I leave her here again with GG she might kill him."

I was only half joking. Tatiana nodded.

"OK. I could use a little more sleep anyway. And maybe a massage. I'm sore after all of that running and swimming."

"Just be careful. And don't spend too much time out of the room."

Tatiana and I left the hotel the next morning, then took a cab to the Athens tram that went south to Piraeus. Less than twenty minutes later we were dropped off in Greece's largest container port.

Founded in the fifth century B.C., Piraeus was the commercial hub of Greek shipping, with most of Greece's shipowners and many oil companies maintaining offices there. Adjacent to the "Athens Riviera," the city was remarkably clean, sporting broad waterfront walkways with picturesque views of the coast and plentiful works of art.

Unfortunately for us, we wouldn't be staying here. Shortly after she'd purchased Janus, Svetlana had moved the headquarters from Piraeus to the nearby island of Salamis. Tatiana and I took the ten-minute ferry ride to Paloukia, the Salamis port, and then a taxi to the Janus headquarters.

Like the rest of the country, most of the buildings were white, or beige, with nothing over three stories. The Janus building stood out. Five stories tall, and constructed largely out of tinted glass, it was easy to see out of, and impossible to see into.

We walked into the lobby, and right away could tell this was not your average, friendly, "c'mon in" kind of corporate headquarters.

A formidable security desk stretched across the entire space, blocking the rest of the floor, including access to the stairway and elevators. A thick wooden gate with a sturdy lock was the only way in. Behind the counter stood two large men in dark suits, both with bulges under their jackets.

Two more men were located in the hallway behind them, next to the elevators. Also with bulges under their coats.

I stepped up to the counter. "Hi, I'm here to see Petros."

"Who are you?" said the standing man closest to the counter, unsmiling.

"I'm Jesse O'Hara."

He punched a few keys on his computer and then shook his head.

"No. Not on list."

"What do you mean I'm not on the list? I have an appointment with Petros, the accountant."

He stepped back from the monitor, and resumed his stance.

"It's Petros. Just call him."

He stared at some spot in the wall above me, and when it became clear that he wasn't going to resume a discussion, we walked back outside and I called GG.

"What the hell? You said you were getting me a meeting with your guy at Janus. They say there's no appointment. They won't even call him."

"Give me a moment. I will look into it."

A few minutes later he called me back. "Do not go back into the building. Petros will meet you at the café across the street."

We walked into a small café across the street and ordered two coffees, then took a seat by the window. Thirty minutes later we were still waiting.

I nudged Tatiana, and pointed across the street. "Hey, do you see that?"

"What?"

"That black car, parked a half block down the street. The one with two guys in the front."

"Yes, so?"

"So, they were here when we arrived, and haven't taken their eyes off of the front door of the Janus building." I pulled out my phone and took a picture. "I wonder if they're—"

The front door to the Janus building opened and a small man in a suit came out. He was walking fast and trying and failing to light a cigarette as he crossed the street and entered the café.

I waved from our seats. "Hey, Petros."

He started, like I'd goosed him, then walked quickly over to us.

"Thanks for meeting with us. Can you give me some info—"

He looked over his shoulder. "Shhh. Not here. Come."

We followed him out of the café and down the street, where he ducked into an alley next to another office building.

"What's with all the secrecy?"

He finally lit his cigarette and took a long drag. "It is not safe. We cannot be seen together."

"What the hell is going on?"

"Our security, it is very strong. And they, eh, do not like it when strangers come to the office."

"Fine, whatever. Look, I just need you to answer a few questions. You handle the budgeting at Janus, yes?"

"Yes."

"Janus was a major sponsor of the International Conference on Law Enforcement and Investigation, yes?"

"Yes."

"Was that new?"

"New?"

"I mean, is that something Janus does regularly?"

"Yes. We sponsor it every year. Although . . ." He looked behind us towards the street, and took another long drag from his cigarette.

"Although, what?"

"There was involvement at the highest level of the company in the program this year, which is rare."

"Involvement?"

"Yes, eh, selecting speakers, choosing the venue, things like that. And this year our allotment to the conference was significantly higher than in past years."

"Why?"

"I do not know. We were told to make sure to donate enough that Janus would be the biggest sponsor."

"Does Janus normally pay for flights, and rooms?"

"Flights and rooms?" He knitted his eyebrows, shaking his head. "No, no, we do not pay for those things, normally."

"Normally?"

"There was one such charge this year. Four rooms at the Celestial Hotel. Very unusual."

So we were the only ones who'd had our flights and rooms paid for. And Janus had selected the speakers, meaning they'd been the ones who'd chosen Gideon and me to give a paper when Jenny and Matt Perkins couldn't make it.

More proof, not that I needed it, that Svetlana was responsible for bringing us here.

"I'm interested in other expenditures. Are there any kind of special accounts, not related to the conference, that seem . . . unusual, or secret?"

Svetlana must have paid out the nose for the guys who shot at us in the market, and at the olive oil mill. And she'd given Platon a bundle to have Loukas distract me while she was bombing our hotel.

He shook his head.

"You know, accounts that aren't earmarked for anything that's obviously related to the company, and no one but Svetlana knows what they're for? They would be significant outlays, in the tens and maybe hundreds of thousands of euros range."

His eyes grew wide. "I must go," he said, turning away.

"No, wait. Please. It's really important."

He threw his cigarette butt on the ground, then pulled out another one and lit it with shaking hands.

"There are accounts like that, aren't there?"

He hesitated, then looked down at the ground and nodded.

"I need to see them."

"That is not possible."

"Listen, if you don't help me I'm going to tell Svetlana you did, anyway. You might as well do it."

"No, no, I do not mean that I will not get them for you. I mean I cannot. The accounts are only viewable on company computers within the facility. The security is very tight. No one may print anything from them. I am not even allowed to look at them from my home. They must be viewed from one of the designated terminals."

"Where are those terminals?"

"There is one in my office, and one in Mrs. Ivashchenko's office."

"Fine. You can escort me to your office."

"No," he said, shaking his head.

"Yes. Look, I only need a few seconds." I'd be able to scan them quickly, and determine if they were what I needed. If so I'd snap a picture and GG would have all he needed to pick Svetlana up.

"Visitors are not allowed into the building unless there is authorization. It is normal to take a week to gain such authorization, if it is granted."

I didn't believe that this guy couldn't get us in. "Well, you're going to try." I stared at him, in what I hoped was a fair facsimile of an Evil Eye.

It must have worked, because he stubbed out his cigarette and walked back to the building. When we stepped into the lobby he went to the front desk, and engaged in a lengthy conversation with one of the meatheads at the counter.

I must have really nailed the Evil Eye thing, because it sounded like Petros wasn't taking no for an answer.

Eventually the meathead sighed and made a call. A few minutes later another man got out of one of the elevators and joined the group. Also in a black suit, also built like a brick shithouse, and also with a bulge under his jacket.

I recognized him. He was one of the guys who'd been at the olive oil farm, the one I'd run into on my way to the car when we'd made our escape.

Unfortunately, he recognized me, too.

He turned to the guys behind him. "Einai afti pou psáxname."

Immediately all five men reached under their jackets and pulled out their guns.

One of them opened the wooden gate and gestured for me and Tatiana to come through. "Come this way."

There was no way I was following him inside. Documents be damned, I was pretty sure if we walked in we wouldn't be walking out.

"C'mon!"

I turned and rushed back out the front door, Tatiana right behind me.

When we got to the street I started running. I wanted to put as much distance between us and them as possible, even though I didn't think they'd follow us down the street waving guns. Not out in public.

I was wrong. I heard yelling and looked over my shoulder. All five of them were behind us, guns pointed our way.

The ferry terminal was too far away, we'd never make it from here. I considered ducking into a store, or restaurant. But the fact that these guys didn't hesitate to wave their guns around in broad daylight suggested they wouldn't hesitate to drag us out of a store in full view of a crowd of people.

Fortunately Tatiana was a marathon runner and I was no slouch, and we were able to pull away from them.

One of them had stopped and was talking into a radio. A minute later a car pulled up and he got in.

We couldn't outrun a car. It was time to get off the street.

I turned towards the water, where there were fewer streets and even fewer buildings, and jumped off of the white pavement and onto the rocky strip of land next to it.

The car had stopped to pick up two of the other guys, then it passed the ones who were still running, and quickly started gaining on us.

Tatiana and I were now running next to a one-lane road on a narrow spit. As we made our way down the road the surface changed from white pavement to gravel, and then to dirt, a rusted metal fence at the juncture of the pavement and gravel. I opened the gate and closed it, hoping that it would stop the car.

It didn't. But the gravel road would end for them in about five hundred feet. That might do it.

It stopped the car, but not the men. They all got out and resumed running after us.

We were faster, but were now running out of real estate. The spit was narrowing, and up ahead I could see the red and white metal tower that marked the end of land and the start of water.

When we made it to the end, the men were still a thousand feet behind us. But there was nowhere else to go.

The closest piece of land not containing guys with guns was an island, directly across the water from us.

The yelling behind us grew louder. Then I heard shots.

So they weren't interested in taking us back, they were going to kill us. I listened in vain for sirens. Where the hell were the cops? I'd assumed that by the time we'd gotten this far that the police would show up.

Tatiana and I looked at each other, and then she dove into the water. I was right behind her, and we both started swimming as fast as we could for the island.

At least there wasn't a current, and this water wasn't freezing. Tatiana pulled ahead of me, but I was going strong. The island didn't look that far away, and while distances could be deceiving on the water, I didn't think we'd have any trouble making it.

The men had reached the end of the spit, and now shots were whizzing over our heads, and occasionally making little splashes in the water. This was the worst kind of déjà vu. But unlike the river, we'd soon be out of range. I dug deep, and swam as fast as I could.

I felt a pinch in my left arm, and then it stopped moving.

Dammit. Blood was flowing out of my arm, and I couldn't make it work.

Bullets were still whizzing over my head and I started up again, using my legs and one arm. Tatiana was quickly outdistancing me.

I was still moving forward, albeit more slowly. But now I had another worry.

Greece had experienced a few shark attacks in recent years. None, as far as I knew, in this vicinity. But with the blood flowing out of my arm I was basically sending out an all-points bulletin to any shark in the region that there was a delicious snack nearby.

I was chum. And not just the bloody, dead flesh kind of chum; I was the tasty, fresher than fresh, thrashing-around kind of chum.

And I was getting weaker. I couldn't tell if it was from blood loss, because the bullet had hit something major, or I was just spent from running and swimming. But whatever the reason, I was slowing down.

I estimated I'd made it over halfway, and recalled from the maps that it was less than a half mile to that island from Salamis. So only about a thousand feet to go. Not easy, but possible, for me. Normally.

But not now. I was giving it my all, but hardly moving forward at this point, barely treading water. At least we were out of gunshot range.

Tatiana would make it, and then she'd send someone for me. I'd be OK. Unless there were sharks around.

I'd always wondered about getting eaten by a shark. A small shark would bite parts of you off, and you'd die slowly, a disembodied torso, while you bled out.

On the other hand, a larger shark would swallow you whole. How long did it take to die in a shark stomach? Probably a while. And it would be terrible, suffocating in a shark's stomach, as you were being slowly digested.

No, I decided, I wanted the shark that killed me to be a medium-sized one, not big enough to swallow me whole, but big enough so its first bite would be a really large, deadly one. That would be quick.

I laid on my back, looking up at the sky, waiting for a medium-sized shark.

# TWENTY-NINE

heard a splash next to me. Tatiana grabbed me around the arms and started to tow me to the island.

It was slow, but she made it the rest of the way in about fifteen minutes, dragging me onto another rocky spit.

I laid on my back, gasping. She wasn't even out of breath.

"You are bleeding. We must get doctor."

She tore a strip off of her shirt and tied it tightly around my upper arm. Then she stood up, grabbing the hand on my non-injured arm to pull me up alongside her.

I started to get up but sank back to my knees. She leaned down and threw my arm over her shoulders and helped me stand. We walked up the short spit to a wooden dock, and then to a one-lane road.

Ahead of us the cross of a church rose above the few buildings scattered near the shore.

"Let's go to the church."

There weren't any people around, and even if there were, I wasn't entirely sure that Svetlana's security guys didn't have influence here, too. They didn't seem to have any qualms about firing guns around Salamis, and who knows how far her influence extended? A church seemed like the safest place at the moment.

We walked towards the cross, a couple of hundred feet away, that turned out to belong to a small chapel. When we got there I sank down on the steps.

Tatiana disappeared inside and came back out shortly with a man.

"You need help?"

I held up my arm, which was bleeding.

He pulled out his phone and made a call. Hopefully to a doctor.

"May I use your phone?" I asked after he hung up.

He shook his head. "No much English."

"Phone." I pointed to it.

He handed it to me, and I called GG's office.

Sophia answered, which was a relief. I had lots to share with GG, but I trusted Sophia more to take care of, well, almost everything, including getting us off of this island as quickly as possible.

"Hey, can you have one of your people pick us up?"

"Where are you?"

"We're on some island."

"Eh, which island?"

"I don't know, it's the one between Piraeus and Salamis."

"Psittalia?"

I looked at the guy. "Psittalia?" I asked, waving my hand around. He nodded. "Ne."

"Yeah."

"There is no ferry service there. Are you with someone? If so please give the phone to him."

I handed him the phone and they spoke, then he handed it back to me.

"Stavros will take you to the dock," said Sophia. "There is a man with a boat who will bring you back to Piraeus. Stavros says you have an injury; I will contact one of our doctors to meet you when you get there."

"Thanks. I don't think I'll need that. He called a doctor on the island."

"There is no doctor on Psittalia. He called a veterinarian."

"Oh. OK. Would you mind picking up a couple of phones for us? Ours got wet."

"Yes, I will do that."

I wished I had a Sophia around. She was probably the main reason GG was ever able to get anything done.

A few minutes later the vet showed up. He took Tatiana's tourniquet off of my arm and bandaged it tightly, then spoke several sentences in Greek.

"Whatever, thanks." I hoped he said that it was nothing serious.

After the vet was done with me, Stavros drove us to a dock, and another guy took us in his boat for the short trip back to the mainland. I looked behind us, comforted that the small island was blocking the view from Salamis.

Sophia's doctor met us on the pier. He examined me on the spot, unwrapping the bandage and examining the wound, before wrapping a fresh bandage tightly around it.

"Tha hriastíte rámata ke ísos hiruryikí epémvasi. Prépi na páte sto nosokomío."

I shook my head. "I don't understand." Damn. I hadn't realized how much I relied on Sam to communicate when we traveled.

"Eh, you must go to hospital."

Normally I would have ignored him, but now that the adrenaline had worn off, my arm was really starting to hurt. We got in his car and he drove us to the hospital, where an ER doctor examined the wound, cleaned it, then put in stitches.

"There is, eh, no bullet pieces inside, and it did not hit any bone. There is no major damage. But you have lost a lot of blood. It will be best for you to stay here for the night."

"No, thanks."

He sighed. "I will give you painkillers. If it starts to bleed heavily you must come back."

"No painkillers, thanks." I wanted a drink, and it wouldn't be a good idea to mix the two.

I called Sophia and she sent a car to take us back to Athens. There was a small bag with two phones in it on the back seat.

We made it back in less than an hour. When we stopped in front of GG's building I jumped out and fast-walked inside. My arm was on fire, but I was excited to share the details with GG. Now that Svetlana's guys had tried to kill us, he'd have no choice but to arrest them, and then her.

When we got up to GG's floor the vibe in the office was noticeably different than it had been previously. People were energized, everyone was walking around with purpose. The muscle hamsters were packing small duffle bags on their desks.

My shoes squished as we walked into GG's office.

Sophia stepped over to me. "Doctor O'Hara, are you OK?"

"Yeah, thanks for your help."

GG was sitting behind his desk, Tiny Joan next to him, both wearing similar expressions of displeasure.

"You were not, eh, to create a commotion," he said.

"We're fine, thanks. And it wasn't me who created the commotion. They shot at us."

"Shot?" he said, looking quickly at Tatiana.

"She's fine. But this is a fucking bullet hole," I said, holding up my arm.

"Oh." He glanced at my arm. "Still, it was important to tread lightly with Janus. It is clear you did not do that."

This was the Mr. Rogers version of a verbal beating. When this was all over I'd have to buy GG a little sweater.

"Eh, I have been asked by the Janus Corporation to arrest you for trespassing." Tiny Joan was scowling at us, and waving her hands at us as he spoke, sending a stack of papers flying off of the desk.

"*Trespassing*? Did you hear me? They shot at us. Which should give you enough now to arrest at least some of Svetlana's people. Unless you're OK having people running around shooting guns all over the place."

"There are no reports of shots fired on Salamis."

"What? Of course there are. Lots of people must have heard it."

"We, eh, have spoken to the local authorities there. They assure us, there were no reports of gunfire."

"You think I imagined this?"

"No, eh, it may be that, eh . . . Janus is a very important company, and they have a lot of money . . ." His voice trailed off.

"Oh, I get it. They paid off any witnesses." *Dammit.*

"Your man Petros confirmed that it was definitely Janus who brought me and my friends to Crete. They hand-picked me and Gideon to replace the original presenters, and paid for our rooms. And Svetlana has secret accounts that she's using to pay off the goons that shot up the market and bombed the hotel."

"Do you, eh, have any evidence of that?"

"I just said, your guy told us that."

He stared at me. "Is that all?"

"What do you mean, 'is that all'? You mean, in addition to getting shot?"

He sighed. "There is nothing but your word, and while I do believe that you have been shot, there is no one who will corroborate your story. And, eh, as I have said before, this is not exactly in our purview."

Tiny Joan nodded her head vigorously at that.

"My *story*? You've got a Russian psycho running around your country, blowing shit up, and shooting indiscriminately at civilians. How can that *not* be in your purview? It's the very definition of terrorist activity."

He spread his hands. If this guy was a country, he'd be Vichy France. "As I said, we cannot arrest Mrs. Ivashchenko. But there is good news," he said brightly.

"What's that?"

"We have found Platon's compound. It is on Santorini."

*Shit.* That's all we needed. I was hoping for a little more time before GG's group went running after Platon.

"So what will you do now?" I asked, dreading the answer. The muscle hamsters weren't exactly negotiators, and they'd been packing go bags.

"We will go to Santorini and arrest him, of course. Dimitrios and Konstantinos will lead the tactical team we are getting from the Special Antiterrorist Unit."

"Wait a minute . . . a tactical team? You're planning to raid the place? Guns blazing and all?" I was hoping for something a little more nuanced.

He nodded, Tiny Joan joining him in rhythm. "I hope it will not come to that. But we are prepared."

*No, no, no . . .* "Gideon's there. If you go in like that he's going to get killed. Can't you do something a little more subtle?"

Even if Gideon didn't get hit in crossfire, Platon had all but assured me that if GG found him, Gideon would be a dead man.

"I am sorry. We will do what we can. But our priority is arresting Platon. We do not expect him to just give up."

"When is all of this happening?" Maybe I could get a warning to Gideon.

"The day after tomorrow."

"The day after—"

GG's phone rang, and he practically jumped out of his chair to answer it. He studiously avoided my gaze as he leaned back in his chair to talk. I expected he'd pretend the conversation was going on long after the other guy hung up, at least until I was gone.

There was nothing left to do here. Sophia gave me a sympathetic look as we walked out. Tiny Joan continued to frown at us.

I texted Sam that we'd meet her in the lobby bar in a few minutes, then Tatiana and I went back to the hotel. After a quick shower I joined Sam in the bar.

"How did it go?"

Sitting in front of the empty seat next to her was a pint of beer and a shot of Redbreast.

"Not good." I downed the shot and put away most of the beer in one sip. My arm was still on fire, but I hadn't lost any function, and the pain was nothing that a few drinks couldn't alleviate. "We got some information; there's definitely something fishy going on at that place, and I'm sure there are incriminating documents. But we couldn't get inside. So it wasn't enough for GG to do anything. And Janus paid off the locals, so they're also getting away with running around shooting guns.

"And it gets worse," I said, waving down the bartender for another round. "GG's figured out where Platon is. They're raiding the compound the day after tomorrow."

"The day after tomorrow? They realize Gideon is there, don't they?"

"Yeah. They don't care. From their point of view, getting Platon off the board is worth one dead American."

Tatiana slipped in next to me at the bar. Surprising, as there was an empty seat next to Sam. Sam handed her the vodka shot she'd ordered for her. Tatiana put it away in one sip and waved to the bartender for another.

"What are we going to do?" asked Sam.

"I don't know."

We needed a new plan. Going after Svetlana would have to wait until we could do something to keep Gideon from getting killed in GG's shootout.

But at the moment I was planned out. And the drinks weren't totally deadening the throbbing pain in my arm.

"I think I need to lay down." I finished my drinks and stood up.

The room spun and I sat back down again.

"I'll go with you," said Sam. "You shouldn't be alone right now." She nodded to Tatiana and they both got up and put their arms around my waist. We shuffled to the elevator and then to my room.

They gently lowered me onto the bed. "Try to get some sleep."

I stretched out and stared at the ceiling. I needed to crash, but as tired as I was, I couldn't get my mind to shut off.

"I don't think I can."

I picked up the Xena action figure from the table next to the bed and took it out of the packaging, idly fiddling with the movable arms.

What would Xena do?

I wished I had a chakram, then I could take off Svetlana's head and all of Platon's men with one move. But Xena had also gotten herself out of a lot of jams even when she didn't have it with her.

"Sam, grab my laptop, will you?"

"What are you thinking?"

"You know what they say. Sometimes the best man for the job is a woman."

"Who's 'they'?"

"Xena. She's a font of wisdom."

Sam handed me the computer and I opened it and started to type.

"You're checking emails? Now?"

"Just sending a message."

She was looking over my shoulder. "Wait a minute. You're telling Gideon to warn Platon about GG's raid?"

"Yeah."

"Why on earth would you do that?"

"You saw those guys in GG's office. They were gearing up for an all-out attack on Platon's compound. And GG's calling in the armed police. They won't care if Gideon dies in the crossfire. The only thing that matters to them is taking down Platon. Trust me. We'll get Gideon back. I just don't want him to die in the meantime."

I closed up my computer. "OK." I laid back down on the bed. "Now we wait."

"Wait for what?"

"For GG and his guys to raid Platon's compound. Don't worry," I said, in response to her stunned expression. "If this works we're going to get two dirty birds with one big-ass stone."

# THIRTY

We ordered room service, and as we ate I filled Sam and Tatiana in on my plan.

"Xena's rules of survival, from season one, the *Dreamworker* episode."

"You have shock, yes?" said Tatiana. "Maybe we visit doctor again."

"Bear with me, both of you. In this episode, Xena tells Gabrielle her three rules of survival. Number one: if you can run, run. Number two: if you can't run . . . surrender, and then run. Number three: if you are outnumbered, let them fight each other . . . while you run."

"I'm calling a doctor." Sam reached for her phone.

"I'm fine. Look, the point is, we get Platon and Svetlana to fight each other."

"That would be great, but how do we do that? They don't even know each other."

"First we have to make sure Gideon doesn't get killed. And –" I turned to Tatiana – "you're going to have to do something you don't like."

"What?"

"Go out on a date with GG."

She shook her head. "I will not."

"You have to. This won't work unless we can get him away from the office, on his own."

She shook her head. "I will not go on date with tiny man."

"Please, it will help us get Svetlana. And save Gideon."

"Gideon? You are sure?"

"Yeah."

She sighed. "OK."

"Great, thanks."

She held up a finger. "One date. And no touching."

"Got it. One date, no funny business. Don't worry. I'm guessing it would take him a few dates before he would even try to hold your hand. And if this goes right, one is all we'll need."

\* \* \*

We spent the next day and a half hanging around the hotel. I slept a lot, Sam and Tatiana went to a few more museums. We got together for meals.

Sam had seemed fine with the plan when I'd initially laid it out, but when it came time for Tatiana and I to leave for GG's office she launched a small protest. "Why do I have to stay here?"

"Because it's not safe for you to be out. We know Platon's got a mole in GG's office; Svetlana might have someone there, too. The safest place for you to be is here. Don't go out alone. Watch a movie or something. We won't be long."

"Why does Tatiana get to go?"

"You know why. We need her for this part."

She didn't argue too much. It wasn't like being in GG's office was a barrel of laughs.

When Tatiana and I got to the office the mood was markedly different than it had been the last time. The silence of failure was broken only by the occasional sound of an office chair as someone shifted position.

GG was in his office, slumped behind his desk, staring at a stack of papers. Tiny Joan was leaning over him, murmuring consolation.

"How'd the raid go?"

"Terrible," he said, not looking up. Tiny Joan shook her head sadly. "There was no one at the compound. It was as if they knew we were coming."

"Was there any sign of Gideon?" I asked, holding my breath.

"No, no one was there. And there were no, eh, bodies, or signs of violence."

*Whew.*

"Well, you did say you have a mole."

He glared at me, as much as he was able. Tiny Joan's eyes stared daggers at me. As she moved away from GG her hand knocked over a glass on his desk, spilling water over his papers. She left the room.

"I must tell you, Doctor O'Hara, this is not a good result. We have paid you considerable money and so far you have not been helpful." He turned to look out the window.

No surprise that he was blaming his failure on me.

"Yeah, I'm really sorry. This has all been harder than I thought it would be."

He looked back, surprised. The last thing he was expecting from me was an apology.

"We're going to extend our stay, on our dime, to help you find Platon."

"Oh, eh, yes, that would be helpful. Do you, eh, have any leads?"

"Not yet. But we're working on it. Something will come through."

He nodded, then looked back down at his desk, expecting us to leave.

I waited, then nudged Tatiana with my elbow.

"Uh, you have dinner with me?" she said, not bothering to hide her apathy.

He looked up quickly. "Dinner?"

"Yes."

"Oh!" His eyes brightened. He'd missed out on corralling the biggest terrorist in Greece, but the prospect of a date with Tatiana was enough to completely change his mood. Her disinterested affect was lost on him.

"Yes, of course. I will find a restaurant—"

I elbowed her again. "There is one I like. It's called Thea. Is, uh, romantic. We meet there at seven thirty."

"Tonight?"

"Yes."

"Oh, eh, yes, of course."

Tiny Joan had returned with a stack of paper towels, and didn't look happy. She probably had her own crush on GG. I'd never seen him without her; she was always there to hand him a folder, or document, or do the million little things he couldn't quite do himself. When and if he got married, whoever he hooked up with would probably have to agree to have Tiny Joan around all the time.

We left, everyone still in a state of depression except for GG, who was pacing around his office, probably pondering what he was going to wear for his date.

On the way out I called Sam to let her know that we'd been successful, and to meet us in the lobby for a celebratory drink.

The call went to voicemail, and I left a message.

When we got to our hotel we went to the bar. Sam wasn't there, so we ordered a round. When she still hadn't shown up we took the elevator to our floor and I knocked on her door.

No answer.

We went to my room. I opened the door and saw a note on the floor.

"Left for a spa appointment. Be back at two."

It was nearly three.

"Dammit, I told her to stay here."

The light was blinking on the room's phone and I picked it up. There was a package for me at the front desk.

We went back down to the lobby and peaked again into the bar, then looked into the spa. No sign of Sam.

Worse, no one had seen her. There had been no drop-in appointments, they'd been fully booked for the day.

I went to the front desk to pick up my package. The receptionist handed me a box, wrapped in brown paper. The contents sloshed around as I took it from him.

I didn't need to open it.

"What is it?" asked Tatiana.

"It's from Svetlana. She's got Sam."

Where the return address was supposed to be, it simply read, "Sam's Place."

# THIRTY-ONE

"I cancel date," said Tatiana, looking concerned and relieved at the same time.

"No, no, you have to keep it. This doesn't change anything. It's even more important now."

"Call police?"

I shook my head. "No. Between Platon and Svetlana we don't know who we can trust there. No, we have to do this on our own. Nothing's changed. Go get ready for your date."

She sighed and went to her room. At seven o'clock I left mine and knocked on her door.

She'd changed, and was now in a stunning, skin-tight black dress, with thin straps over her shoulders, and cut up the side almost to the hip. She looked like a model.

"You look, uh, great," I said. "Where'd you get the dress?"

"Shopping. Is date, yes?" she said.

"Yes," I said, wondering how GG would react. Probably with an aneurism.

We left the hotel and took a cab to Thea.

Thea was small, and unlike a lot of the restaurants we'd seen here, dimly lit. Soft curtains adorned the walls, surrounding dark wood tables and booths. Per our request we were seated in the back.

GG showed up just before seven thirty, his standard black business suit replaced by a silk dinner jacket and a white shirt that was open at the collar. No pocket square tonight, and his hair looked like he'd used the entire bottle of gel on it. He was carrying flowers.

Most importantly, there was no phalanx of guards, Sophia, or Tiny Joan.

The host brought him back to our booth. As he approached he saw Tatiana and smiled broadly.

"Hello," he said to her. "You look very beautiful tonight."

"Hello, thank you."

"Uh, hello, Doctor O'Hara. Are you, eh, joining us for dinner?"

"Unfortunately, yes."

"Oh." He looked around, his smile fading. "Eh, so, this is not a date?"

I was almost sorry to burst his bubble. He'd looked so happy. "No, we had to get you alone."

He sighed, his shoulders slumped.

"Please, sit down."

"No. I think I will go home." He set the flowers on the table and started to turn away.

"It's about Platon."

He stopped.

"Please, sit down, hear me out. Let's get a drink." I gestured to the waiter, who took our drinks order. Vodka for Tatiana, whiskey for me, and wine for GG.

"I know where Platon is going to be, and when."

"How do you know this?"

"You paid me to investigate, that's what I did."

"So you have been keeping information from us?" he said, his face darkening. He was already mad that his sexy plans for the night were not going to happen. "And, I wonder, if it was you who warned Platon about our raid on his compound?"

No way was I going to cop to that. "No, definitely not. You said you think you have a mole; I'm sure of it. That's why we had to get you alone tonight."

He calmed a bit at that, and took a long drink of his wine. The waiter set an entire bottle on the table, and it looked like GG planned on finishing it by himself.

"Where is he?" he said, staring at the table.

"I will find out exactly where, soon. But before I agree to tell you, you need to agree to do some things for me."

"You know, I could have you arrested for withholding information about him. He is a threat to our national security."

His threat had more to do with his date going awry than me withholding information, I knew, but I needed him agreeable. I nudged Tatiana under the table with my leg. "Say something nice," I whispered.

She stared at him. "You are Greek. Greece is one of the foundations of civilization, like Russia."

*"For Christ's sake*, say something nice about him," I hissed. "And ask him for his help."

"Please, you are important man, you must help," she said, in her best version of a pleading, "save me" voice, which was about as authentic as an email from a Nigerian prince. Nevertheless, it seemed to work.

He looked up. "What is it you want me to do?"

"I want you to arrest him."

"Oh, yes, of course." He looked confused. This wasn't a concession.

"And you can't tell anyone on your staff."

He frowned. "What do you mean?"

"You have a mole, at least one. Whoever it is warned Platon when you were going to raid his compound in Santorini. You can't tell anyone in your office about this."

"Yes, certainly. Of course, I will need to tell Sophia, and Cora, because they—"

"No one."

"I must tell someone. I cannot bring in Platon by myself."

That was the understatement of the century.

"You don't know who the mole is, or how many there are. No one on your staff, or even in your department, can know. Go directly to your Antiterrorist Unit. Ask for their help, but don't tell them you're going after Platon, either. Lie to them, say it's top secret, do whatever you have to do to get them to help without naming him."

He finished his glass of wine and poured another.

"Eh, yes, OK." He knew I was right. But the prospect of having to set something up himself was giving him pause. I wondered when the last time was that he'd done anything on his own.

"And there is one other thing."

"Yes?"

"Platon will be with Svetlana. If I help you, you have to agree to arrest them both."

"How do you know that?"

"Never mind. I just know."

He shook his head. "I cannot promise that. I have told you, we need strong evidence to arrest her."

I sat up and leaned across the table, my face inches from his.

"If I'm not one hundred percent convinced that you're going to arrest her, when I leave here I'm going to warn them both that you're coming."

He snorted, a pitiful, weak sound. "I could arrest you for that."

"Go ahead."

I knew he didn't have the cojones to arrest me.

He knew it, too, and after a moment, said, "If I agree, you will tell me where Platon will be?"

I nodded.

"Yes, I agree."

I stared at him. "I mean it. If you don't do as I ask, things will go very badly for you. Very badly. You can't even begin to imagine how I can make your life a living hell."

"Yes, yes, I agree. I swear on my mother."

He finished his glass and poured another, then slid a look at Tatiana. "Is that all?" he asked, maybe hoping that she'd still be up for their date.

I couldn't blame him, she looked terrific.

"No, that's not all. Sam's been kidnapped."

"Miss Hernandez? Kidnapped? By who?"

"Svetlana. I need you to let everyone in your office know, right away."

"Why?" he asked, confused. "You asked me not to tell anyone about this."

"Yes, don't tell anyone about the raid. But make sure they all know that Svetlana's taken Sam. Tell every one of them, tonight. Never mind why, just do it. I'll send the details about the time and place of Platon's location as soon as I have them to your cell. Delete the message as soon as you've read it, in case the mole is going through your personal stuff as well."

His eyes widened. He hadn't considered that the mole might be digging into his private life.

"How do you know this, where Platon will be?"

"I told you. I'm an investigator. It's what I do."

Tatiana and I got up, leaving him sitting at the table. When we walked out the door I turned to see him pouring the last of the bottle into his glass. I hoped he wasn't driving home.

We returned to the hotel, where she changed into her normal attire and then met me in my room.

"You know where Platon and Svetlana are? You know where Sam is, also?"

"Not quite yet, but I will."

"Sam is safe?"

"Yes."

"And you not tell GG this?"

"No, not yet."

I appreciated that she didn't flood me with questions, trusting that I knew what I was doing.

I hoped I did. Dealing with GG had been the easy part.

I'd sent Gideon an email the night before, and now we were waiting.

I opened the minibar and pulled out whiskey and a beer for me, vodka for Tatiana. We sat on the bed, drinking.

After an eternity the phone rang. It was the front desk, I had another package.

I took the stairs down two at a time, not wanting to wait for the elevator, and picked up a small, nondescript brown box at the front desk. There was no return address.

I ran back up the stairs and tore it open.

It was a burner phone. I called the single number listed in the contacts.

After one ring it picked up.

"I told you what would happen if you told the government where we were," said Platon.

"I didn't tell anyone. They found you on your own. I tried to warn you, remember?"

"Yes, that is the only reason that Gideon is still alive. He was not to have any contact with anyone outside of the compound."

"And I'm sorry about your estate."

"It is of no importance. Sacrifices must be made. And I have many homes. What is it you want? I am a busy man."

"I want you to help me. Svetlana's kidnapped Sam."

"Svetlana?"

"Svetlana Ivashchenko. You know, the woman who paid you to have Loukas lure me away from the hotel, and then had it bombed."

"How do you know this? Why would she kidnap Salbatore?"

"She left me a note. And it's a long story. The short version is that Svetlana hates me, and has been trying to kill my friends to hurt me."

There was a long pause. "How do I know you are telling the truth? It could be that Salbatore is fine, and you are just trying to get me to help you."

I was ready for this. "You have lots of informers, and people all over the country. Check it out. If what I'm saying isn't true, then, well, you do what you have to do."

He hung up.

We waited again, long enough to require a call to the front desk to restock the minibar.

After another eternity the burner phone rang.

"I have confirmed that Salbatore has been kidnapped by Svetlana. And that she is behind the bombing at the hotel."

His voice, normally resonant and soft, was clipped. He was angry, more angry than I'd ever heard him. In addition to his feelings for Sam, he detested the idea of a foreigner blowing up Greek citizens.

And then he said the words I was waiting to hear.

"We know where Mrs. Ivashchenko is. We will go there and pick Salbatore up tomorrow."

"Pick her up" sounded like they were going to get some takeout, not engage in what might end up being a bloody battle. But he'd found Svetlana, that was the only thing that mattered.

GG had said Platon had supporters all over the country, and he'd used his network to track down Svetlana's whereabouts. I wasn't surprised that he'd pulled out all the stops; Sam was the face that launched a thousand ships, and he'd fallen head over heels for her.

She'd been right, too. All of that flirting with him had paid off in a big way.

"Where is she?"

"She has an estate on Salamis Island."

Of course, that made sense. No wonder she'd moved the Janus headquarters over there; she wanted it near her home.

"That's great." I didn't have to fake a sigh of relief. "I just have one, uh, request."

"I am not in the habit of taking requests."

"I want to be there when you go."

"I see no reason for that."

"Svetlana may want to exchange Sam for me. And even if not,

Sam could get hurt if things turn violent. And, uh, it's more likely that things won't turn violent if you do an exchange."

He paused before he spoke, a long moment. "You would do this? Exchange yourself for her?"

"Of course I would."

It took him a microsecond to decide that he was completely fine with exchanging me for Sam.

"Yes, you may join us. You alone. But once Miss Hernandez is safe, you must leave if you can. We will, eh, have further business with Mrs. Ivashchenko."

I had a good idea what his "further business" was. She'd stolen his woman; there was no way he was letting her out alive.

Part of me would be just fine with that. But I texted GG the details, even though I was sorely tempted to let Platon do his thing with Svetlana. Then I did my best to get some sleep.

# THIRTY-TWO

As agreed, I met Platon and his men at the ferry dock on Salamis. They were in a small fleet of black Volkswagen T-Roc SUVs, there being no Greek car brands, nor even any manufacturing of other models, in the country.

I got into the back of the last one in the line and we drove out of town.

The road transformed quickly from multiple lanes to a single one that wound upwards, between scattered homes and large empty patches of short trees, scrub brush and rocky banks.

We climbed for a few minutes until the road dead-ended at a thick metal gate, the only opening in a sturdy fence that appeared to ring the entire top of the mountain.

On the other side of the fence was a newly paved road that continued up. At the top I could see a house, and the blades of a helicopter, no doubt ready and waiting to take off at a moment's notice.

The cars emptied, fifteen men piling out at once, all carrying guns on straps around their necks. Platon was the last to step out. His men made a semicircle around him as he strode to the gate.

Normally the model of placidity, his face was contorted in barely concealed fury. He didn't say anything into the intercom at the gate, just stood as close as he could to the camera, staring into it.

He looked like a sociopath. But he was my sociopath, at least for the moment.

He stood there, stock still, for several minutes, until we heard the sound of a small engine. From the top of the hill came a fleet of compact golf carts, each carrying two men, all with guns.

They stopped and lined up facing us on their side of the gate. A moment later another cart rolled down the hill, containing one man with a gun. Sitting next to him was Svetlana.

When they made it to the bottom of the drive, Svetlana said something to her driver, and he pointed a small box at the gate. It slid open slowly, the metal creaking.

She stepped out of her cart and walked forward, her men closing around her, all with their guns trained on Platon.

She stopped at the gate, a few feet from him. "The man around town, as they say. To what do I owe this pleasure?"

"You have taken something that doesn't belong to you."

"Everything I have belongs to me."

She turned to me. "Hello, Doctor O'Hara."

I stepped forward, immediately garnering the attention of all of her men, who now trained their guns on me. "Hey Svetlana, nice to see you," I said, holding out my hand to shake. "Oh, sorry," I said, nodding to her mangled right hand. "I forgot."

Svetlana's hand had been mauled by Sam's dog Chaz on the cruise ship we'd been on in Bilbao. It had gotten infected, which was no big shock to me; Chaz was the nastiest dog I'd ever encountered.

But in this case, his grossness paid off: she'd had to have the hand amputated. A light blue cloth matching her current old lady skirt suit covered the stump.

Her eyes narrowed, and she turned back to Platon. "What is it you want?"

"I want Salbatore Hernandez."

She frowned. "She is not here."

"Please do not insult my intelligence. If she is not here, you will tell us where you are keeping her."

She shook her head. "I have no idea where she is." She looked at me, still talking to him. "You have been misinformed. I do not have Miss Hernandez. But I will take Doctor O'Hara." She murmured something to one of her men, who stepped forward and grabbed my arm.

"You may have Doctor O'Hara. But not until I have Miss Hernandez."

Boy, that didn't take long, for him to give me up. He didn't even try to negotiate.

Platon said something to his men, who raised their guns, now all pointing at Svetlana. She barked something and her man let go of my arm.

"You are making a very big mistake. I do not have Miss Hernandez." She pointed a finger from her good hand to me. "She knows where she is, and has used you to find out my location. You have been fooled."

Platon turned to me, rage turning his face even redder. "Is this true?"

"Of course not. She's stalling."

I'd need to do the same in a minute. Twenty-five guys with guns locked and loaded and aimed at each other. We were one involuntary finger twitch away from a bloodbath.

"I will ask you one more time, where is Salbatore Hernandez?"

*Jesus, GG, take your time*, I thought, trying not to be too obvious as I looked around.

Then it occurred to me that even if GG did come, everyone here would have ample time to see him and his men drive up the road.

On the one hand, it meant that no one would be able to escape.

But on the other, if anyone opened fire, I was going to get shot. I looked around for something to hide behind if the bullets started flying.

Too late. Everyone turned to the road, to the sound of engines.

Seven black SUVs and a bus trundled up the hill. Once they reached the top they emptied out. Thirty-two men with guns formed a perimeter outside of the gate, ringing Platon and his men.

GG got out of the last vehicle and walked towards us, stopping short of the front of the line. His man in front stepped forward and addressed the group. "Óli, válte ta ópla sas sto édafos kai válte ta héria sas píso apó ta kefália sas."

Platon's and Svetlana's guys looked around, doing the math. One by one they each laid their guns down on the road, and put their hands behind their heads.

"Ksaplóste sto édafos."

Each of them lay down on the ground. All except Platon and Svetlana.

"Den ksaplónome ya kanénan," said Platon.

He spread his hands in a welcoming gesture. "Htízume mia néa Elláda, pu tha anaktísi ti thési pu mas axízi ston kósmo. Boríte na íste óli méros tis. Eláte mazí mu," he said, looking at each man in turn.

He was making his pitch, to what had to be a target-rich audience. As evidenced by far too many nodding heads, a lot of them were buying it.

GG's lead man was having none of it. "Válte tus hiropédes!"

Two of his men stepped forward, grabbing Platon roughly and putting his hands behind his back.

"I don't know which one of you is responsible for this, but you will both be very sorry," Platon said, taking his time to stare at me, and then at Svetlana. "There are many people in law enforcement who support the Megali Titans. I will be out soon. And neither of you will be safe."

He continued his rant in Greek as the two men escorted him to the lead car and put him in the back, taking seats on either side of him and closing the doors.

The rest of Platon's and Svetlana's men were zip-tied, and then marched to the bus where they were loaded in. As they did, GG walked over to me.

"Thank you for your help."

"You're welcome. You have Gideon?"

"Our men will pick him up as soon as we find out where he is being held."

Platon's men wouldn't dare do anything to Gideon without a direct order from him, and now that he was incommunicado, GG's guys could pick him up without fear that he'd be killed.

"Good bye, Doctor O'Hara." GG turned towards the cars.

"Hey, wait a minute, aren't you forgetting something?" I gestured towards Svetlana, who was still standing on the other side of the gate.

"I am sorry, I cannot arrest Mrs. Ivashchenko."

"We had a deal."

"Yes, and I have tried. I spoke to my supervisor, and also his supervisor."

He shook his head; he looked genuinely sorry. "Janus is a very important company. Without more evidence of significant wrongdoing I have been told to leave her alone."

He looked up the driveway to the house. "Where is Miss Hernandez? If we can prove that Mrs. Ivashchenko has kidnapped her, that would be enough evidence." He looked at me, hopefully. "Is it possible she is in the house?"

"No, she's not."

"How can you be sure?"

"Because I am."

I turned to join everyone else in the SUVs. Over the creaking of the closing gate Svetlana drew her finger across her throat, and hissed, "Ty mertvets zhenshchina."

# THIRTY-THREE

On the way back to Athens I sent a few messages, and by the time I made it back to the hotel Sam and Tatiana were together in the lobby bar.

If looks could kill, I'd be dead, based on the glare I was getting from Tatiana.

"You did not tell me, Sam was not kidnapped."

"I'm sorry." I was doing my best to get the attention of the bartender. "I didn't want to risk anyone finding out. And by the way, for the record, I can keep a secret," I said to Sam.

"You're right, I was wrong."

"Hey, you know, Sam was in on it, too," I said to Tatiana, who was scowling at me. "Why aren't you taking it out on her?"

She shrugged. It was a dumb question. No one could stay angry at Sam.

"It hasn't all been fun and games for me too, you know," Sam said, trying to defuse the tension. "I was in a tiny hotel on the outskirts of the city, and confined to my room the whole time."

Tatiana shook her head. "It is your plan," she said to me, her voice louder. She'd been really worried about Sam.

She looked like she was getting ready to stand up and take me on, when Gideon walked into the bar.

Tatiana jumped up and threw her arms around him. After giving her a moment, Sam and I joined them in a group hug.

I stepped back, holding onto his shoulders.

"Are you OK?"

"Yes, fine. Just a little tired." His eyes were red, and he had dark bags under them. Platon had granted him every hospitality, but that didn't change the fact that Gideon had been held captive for over a week.

"How was it, when GG's men showed up? Was there a gunfight?"

"No, nothing like that. They just drove up and Platon's guys opened the gate for them. None of them were carrying guns, so they didn't get arrested. His guys just let them walk in and escort me out."

Part of me wasn't surprised. Without Platon giving them orders they wouldn't know what to do.

And despite his warning, I didn't think he'd be getting out any time soon. GG already had him on a number of serious charges, and they would be adding more.

I hadn't asked GG for any details, and didn't even know where they were keeping him. He was playing it all close to the vest, even limiting the number of people in the government and law enforcement who knew where he was being held. The one thing that he'd already let out publicly was that one of the charges against Platon was aiding and abetting a terrorist act, related to the bombing of the Celestial Hotel. As much as they might want a "Greater Greece," most Greeks weren't supportive of hotel bombings. It was smart; releasing that tidbit would thwart any groundswell of support for Platon.

"What about Loukas?"

"He wasn't there. Wasn't he at Svetlana's?"

"I didn't see him." Platon probably had him squirreled away somewhere, just in case. "Wherever he is, it's just great to have you back. Are you hungry?"

"Yeah, all of a sudden I feel like I could eat a horse."

We ordered food at the bar, and while we waited the three of them chatted away, Sam and Tatiana telling Gideon every detail of what had happened in his absence, barely slowing down when the food arrived.

"You were right," he said, digging into his second plate of souvlaki. "About the on-the-ground stuff. It's tough being in the field. I'm going to stay behind my computer from now on."

"You did really well," said Sam. "You kept your head."

"It is not surprise." Tatiana was glowing.

We finished dinner and were now nursing drinks, everyone comfortable and happy, for the first time in what seemed like a very long while.

Everyone but me. I wasn't nursing so much as pounding, already on my fourth shot of Redbreast, barely tasting it at this point.

We were all together, and safe. But for how long?

Gideon stood up. "I need to hit the hay. Thanks, all of you, for getting me out. When are we going back?"

"Our flight leaves the day after tomorrow."

"Good, I might sleep until then."

He walked out of the bar, and I waved my hand at the bartender for another round of drinks, staring sullenly at my glass when he brought it.

"What's going on? You're acting like your favorite bar just closed down."

"We're not going to be able to get her. She's going to follow me around until she kills all of us."

"Svetlana? She hasn't gotten to us yet. She did everything she could this time, and she barely avoided getting arrested."

"It's only a matter of time. Think about all of what she went through to get to us here: gathering a bunch of goons to bomb a hotel, then paying a ridiculous amount of money to one of the most high-profile gangs in the country to keep me away while she was doing it. She even bought a damn olive oil mill to ambush us."

Gideon had confirmed that he'd been looking into the olive oil mill just before he'd been taken by Platon, as it had recently been purchased by Janus.

"She can do whatever she wants. She has unlimited funds, and if she was mad before, she's furious now." I finished my drink and gestured to the bartender for another.

"Yes, she spent all of that money, and she failed. How eager do you think she's going to be to start it all up again?"

"Very. You didn't see her face, Sam, when we were in Salamis." I hadn't imagined that much hate could be in one person. "She's the kind of person to completely ignore the sunk cost fallacy. She's going to try even harder now. She loves money, but she hates me even more."

"It's not a complete loss, you know. You did help take down Platon, and not only that, you helped GG put away a lot of other criminals as well."

I drank the next shot the bartender put in front of me in one sip. "She's never going to stop. She's going to kill you, and Gideon, and you," I said, looking at Tatiana. My attitude towards her had undergone a seismic shift on this trip.

"And it will be because of me." I waved at the bartender again. "I should just let her do it."

"Do what? Kill us?"

"No. Me. At least then I'll know that the three of you will be safe."

"You're smarter than she is. You'll figure it out."

"I used to think that. But she's untouchable."

"Is she?"

"What do you mean?"

"I mean, just because GG hasn't arrested her doesn't mean that he won't. He told us, he is looking into Janus."

"Sure he is," I said, my head down. I wasn't going to hold my breath that he'd get very far with her. Large corporate entities had a way of avoiding trouble. "They're not going to touch her unless there's unimpeachable evidence of wrongdoing. Besides, once we leave Greece, all of that shit will stop. He'll have no reason to go after her. She'll just track us to the next place. And if she can't get us while we're traveling, she'll eventually come to the US. She's got infinite wealth, she can buy whoever and whatever she wants, for as long as she wants."

Sam didn't say anything. She knew I was right.

I brought the next glass of whiskey up to my mouth and stopped. Something Sam said was niggling in my brain.

"You're right; GG was able to pick up a bunch of criminals. Greek criminals, that Svetlana hired."

I put my drink back down on the bar. "And do you remember, when we were at the olive oil mill? Those guys that tried to ambush us there? They were Greek, too, weren't they?"

"Probably. They were speaking Greek."

I nodded. "Yeah. And the guys at the market? Not Platon's guys, the other group – the ones that shot at you, and then chased me. Greek too, yeah?"

"Yes. She did the same thing in Spain. We know Svetlana uses locals for her dirty work."

"The guys at her compound, the ones that GG arrested, they were Greek, too . . ."

"So?"

"So, who're the Russians that have been following us?"

"What Russians?"

"When you and I were in Gazi? And I pointed out the guy that was following us? I saw him before that. He was Russian."

I'd noticed him when we were outside at the café in Heraklion, where Gideon had been cruised.

"Our second night in Heraklion, after our presentation. He was sitting at a table not far from us, with another guy." I wasn't multi-lingual like Sam, not even close. But I'd spent enough time around Russians in the last two years to recognize it when I heard it.

"Why didn't you say anything?"

"I didn't want to worry you." She rolled her eyes. "And I didn't think anything of it at the time. I thought maybe she'd just hired a couple of Russians to help her. I saw the two of them again, when we were in Fira. And they were in Salamis, too, outside of the Janus building." I turned to Tatiana, who was barely listening to us. "You remember, don't you? There was that car, outside of the Janus building, on the side street. There were two men in it. I took a picture of them."

"So? It was just more of Svetlana's guys, keeping an eye on you," said Sam.

I shook my head. "No. Those two guys were there, already, watching the building, when we got there. They weren't there for us."

"I'm not sure what you're getting at. Maybe Svetlana hired some Russians, to augment the locals?"

"To spy on her own building? One that was already filled with an entire platoon of armed security men?" I shook my head. "No. And neither he nor his partner joined in when they chased us into the water, either."

Maybe one good thing had come out of that shitstorm in Piraeus.

"So if these Russians, whoever they are, have been following you, how did they know where you'd be all of those times?"

"That's a great question. How did they know? C'mon," I said, getting up from the bar. "Time to put Gideon's skills to good use. And we're going to have to delay our flight. I'll be back in a minute."

I called Gideon in his room, and when there was no answer, I took the elevator up and knocked on his door. Then I pounded on it.

After a few minutes he opened it, sleepy-eyed, wearing just his boxers. "Jesus, Jesse. Can't a guy get some sleep?"

"Later." I brushed past him into his room. "Put some clothes on. We're going out," I said. "Meet me in the lobby. Bring your computer," I whispered.

"What are—"

I put my finger to my lips and left the room.

A few minutes later Gideon joined me, Sam and Tatiana in the lobby.

"Fire it up."

He grumbled and opened up his laptop. "What's with all the secrecy?"

I put the picture I'd taken in Salamis of the two guys in the car in front of him. "Can you find out who these guys are?"

"Is this all you have? A license plate, and a blurry picture of two guys?"

"I think I can narrow it down. They work for the Russian government."

He rolled his eyes. "Oh, yeah, that really narrows it down."

I stared at him until he sighed. "Fine. I'll need some time. Can you get me some coffee?"

I went to the hospitality station and grabbed him a couple of cups, returning and setting them down on the table next to him while he tapped away on his keyboard.

"Now leave me alone. I'll call you if I get anything."

I joined Sam and Tatiana back at the bar, and two very long hours later my phone buzzed. Gideon had something.

We went to the lobby and Gideon gestured towards his laptop. On the screen were pictures of two men. Maksim Sokolov and Yaroslav Zaitsev.

"You were right. They're both with the SVR."

"SVR?" said Sam.

"Russian intelligence and espionage. For the most part the FSB handles domestic intelligence, like our FBI; the focus of the SVR is outside of the country."

"So, like the CIA?"

"Yes, although they're known for being a little more . . . active."

"Active?" said Sam, frowning. "What are they doing in Greece? And why would they be following us?"

"They're not following us. They're following her."

"Who?"

"Svetlana."

"Svetlana? Why would the SVR be following her?"

"I can guess, but the why doesn't matter. We can use it to finally get to her."

"How can you be sure? It seems a little far-fetched, that her own country's intelligence agency is following her, especially overseas," said Sam.

"It's not far-fetched, it's part of their remit. But I can't be one hundred percent sure, not yet. That's why we're going to test it out. Thanks," I said to Gideon. "You can go back to sleep now."

Tatiana stood up. "I walk you to room." I mentally wished him luck keeping her out of it.

Sam followed me up to my room. Going in I held my fingers to my lips, then picked up the pad of paper in the drawer and wrote something on it.

"I can't believe we found Svetlana. GG's going to have to listen to us, now," I said loudly, showing Sam what I'd written on the paper.

She stared at it, until I waved my hand at her.

"Yes. Uh, how did you get her to meet with you?"

"I told her I was going to give myself up. To save the rest of you."

I wrote something else down on the paper and held it up.

"Uh, that's very gracious of you. You are a great friend. The best." She rolled her eyes.

"That's me, sacrificing for my friends."

She looked down at the pad. "Where is she going to be?"

"At the *Nisiá Café*, at nine tonight. Do you want to get a drink before I go? It might be our last one together."

"Uh, OK." We left the room and headed downstairs.

"What was all of that?" she asked me in the elevator.

"I think our rooms are bugged. That's how they knew where we'd be."

"Didn't you say they were following Svetlana? Why would they care where we were going?"

"They are, and they don't. But they know she's after us. They've been using us to get to her."

"So where are we going now?"

"To just outside the *Nisiá Café*. I want to make sure I'm right."

We left the hotel and took a short cab ride to the café, then crossed the street and went into a bar, sitting at the window where we could watch the street in front of it.

At ten minutes before seven, Maksim Sokolov and Yaroslav

Zaitsev appeared on the street in front of the café. They walked past it, crossing the street and stepping around the side of a corner business that had a clear line of sight to the café's front door.

I got up and went outside, then walked by them. I disappeared around the corner, then after a few moments went back to the bar and sat back down next to Sam. "Did they try to follow me?"

Sam shook her head. "They weren't the least bit interested in you. They never took their eyes off the café."

We watched the two men wait another forty-five minutes before they left.

"Do you believe me now? That my room is bugged? And that they're here for Svetlana?"

She nodded. "OK. So what do we do now?"

"Now we poke the bear."

# THIRTY-FOUR

"Our problem is that we have to find a way to get Svetlana out in the open, by herself," I said.

Sam, Tatiana and I were in my room. I'd decided to let Gideon sleep.

"How do we do that?"

"I don't know. As far as I can tell she lets her goons do her dirty work, and most of the time she's holed up in her compound. I doubt she even goes into the Janus building, at least not very often."

"She does have fewer guys now. Didn't a lot of them get arrested when GG raided her place?"

"Yeah, but she's probably replaced them by now."

I turned to Tatiana. "Tell us what you know about Svetlana." She'd spent more time than any of us with her, including a week on a cruise ship where she'd been forced to pretend to be Svetlana's granddaughter.

"She is bitch."

"Yes, we know that. I'm trying to figure out what would get her to go out by herself. Something she would want to do alone."

She shook her head. "Never. Always with security."

"Always? C'mon, there've got to be some situations where she wants to be by herself. Or, at least, not surrounded by security right next to her. Think back, when you were in Russia," I prompted her. "When did Svetlana come out in public?"

"For big events. Svetlana is . . ." She put her hands up to her head and moved them apart.

"She has a big head? A big ego?"

She nodded. "She buys company, she talks to newspaper, she gets awards. She is alone then."

That made sense. Svetlana liked to gloat, I'd seen it up close and personal. "OK. So what would make her think she had reason to celebrate?"

"She wants to kill everyone close to you, to make you suffer.

Maybe if she thinks we're all dead, she'll want to rub it in your face," offered Sam.

"You might be right, but all of you dying to get her to show herself sounds a little extreme."

"She is angry woman. More angry now," said Tatiana.

*No shit, Sherlock.* She was already furious with me for ruining her bombing plans in Spain, and had been apoplectic when I'd teased her about her lost hand at her compound. Whatever rage she'd associated with me before was ramped up to eleven.

"Do you think she could get so angry, she'd let her guard down?"

"No." Tatiana shook her head. "She is careful. Always planning to be, eh, safe."

"Safe. Like, at home?"

"Yes."

"OK. We might be able to get her alone at her home. So what does she want, more than anything?"

"That's easy. She wants to see you suffer. And then die," said Sam.

"Right, and her way of getting me to suffer is to hurt all of you. But maybe, maybe now, she's running out of patience. She knows she's got to start all over again, if she wants to get to you guys. But what if she's presented with a golden opportunity to just kill me? Would she take it?"

"I don't like where this is going," said Sam.

"Don't worry. I'm not intending on sacrificing myself."

"Then, maybe. She has been after you for a while."

We both looked at Tatiana, who nodded.

"All right. So we need to ramp up her anger, to increase her impatience. What would make her so angry that she'd let her guard down, for the chance to get at me?"

Tatiana was looking thoughtful.

"What? What are you thinking about?"

"There is one time. Rumor that husband was cheating."

"Her former husband? The dead one?"

"Woman who was cheating with him was found dead, by mugging."

"Didn't he die, too, shortly after that?"

"Yes. Papers say is accident. Is not accident."

"So she might have killed him, because of the affair?"

She nodded.

"I'm not sure how that helps us. Unless Svetlana marries Gideon," said Sam, causing Tatiana to scowl.

"What else?"

"Newspaper, shows story about her, once."

"Let me guess, it wasn't flattering?"

"No. They write that she is ruthless monster, and say that she killed husband."

"What happened?"

"Newspaper office is set on fire. Man who wrote story was found dead."

"Extreme, but how does that help us?"

"Police find fingerprints. Only Svetlana's."

"So she did it herself? And didn't get arrested?"

"Yes. She has too much money for arrest in Russia."

"So when she's *really* angry, she does it herself." I nodded. "Now we're getting somewhere. I need to make her really angry, so angry that she throws caution to the wind."

"Well, we can't put something in the newspaper," said Sam. "I'm assuming you don't want to get a journalist killed."

"Maybe it's as simple as that . . ."

"As what?"

"If I let her know that I think I've won, you know, that she's pulled out all the stops, and still hasn't hurt me, or any of you . . . if I shove that in her face, that I'm not afraid of her . . . Whatever level of anger she has will go through the roof. She loves to gloat, and she'll hate it when I do it to her."

I opened my computer and typed out an email:

Let's finish things up. I'll come to your place tomorrow afternoon.
Maybe while I'm there I can give you a hand with something?

With the email I attached a picture of Chaz, a disembodied hand I'd found on the internet, and the video I'd taken of Sam shooting up Svetlana's Crystal Head vodka.

"Wow," said Sam. "But, isn't this a little, you know, obvious?"

"I'm counting on her belief in her own infallibility."

Tatiana nodded. "Is good."

"How will you get it to her?"

I'll send it to the general info contact at Janus, with "For that bitch, Svetlana" in the subject line. "I'm pretty sure they'll forward that along to her."

"OK, then what?"

"Hang on," I said, pulling up a map of Greece, and zooming in on Salamis. I brought up the little yellow man in Google Maps and examined some of the ground-level photos of the island.

I closed the laptop. "So," I said, loudly. "To summarize, I'm going to be at Svetlana's place on Salamis tomorrow, at two in the afternoon. I'll try to meet with Svetlana in the driveway in front of her house. You know, the one with the great view of most of the island, and in particular from the slightly higher, beautiful peak to the west of it. That's the one that's outside of Svetlana's fence, about five hundred meters from her house, and accessible from the western side of the island."

Sam was frowning. "What are you—"

"Uh, I know we've talked before, about Svetlana being at the *Nisiá Café*, and she didn't show up there. We were just, uh, doing a little test. This time it's for real. Seriously. She'll be there, and she'll be out in the open."

Sam was shaking her head, realization dawning about what I intended to do. "Gosh, I'm trying to imagine something more risky and speculative than this, and I can't. This is by far the most dangerous thing you've ever done."

"I doubt that. But even if so, I can't stand it any more. She's making me nuts. I'm not safe at my own house, not at yours, not anywhere. Everywhere I go she's going to be there.

"If it were just me, that would be one thing. But knowing that she's targeting all of you, I can't live like that. I can't stand the thought of you not being around, and me being the reason for it. No, this is our chance. I have to take it."

The next morning I rented a car in Athens and drove to Piraeus, then took the ferry to Salamis.

Sam offered to go with me, but I'd turned her down. I didn't want anyone else getting in harm's way, in case things didn't work out. And I'd have a better shot with Svetlana if I was alone.

I drove up the one-lane road to her compound and parked in front of the gate.

I waited in the car for a few minutes, then got out and walked to the gatepost. I stood, staring up at the video camera.

"Empty your pockets, please." Svetlana's voice was tinny through the intercom.

I pulled out my pockets and turned around, lifting up my shirt to show I wasn't carrying a gun.

The gate opened, just a little, barely enough for me to get through.

I parked the car and walked up the winding hill to the large circular driveway that was next to her house.

Her estate, like Platon's, sat at the top of a hill. That's where the resemblance ended.

Platon's house and environs were festooned with flowers, gardens, and olive trees, giving it a vibrant, alive feel. Svetlana's place looked like someone had airlifted an empty house down on top of a barren hill.

There were no plantings, of anything, around the plain house, just rocky outcrops, interspersed by low grass and the occasional shrub. Where everything about Platon's house looked artsy, and cultivated, hers had the look of someone who'd never moved in.

Her compound was on the highest mountain on the island, the house itself on the second highest point, the only higher one a bare hill a half kilometer to the west. In all directions were views of the ocean.

A hundred feet away from the south side of the house was the helipad. A helmeted man that I assumed was the pilot was packing bags and suitcases into the helicopter.

I waited outside in the center of the driveway. After a few minutes the front door opened and Svetlana stepped outside.

She was dressed as always, in an expensive-looking, conservative skirt and jacket, with a white blouse. A matching coat and purse hung from her right arm, the one without a hand. A covering, this one light green, matching her suit, covered the stump.

I'd been amazed at her ongoing rage directed at me. After all of this time, I'd expected she might have been able to let go of the things I'd done to her, and get on with her life.

But that lost hand was a constant reminder of how I'd bested her, one that made her life difficult, every single day. No wonder she was so determined to hurt me.

"You going somewhere?" I asked, nodding towards the helipad.

"My time in Greece is over."

"And how'd that work out for you?"

"Not exactly as I had planned. But it is ending, as you say, on a high note."

"Oh yeah? How's that?"

She gestured toward the front door. "Why don't we step inside?"

"No thanks, I'm good right here."

She shrugged. "Suit yourself. You know that your friend in the government is not coming, yes?"

"What do you mean?"

"You have no doubt told him about our meeting, and you must believe he is in the process of following you here. Unfortunately for you, his group is currently engaged in dealing with another bomb threat. One that will keep them busy for some time. A great coincidence, yes?"

She'd assumed I'd arranged with GG to bring his people here, and had set up a bomb threat as a distraction. At least, I hoped it was only a threat. Regardless, after the bomb in Heraklion she would know that law enforcement would take any threat seriously.

It was a good assumption, but I hadn't. GG didn't know anything about me being here.

"No, Doctor O'Hara, no one will be joining you. So whatever it is you have planned, I can assure you, it will not end the way you had anticipated."

She pulled out a gun from her purse and pointed it at my chest. It was in her left hand, but even though it was her off hand, she couldn't miss from this distance. "Do not move."

I slowly raised my arms over my head and waited.

# THIRTY-FIVE

"Y ou do not need to put your hands up. I could shoot you before you could move."

"I just don't want you to think I'm going to try anything. I wouldn't, given that you have the upper hand, and all."

She frowned, and raised the gun until it was pointing to my head.

*Yikes.* I needed to keep her talking, but not antagonize her any further at this point. No more hand jokes.

"It will be a pleasure killing you. I only wish I could make it last longer."

"What's the rush? Let's have a meal together. I'd be happy to give you a hand in the kitchen."

*Arghhh.* I mentally double face-palmed myself.

"You think you are funny. You will not think so, while you are bleeding to death. Maybe I will shoot you in the stomach. I understand it takes a long time to die that way."

"C'mon now, let's not let things get out of hand."

*Dammit.* I had no self-control. Maybe it would be better to just let them all out at once.

"You're the most evil person I've ever met, hands down. Especially now that I see you taking matters into your own hands. I did hear that you liked to do that, but it was only second-hand information. You've had your hands full with me, and I'm sure you'll be relieved to wash your hands of this whole situation. I know the government would love to take you down, but their hands have been tied, and they don't want to bite the hand that feeds them. I don't want to tip my hand, but everyone will know that you had a hand in all of this."

I took a deep breath, then blew it out. "OK. I think that's all I've got. Oh, wait. Hang on, I've got one more. Nicely done. Give yourself a hand."

She'd been relaxed and gloating when I'd arrived. Now her face was stormy. I snuck a look at the helipad. All of the bags were loaded and the pilot was in his seat.

This was all taking longer than I'd expected. The *whoop whooping* came from the helicopter as the blades began to rotate. Maybe I'd been wrong.

All I could do at this point was keep stalling.

"So this is it? After all you've done, mailing vodka to me for months, luring us to Greece, blowing up a hotel, setting up a gunfight at the market, arranging an ambush at an olive oil mill . . . you went to all of this trouble to kill my friends, and now you're just going to shoot me in your driveway, and fly away? Seems like a little bit of a let-down."

"No, not so much. I have enjoyed how easily it is to manipulate you. Is like dealing with child." She grimaced, attempting and failing to smile.

"A child that managed to stop you."

"Stop me? I do not think so." She waved the gun at me for emphasis.

"Yet here we are: you pulled out all the stops, and spent a fuckton of money, to try to kill my friends, but they're still alive, and all you can do is point your little gun at me. With your one working hand."

Her eyes narrowed. "You will die here today," she said, frustrated at me not being more upset about that.

"I know. If you want the truth, I never expected to make it past thirty, anyway. And it's been a good ride. Not to mention that I'll die knowing that my friends are safe, and you're ruined."

"Safe?" She laughed, a wretched sound. "No, they are not safe. Please know, I will not stop until I track them down and kill them all. You can die knowing that you caused the death of the people who mean the most to you. I already came very close to killing Miss Hernandez in that bar; the next time you will not be around to watch out for her."

"And ruined?" She shook her head. "Not at all."

"Yes, ruined. They found the guy you used to plant the bomb at the hotel. And guess what? He's talking. You've been designated a terrorist, Svetlana Ivashchenko. And all I can say is, it's about damn time. While we speak my buddy GG is in the process of transferring Janus to the Greek state. Your company is gone. And you'll be on the terrorist watchlist. Your days of globetrotting to fun places are over. Enjoy North Korea."

This was all a complete lie. I'd never given GG enough information to look into Janus, and they hadn't caught the guy who set off the bomb in the hotel.

She smirked and shook her head. "Janus is only one of my companies. I can lose ten more and it will not matter. And I do not need airports, or ports, to go where I want to, as you know." She waved the gun again at the helicopter, whose blades were now rotating at full speed.

"No?" I said, looking at my watch, and then around us.

"Are you expecting someone? No one is coming. You are alone, and you will die alone."

She started to laugh, then raised the gun again and pointed it at my head.

There was a soft *pffft* like something plopping into a wet pile of dough. Svetlana stumbled.

I heard the crack of a gunshot.

The smirk on her face disappeared, and the gun dropped from her hand, now hanging limply at her side.

She looked down at her blouse. A bloom of red was growing, just under her shoulder.

"You lose, you crazy, one-handed, loathsome, murderous, vile, loathsome, virulent, sociopathic, shitty excuse for a human being. Did I say loathsome twice? That's because you really, really are loathsome."

Another crack, and another bloom of red, this one in the center of her chest. She fell forward, her head bouncing on the gravel.

I waited, to see if she would get up. When she didn't move I did that thing they always do on cop shows, and kicked the gun away from her body, then leaned down to put my fingers on her neck.

No pulse.

"See you never, you fucking bitch."

I stood back up, putting both of my hands up, wondering if a bullet would come for me, too.

After a few moments I turned around to face the high western peak, where I'd seen a glint of light earlier. I closed all of my fingers into fists, leaving two thumbs up.

Then I turned and walked back down the hill.

# THIRTY-SIX

On my way back to the ferry I called Sam, letting her know I was fine, and to tell everyone we'd be checking out in the morning. Then I called GG and told him what happened.

I was done with Greece. Svetlana was dead, and Platon was in jail, but he hadn't been convicted yet, and I wasn't a hundred percent sure his followers wouldn't come after us.

Not to mention that Loukas was still out there. Best to put some distance between us and them for the time being.

Once I made it back to Athens the four of us spent the evening packing, and then had one last dinner. The next morning we checked out early and walked to GG's office.

He was sitting behind his desk, Tiny Joan next to him as always. Sophia was talking to a man in a suit.

"Eh, Doctor O'Hara, this is Lieutenant Detective Antonis, from Salamis. He is, eh, responsible for investigating the death of Svetlana Ivashchenko."

Detective Antonis didn't bother with niceties. "You were with Mrs. Ivashchenko yesterday, when she was shot?"

"Yeah. But it wasn't me that shot her."

"Eh, yes, so, it is a coincidence, eh, that she was shot while you were there?"

"No, not at all."

He frowned. "So, you are saying that you did shoot her?"

"No. The SVR did."

He frowned again, deeper this time. "The SVR?"

"Yeah, you know, Russian security. There were two of them, Gideon can give you their names if you want." By the time they got around to looking for them, Cheech and Chong would be out of the country.

Now he looked confused. "So, eh, you were working with them? This does not absolve you of responsibility for Mrs. Ivashchenko's death."

"I wasn't working with them, and I've never had any contact with either of them. They did it on their own, for their own reasons."

He shook his head, exasperated. "This is, eh, hard to believe," he said, turning to GG, "that Russia's security service would want to assassinate one of their own people, outside of their country."

"Are you kidding?" I said. "They do it all the time. They push them off of buildings, hang them in their homes, poison them, and frequently shoot them, often in broad daylight. Leonid Rozhetskin disappeared in 2008 in Latvia after selling some of his assets that the Kremlin thought were strategic. Aleksandr Litvinenko, a former KGB agent, was poisoned in 2006 with radioactive polonium while living in England. Do I need to go on?"

"No, no. But I still do not understand why they would shoot Mrs. Ivashchenko. You are the one with the motive. Mrs. Ivashchenko has been threatening you, and your friends, yes?" He looked at GG again, who made a point to avoid eye contact with me.

*Dammit*, after all I'd done for him, he could have kept his mouth shut for one day, and not mentioned my name to this guy. I'd basically handed Platon to him on a platter.

"They have a huge motive. She's hired people to run around and shoot up your country, blow up a hotel, and assassinate tourists. And she's using company funds to support all of it. She's completely out of control, and is a huge embarrassment to Putin. They needed to get rid of her, and it's easier for them over here than on Russian soil. Less bad publicity at home, which is all they care about.

"The SVR have been here at least since we've been here, trailing her. And they don't send out guys like that unless there's something really important to take care of."

"How do you know all of this, if you were not working with them?"

"I recognized them, they were following us around."

"How could you be sure it was them?"

I sighed, and he looked at GG, who nodded.

"If you need proof about these guys, check my room at the hotel. You'll find a listening device."

Antonis didn't say anything, just stood there with his little notebook.

*Jesus.* "If you need more proof, find the bullets they shot her with, and then take a look at the gunshot wounds. You'll see she was shot from a distance, with a Russian sniper or marksman rifle, like a Dragunov."

That finally got him to close his notebook.

"We will need to verify all of this. Please do not leave Athens until you hear from us."

"What?" I glared at GG, who quickly exchanged a few words with Antonis. I didn't know what they were saying, but I imagined it was something like this:

*"You must let them leave."*

*"I cannot. It is obvious she had something to do with this murder. And besides, I do not like her."*

*"Nor do I. But she is telling the truth. And she is the one who helped us bring in Platon."*

*"OK. I will let them go. Only because you are a friend."*

*"Thank you. Now, if you can find a reason to detain Miss Alekseeva, that would be a different story."*

*"Miss Alekseeva? No, there is no reason to detain her."*

*"Are you sure? Perhaps she can be found to have some kind of connection with the Russians who shot Mrs. Ivashchenko? Or maybe her passport has a problem. Something like that . . ."*

*"Yes, I am sure. And you really need to find a wife. You do this all the time, and it is getting pathetic. A wife will help you dress more normally, and perhaps convince you to use less gel in your hair."*

*"Who are you calling pathetic? At least I do not live on that shitty island."*

They shook hands and Antonis left, not bothering to say anything to us.

"Eh, you are free to go," said GG. "He agrees that it is best that you be allowed to leave."

"Why in hell did you have to tell him about me?"

"I am sorry. It is better to be forthcoming with these kind of things. But it is of no importance. The Greek government is not interested in spending resources investigating the death of a Russian citizen, one who may have had a hand in terrorist activities."

"Whatever. We're out of here. Good luck with your stuff."

"Oh, eh, I had hoped you might stay for a few days."

"Sorry."

He stood up and came from behind his desk. "Well, eh, on behalf of the Greek government, I thank you, Doctor O'Hara, Miss Hernandez, Mr. Spielberg, and Miss Alekseeva, for your help." He shook each of our hands, using two with Tatiana. "It was, eh, an interesting experience to work with you. If you ever come back to Greece, please let me know," he said, looking at her.

"Thank you," said Sophia, also putting out her hand.

We all shook hands and walked out of the office.

"Oh, yeah," I said, turning back when I was in the doorway. "There is one more thing."

"Yes?"

"I know who your mole is. Or, at least, one of them."

His eyebrows went up. "Who?"

I turned to Tiny Joan. "Say it ain't so, Tiny Joan."

She looked up quickly from the folders she was scattering on GG's desk.

"Take a look at her phone."

GG looked at her, and then at me, aghast. "No, it is not possible. Miss Gataki has worked for me for over five years."

"That may be, but she's got a serious nationalistic streak to her, don't you? Enough to be an informant for the Megali Titans."

If I wasn't sure I'd gotten the Evil Eye before this, I knew I was getting it now from Tiny Joan.

"While you're at it, you might want to check out her apartment. I'm guessing there's some interesting stuff in there, too."

"Impossible," said GG.

"OK. Why don't you just check her phone, and then you don't have to worry about it?"

"Fine. I am sorry," he said, turning to her. "May I please look at your phone?"

She continued to glare at me while she handed him her phone.

I shook my head. "Not that one. Her other phone."

"Other phone?" asked GG.

"She's got another one, in her bag. On it you'll see calls to Santorini just before you raided Platon's compound, as well as calls before the market shootout, where Christos was killed. And then one from

Platon to her, just after you learned that Sam was kidnapped." I turned to Tiny Joan. "Thanks, by the way, for passing along that little tidbit of misinformation. We couldn't have done it without you." I pointed to her bag, which was sitting on the floor leaning against the wall. GG nodded to Sophia, who picked it up and went through it, pulling out a phone and handing it to him.

He held it in his hand, and looked at Tiny Joan sadly.

They already had Platon's phone, and it would be a simple thing to verify calls between Tiny Joan and him, all occurring before something big was going to happen.

Tiny Joan must have realized the jig was up. Now she stood up straight and started to talk very fast.

"Elláda ítan kápote o megalíteros politismós ston kósmo! Tha kánume tin Elláda ksaná megáli, énan politismó pou prépi na timáte, ópu káthe Éllinas, káthe ándras ke káthe gyneka, íne sevas?" she said, looking pointedly at GG, who was too shocked to react.

This was the first time we'd ever heard her speak. "What's she saying?" I asked Sam.

"She's talking about restoring the greatness of Greece, and respecting both men and women."

"Íne timí mu pu sinergázome me ton Pláton! Óla afá ta hrónia me férthikes san skílos. O Plátonas me antimetopízi san énan polítimo protathlití. Eíse énas adínamos hazós, morós ke malákas!"

"Oh!" said Sam.

"What?"

"Now she's on about GG. About how he's treated her like a dog all these years, and she was proud to be working for Platon, especially since GG was such a . . . hmm . . . I'm not sure how to translate this. Maybe, a weak moron? And there's something in there about masturbating."

That sounded about right.

It was time to go, and we brushed past the muscle hamsters and other members of GG's team who were crowding around the door to get a better view. The sound of Tiny Joan's ranting stayed with us until the elevator door closed.

None of us said anything until we were back down on the sidewalk.

"How did you know?"

"Process of elimination, along with a few other things. GG's group is already down to a handful of people. But mostly it was her bag."

"Her bag?"

"Yeah. How many times did we see her drop folders, spill drinks, and dump her phone and other shit on the floor?"

"Too many to count."

"Yeah. And how many times did she drop her bag? Never. She never even opened it when we were around. Not for tissues, or glasses, or anything.

"And that explains how she got away with it for so long . . . she came across as a bumbler, no one could believe anyone like that could have strong ideas, or be working directly with someone like Platon. GG wouldn't have even thought about checking into her; I doubt he ever considered she had a life outside of the office. He barely acknowledged her as a person."

"There's something else I don't understand," Sam said. "How did you know they would kill her?"

"Svetlana?"

"Yes. They could have just been keeping an eye on her."

"No, I was sure they wanted to take her out."

I hadn't been sure at all. But I didn't want Sam to know that.

"Think about it. Russia's got enough problems right now, without one of their most famous oligarchs running around in another country trying to assassinate people. They're on very tenuous footing; Greece could decide any day that appropriating Janus Oil was in the best interest of the country. Russia can't afford to add to their current international shitstorm, especially not related to their energy industry. It was a no-brainer," I said, giving her my most reassuring look.

I could tell she wasn't buying it. But she let it go; nothing could be gained by making me relive how close I'd come to getting killed.

We picked up our bags from the hotel and took a cab for the airport.

The car was silent, Gideon taking another opportunity to catch up on his sleep, and Tatiana staring out the window.

My phone buzzed. Another one from my dad. He'd been calling me incessantly the last few days, leaving voicemails each time. I'd deleted all of them without listening.

I swiped left and put it back in my pocket.

# EPILOGUE

We'd been back in the US for a week when Tatiana announced she was heading back to Russia. Now that Svetlana was gone, she'd be safe there. And while her dad was still in prison, there were signs that he might be let out early. In the meantime she was going to stay with cousins in St. Petersburg.

"That'll be nice for you," I said, trying to sound positive about her leaving. "Reuniting with your family."

"Yes. But it will be difficult. My cousin Olga is negative person. She is very . . . bitchy. And they have never been out of Russia, they do not know of things outside of Russia. For them Russia is everything."

Wow. I'd sprained every muscle in my face trying not to roll my eyes.

Nevertheless I was sad to see her go. A month ago I'd have been thrilled, but since Greece I'd softened on her. Almost getting killed together multiple times had brought us closer. We'd not had a single argument since our trip to Salamis, and she'd actually smiled at me once.

The evening after Tatiana had made her announcement the four of us were sitting around Sam's kitchen eating takeout shawarma when I let them know I was moving back home, too.

"Was it something I said?" Sam joked.

"No, no, it's just . . . I never liked the idea that she forced me to move out of my own home." Now that she was dead we had an unspoken agreement not to utter Svetlana's name.

"I know. It's fine. But it's going to feel empty around here without you guys."

"It's not like she's moving out of the city," said Gideon. A few long nights of sleep and he was back to normal, although I knew he wouldn't be eager for more fieldwork any time soon.

I loved Sam, and it was fun to live with her, but the truth was that I didn't want to wait another minute to move back into my own house. Svetlana was dead, but I needed to be in my home to make it feel real.

I left the next night, saying my goodbyes to Tatiana, possibly for the last time, and drove home. I was relieved to see it was dark and quiet, half expecting my dad to be here waiting for me.

I opened the door and set my bag on the floor, turning on the lights.

The house looked like a bomb had gone off in it. Everything that had been on a shelf was on the floor, all of the things that could be broken, were. The stuffing from every seat cushion and the couch was laying around the room like chunks of snow.

I walked around the house, checking windows and doors.

Everything was locked, and I'd used my key to get in the front. Dad.

He hadn't believed me when I'd said that I'd given his money away, and he'd torn the house apart looking for it.

He was the gift that just kept on fucking giving.

I called him. It went straight to voicemail. This time I left a message.

"Listen, you pathetic loser. How dare you trash my house. If you're looking for your fucking money, I told you, it's already been spent by the women's shelter I donated it to. So fuck you. And by the way, I'm going to have a discussion with your parole officer in the morning. I'm sure he'll be interested to know what you've been up to. Breaking and entering is a parole violation, isn't it?"

I hung up, wishing there was a cell phone equivalent of slamming a receiver down. I went to the kitchen and grabbed a beer out of the refrigerator.

At least he hadn't trashed the kitchen, or the liquor cabinet, I noticed, as I opened to see my bottles of Redbreast intact. I poured myself a shot and sat down at the table.

My phone buzzed.

Dear ol' Dad. This time I answered.

"Hey, fuck you, Dad. I meant what I said about calling your parole officer. Enjoy your last night of freedom, you—"

"Jesse, please, stop."

"*You* stop, you pathetic, son of a—"

"It's your sister."

"Shannon?"

"She's gone."

"Gone?"

"She was taken."

"Taken by who?"

"By the man who's after me. The man whose money you gave away."

"Danny Ryan."

# Acknowledgements

I should state for the record that I've never been in a Turkish prison. At the time I wrote *Murder in the Greek Isles*, they were offering conjugal visits, even in the highest security facilities. This may not be the case at the time of publication.

Those who have been to Santorini know I took a few liberties with the landscape, but Platon's compound is modeled after a real place, called "Artspace." It was one of the coolest places I've been to in Greece, and I highly recommend it to anyone visiting the island.

The Golden Dawn was a real organization. It's now defunct, and its leaders are in jail. Descriptions of their attitudes and actions are accurate. The Megali Titans organization is entirely fictional, and was a result of my wondering what would happen if a far-right group formed that didn't have the attendant homophobia, misogyny and racism as part of its belief system.

Many, many thanks to Tina, Martin, Sianna, Anna and the rest of the team at Severn House for your ongoing support! You are terrific.

I'm eternally grateful to my beta readers, Lynne, Twila, George, Stuart, and Anna for your critical comments on early drafts, and to Jennifer for your ongoing support. Cindy Gaines, you're absolutely the best.

Thanks to Trace for input on law enforcement, Kristen for being my BFF, and as always, Anna.